THE MIRACLE OF LOVE

Book of Love, Book Fifteen

Meara Platt

ARE YOU SIGNED UP FOR DRAGONBLADE'S BLOG?

You'll get the latest news and information on exclusive giveaways, exclusive excerpts, coming releases, sales, free books, cover reveals and more.

Check out our complete list of authors, too!

No spam, no junk. That's a promise!

Sign Up Here

www.dragonbladepublishing.com

Dearest Reader;

Thank you for your support of a small press. At Dragonblade Publishing, we strive to bring you the highest quality Historical Romance from some of the best authors in the business. Without your support, there is no 'us', so we sincerely hope you adore these stories and find some new favorite authors along the way.

Happy Reading!

CEO, Dragonblade Publishing

Additional Dragonblade books by Author Meara Platt

The Moonstone Landing Series
Moonstone Landing (novella)
Moonstone Angel (novella)
The Moonstone Duke
The Moonstone Marquess
The Moonstone Major

The Book of Love Series
The Look of Love
The Touch of Love
The Taste of Love
The Song of Love
The Scent of Love
The Kiss of Love
The Chance of Love
The Gift of Love
The Heart of Love
The Hope of Love (novella)
The Promise of Love
The Wonder of Love
The Journey of Love
The Dream of Love (novella)
The Treasure of Love
The Dance of Love
The Miracle of Love
The Remembrance of Love (novella)

Dark Gardens Series
Garden of Shadows
Garden of Light
Garden of Dragons

Garden of Destiny
Garden of Angels

The Farthingale Series
If You Wished For Me (A Novella)

The Lyon's Den Series
Kiss of the Lyon
The Lyon's Surprise
Lyon in the Rough

Pirates of Britannia Series
Pearls of Fire

De Wolfe Pack: The Series
Nobody's Angel
Kiss an Angel
Bhrodi's Angel

Also from Meara Platt
Aislin
All I Want for Christmas

CHAPTER ONE

London, England
December 1821

DEKLAN QUINTON HAD just fallen exhausted onto his bed when he felt something more than a lump on the mattress. In the next moment, a piercing shriek resounded in his ear and someone began hitting him with a book. "Help! Help! Intruder!"

Holy Mother!

It took him mere seconds to subdue his assailant, a young woman with delicious curves. She shrieked and hit him again when his hand accidentally cupped her breast. He had meant to reach for her arm, but it was dark, and she was squirming and kicking.

How was he to know that exquisitely soft, fleshy bit was not her arm?

Thwack!

Bollocks, she hit him again with that book.

He covered her mouth with his hand as she was about to scream again, then rolled her flat on her back and used his weight to hold her down. Lord, she smelled delicious, like fresh strawberries you wanted to lick all over.

Well, he wasn't going to do anything to this obvious innocent other than try to calm her and find out what she was doing in his bedchamber, and more specifically, in his bed.

Her screams continued, but were now muffled under the

pressure of his palm.

However, the damage had been done.

That first banshee shriek must have carried into the hall and woken up those in the adjoining bedchambers.

She was still wriggling beneath him, and he was naked.

Thank goodness he had bothered to lock his door or else his family would now be upon them and gawking at the tattoo on his arse, the one he'd drunkenly acquired two months ago. It would also escape no one's notice that he was atop this delicious girl while wearing nothing at all, not a stitch, even though it was winter, and the night air was cold and crisp.

As for her, she was wearing a nightrail of thickest linen that had ridden up her legs as she kicked him in an attempt to unman him. A failed attempt, and now she was desperately trying to tug it down.

One slender leg rubbed against his privates, and she suddenly realized what she had just grazed.

She shrieked again, the sound completely muffled by his hand. "Stop screaming," he said in an urgent whisper, hearing footsteps down the hall. "My name is Deklan Quinton. Miranda…Lady Grayfell is my aunt. Do you hear me? She is my aunt. This is my bedchamber when I visit her. I promise you. I had no idea anyone was in here. She never puts anyone in here but me. Why are you here?"

The girl was no longer shrieking but her mouth was moving. *"Hummph, bummph."*

"Stop. I cannot understand a word you're saying."

"Hummph, glummph, clothes."

Ah, he'd caught that last bit about clothing. "I am going to take my hand off your mouth, but you must promise not to scream again. Nod if you promise."

She nodded.

"Good." He eased his hand away the littlest bit but dared not fully remove it off her achingly soft lips just yet. "Now, I need you to close your eyes and count to ten."

"Why?" Her voice was only slightly muffled and sounded much less hysterical.

"So I can find my clothes and put them on. That is for your sake, not mine. I have no delicate sensibilities whatsoever. Go ahead. Close your eyes and start counting quietly."

To his relief, she appeared to do so.

"One. Two. Three."

She had an angel's voice, sweet as a melody.

He groped for the candle always kept on the small night table beside the bed and lit it to search for the trousers he'd tossed on the floor. He then whipped them on and buttoned the falls. This left him five seconds to get a good look at her beyond what he could make out under the silvery rays of moonlight slanting in through the window.

It took him much less time.

Holy Mother.

He held the candle up so that it shone over the bed.

He'd never seen a prettier girl in his life.

Someone pounded on the door. "Grace! Grace! Are you all right?"

She opened her eyes and rolled to her knees. Her dark blonde curls swirled about her shoulders, cascading in soft waves down her back. Her big eyes, laden with fear, were as green as the Irish hills. "What shall I say, Mr. Quinton?" she whispered. "You cannot be found in here!"

He sank to her side.

The mattress dipped from his weight, causing her to slide closer. She had to catch his shoulder to steady herself, but not before that luscious body of hers fell against him and left him feeling as though he had just been struck by a bolt of lightning. "Tell them all is well, you were simply frightened by a mouse."

"Oh, that is very good." She cleared her throat and released him now that she had regained her balance. "I'm fine, Lady Miranda. Just a mouse. He startled me. He's gone now."

"He?" his aunt intoned.

The girl's eyes widened once again.

She looked at him in panic.

Deklan grinned, liking that she was not a practiced liar. "*It*. Refer to the mouse as an *it*, not a *he*," he whispered.

"Oh." The little apple in her throat bobbed. "Um…er…perhaps *it* was a rat. A big, dark, furry thing. As I said, *it* is all gone now. Yes, I must have chased *it* away. I'm so sorry I disturbed you. Please, go back to bed. Crisis has passed. All is well."

Miranda rattled the door.

The girl looked about to faint.

But the door held as Deklan knew it would.

He heard another female voice now calling out to this angelic vision and knocking at the door. "Grace, open up and let us make sure. My dear, you sounded dreadfully overset."

Bloody hell.

His mother.

Could this get any worse?

He was still holding the candle and now glanced at the book the girl had been hitting him with. He waited for Grace to finish babbling some more assurances about the mouse that no one was ever going to believe had come into her room.

A moment later, she let out a breath and groaned. "Do you think we fooled them?"

Was she serious?

This girl could not lie her way out of a sack of grain.

But he nodded. "I'm sure we did."

When the footsteps receded down the hall, Deklan picked up the book to read the title. *The Book of Love.* "What in blazes are you reading?"

"I don't know. It simply appeared atop the bureau earlier today. Is it yours?"

"Hell, no. Why would I want to read that book? I don't need anyone telling me how to seduce women."

"It isn't that sort of book. It is about finding true love, the forever and abiding sort. Nothing whatever to do with the lewd activities you indulge in with your sordid paramours. And what was that dark splotch on your backside? It looked like a snake curling around your thigh and its face imprinted on the...um, cheek of your derriere."

"You peeked at my arse?"

She blushed furiously. "Of course, I did. I wasn't going to close my eyes all the way just because you told me to do it. For all I knew, you could have had a hatchet in hand and intended to murder me."

"I am not in the habit of murdering my aunt's guests, and that dark splotch is a cobra, to be precise."

"A cobra? What an idiotic thing. Who paints a snake on their rump?"

"I did, obviously. And it wasn't idiotic. It was..." Well, it certainly hadn't been his brightest idea. "Grace, are you trembling?"

"Apparently so." She clasped her hands together and nodded. "You gave me a scare."

"I'm sorry. I mean it sincerely. I had no idea you were in here. I was exhausted and merely slipped in to what I thought would be my empty bedchamber. I was desperate for sleep and to let down my guard or else I would have noticed you curled in my bed. Do you never toss about? I've never seen a bed in such pristine condition before."

She nodded. "I do sleep rather soundly."

"Like the dead," he muttered. "I never meant to frighten you. Please know, I will not hurt you. You will always be safe with me."

He wanted to reach out to the lovely girl and take her hand, but she did not trust him yet, and he did not want her screaming again. "I promise. I will never harm you. However, I am disappointed. You gave me your word and then you broke it."

She tipped her head and looked up at him in indignation. "Why are you so offended? Would you not do the same if our roles were reversed and I was nakedly slipping between your sheets and…well, never mind. I don't suppose it works quite the same way in reverse. Stop grinning at me. This is serious. Rest assured, I will not be taking off my clothes around you ever. Do you hear me? Not ever. My point is, would you not say anything to save your life?"

He raked a hand through his hair. "I suppose. Yes, I would. You are forgiven."

"I have done nothing that requires forgiving. But I will be generous and forgive you. Do not sneak into my bedchamber naked again." She paused a moment and gave her lip a light nibble. "Well, do not sneak in here clothed either. By the way, I will not stop you if you wish to put on your shirt."

He grinned again. "Who are you exactly? My aunt and mother referred to you as Grace, but Grace what?"

"That was your mother? Of course, Mrs. Quinton. She's lovely, but I suppose you know this. So is your nephew, Sam. He is quite adorable." She covered her face with her hands. "Oh, why did you not stop me? I've just lied to your mother."

"Believe me, she doesn't really want to know the truth." Deklan set the candle on the night table. "Sam is here?"

She nodded without looking at him, causing her lively curls to bob upon her slender shoulders. "Yes, at the opposite end of the hall with the older children. The youngest are upstairs in the nursery. Miranda has a full house just now."

He reached for his shirt. "Then where am I supposed to sleep?"

"Well, it cannot be in here. Try the library. There is a sofa and several comfortable chairs." She scrambled off the bed and tiptoed to the door to place her ear to it. "I think your aunt and mother have disappeared back in their rooms. Gather your things and go. Shall I help you?"

He joined her by the door but kept enough of a distance so as not to alarm her. Still, he was close enough to inhale her strawberry scent. Lord, she smelled nice. "You haven't answered my question. What is your family name?"

To his surprise, tears welled in her lovely eyes. "I am too ashamed to say. Please go. I suppose we shall see each other at breakfast, and your aunt will tell you everything. You mustn't forget to pretend we have never met."

"I can keep my stories straight. You're the one who needs to remember."

"I know. I am not very good at deception." She nodded. "How did you acquire those scars on your body?"

"Ah, that is a sensitive question. I am not at liberty to say. You mustn't ask." He tossed on his shirt, then moved away to don his boots and stuff his jacket in his travel pouch. He grabbed the pouch and his hat before striding back to her side.

Grace watched him the entire time. "You move about so silently."

It was a trait he had acquired by necessity for survival. "Hush, Grace. I am going to open the door now. Do not say a word."

"All right." She took a step back. "I'll lock it behind you."

"You're still talking." But his heart surged in his chest as she gazed up at him with those big green eyes.

Oh, hell.

What was he going to do about her?

They were probably caught anyway. Miranda and his mother would know he had been the *rodent* in Grace's bedchamber the moment they found him asleep in the library.

He ran his thumb across the line of her jaw. "Close your eyes."

"Why?"

"Fine, don't close them." He drew her into his arms and kissed her full on the lips, sinking his mouth deeper on hers than intended. But who could resist the soft give of her luscious mouth? "Sweet dreams, Grace. I'll see you in the morning."

What was it about this girl?

The only thing wild about her was her glorious tumble of golden curls. Otherwise, she was shy and modest, standing there looking utterly beautiful in her nightgown primly buttoned to her throat and the most confused look he had ever seen on anyone's face.

A knot formed in his stomach.

Had she never been kissed before?

And now he'd gone and done it, stolen a first kiss without the slightest care, a kiss that ought to have been something special and treasured for her.

Perhaps this is why he was still feeling the lightning-bolt impact of it.

How was it possible?

He had hardened himself to all feeling years ago.

For this reason, he was the Crown's most lethal agent.

"Mr. Quinton, why are you staring at me so oddly?"

Indeed, icy calculation was necessary in his line of work, and he was effective because he was impervious to all sensation.

Or so he thought.

Apparently, he had no defense against Grace.

How had this innocent managed it?

Heaven help him, she shot fire through his blood.

He did not even know her family name.

What was so awful about it she would not tell him?

CHAPTER TWO

GRACE MONTFORD HELD her breath as Deklan Quinton, easily the handsomest man she had ever beheld, unlatched her door and silently slipped into the hall. She followed, her only intention to stand in the hallway and watch him disappear downstairs. But he stopped suddenly, and she slammed into his broad back with an *oof.*

"I might have known," he grumbled.

At first, Grace thought he was muttering to her and was irritated she had followed him out.

Then she saw his mother and aunt standing there with their arms folded and gloating expressions on their faces.

"We thought you might have been the big rat Grace was shrieking about," his aunt said, her smile quite smug. "Glad you made it home in time for Christmas, dear boy. Why is your shirt undone?"

Grace's heart sank into her toes. "Lady Grayfell. Mrs. Quinton. It is not at all what it appears." She could not blame them for imagining the worst. Deklan had not bothered to properly button his shirt, and his finely rippled torso was still on dazzling display.

Blessed Mother.

This gorgeous beast of a man had kissed her.

Stars were still bursting behind her eyeballs.

Heat shot into her cheeks as she tried to stammer out an explanation and only made things worse. "He did not realize I was already tucked in there when he fell onto the bed atop me."

His mother gasped. "Atop you?"

"What? Oh, no...well, yes. Purely by accident, and he immediately apologized and put his clothes back on because–"

"He took his clothes off?" His aunt scowled at him. "Wretched boy."

He merely arched an eyebrow.

Grace coughed. "He cannot be blamed for the manner in which he sleeps. But he wasn't looking at me, and I was not looking at him. Well, not on purpose. That is, how could I close my eyes when I had no idea who he was or what he was doing in my bed...um, bedchamber?"

She took a deep breath and continued because everyone was looking at her and not saying a word, not even this man who was having far too much fun watching her struggle. Obviously, it was as he had told her. He had no delicate sensibilities whatsoever and did not care if the entire household knew he slept naked.

Or had accidentally fallen into bed with her.

But she cared.

How would she survive another scandal?

She wished someone would say something and let her out of her misery. But the air remained thick and charged, the older ladies still staring at this magnificent form of a man while they awaited his explanation.

He obviously had no intention of giving one, no matter how reproving their looks.

Grace hated the silence, so she tried to fill it. "But I do hope you will forget this unfortunate mishap ever occurred and not breathe a word to anyone...please. This will destroy my reputation if so much as a hint of it gets out. Although I suppose it is already shattered beyond repair and cannot possibly get any worse."

She turned to Deklan Quinton, melting under the force of his stare. He had leopard eyes. Perhaps this is why she was thinking of him as a beast, but he was not an ungainly sort of animal. No, he was the sleek, lithe sort who moved with the graceful power of a predator.

His eyes were beautiful, an enrapturing, icy blue with hints of amber. Dangerously seductive. She could swear he looked upon her as prey and wanted to eat her.

Devour her if that hot look was any indication.

But in a deliciously enticing way.

Goodness, how did women keep their clothes on when he looked at them with that hunger in his eyes? Well, she supposed goodness had nothing to do with it.

He was still staring at her, his body now taut.

He resembled a leopard about to pounce.

She had seen one once in a royal menagerie and had been enthralled as well as frightened.

She blinked to banish the vision of him savaging her body in a highly improper and yet thoroughly delightful way. "You see, Mr. Quinton, I am considered unfit for good society. But kindly wipe that grin off your face, for I have done nothing wicked myself. Nor will I ever do anything wicked with you."

He arched a dark eyebrow once again. "Did I ask you to?"

"Well, no. But on the chance you were thinking it…the answer is no. Nor will you want to have anything to do with me once you know who my family is. Your aunt will tell you."

She hoped Lady Miranda would now take over the explanation, for she felt tears well in her eyes again and did not want to be seen crying. Indeed, she had done nothing but cry these past few months while every possession had been stripped from her parents, her siblings, and herself. Now, her father and brother were held somewhere within the walls of old London. She did not know where, and those in authority who did know refused to tell her or allow her to visit them.

Mr. Quinton caught her arm when she tried to return to her bedchamber. "Grace, it is all right."

She shook her head. "No, how can I make you understand? It isn't all right. It can never be."

He frowned thoughtfully. "Who in blazes are you?"

The response constricted in her throat.

Yet again, neither Lady Miranda nor Mrs. Quinton spoke up.

She tried to slip into her bedchamber, but he was at her door and blocked it before she could step through. "Do not run from me."

He took her by the shoulders, his touch surprisingly gentle but firm enough not to let her get away.

"Please, just let me go. You will want nothing to do with me when you find out, so why put me through the humiliation?"

"Let me be the judge. Just tell me, will you?"

What was she going to do about this man?

She understood why his family spoke his name in hushed, reverential tones whenever he came up in conversation. *Deklan.* He moved with the stealth of a wraith in the night. He exuded heat and power. Even his voice had a sensual growl to it.

His eyes had the power to penetrate her soul.

In truth, to shatter her soul.

She did not want anything to do with him, and yet she could not bear to see him repulsed by her. "My family name is Montford. Sound familiar? And yes, I am from *those* Montfords."

His fingers tightened on her shoulders. "I see. You are the daughter who was about to have her society come-out?"

"Yes, the very one. But it will never happen now. Who would ever sponsor the daughter of an art thief and forger? At best, I am a laughingstock. At worst…" She was unable to hold back a light shudder. "I cannot repeat the horrible things they are saying about me. Now will you let me crawl back into my bedchamber?"

"Grace–"

"Just leave me alone. I do not require your condescension to remind me my life is in ruins. Nor do I need your comments. You cannot possibly make me feel worse than I already do."

"Blast it, I would never hurt you. You must trust me."

"Why?"

"Because…well, it will take some explaining. What on earth

are you doing here? Under this very roof? How do you know my family? I don't suppose it matters. But you had better prepare yourself."

"What are you talking about? Prepare myself for what?"

He sighed. "Unfortunately, the worst is not over yet."

His aunt, who had remained in the hall and was listening to their conversation, snorted in dismissal. "Honestly, Deklan. What a thing to say to poor Grace. You can see how distraught she is over this sad affair. Why add to her worries? I'd hit you with a rolling pin if I had one close at hand."

His gaze swept over the three of them, for his mother had also remained beside them and regarded her son dubiously. "I'll explain in a moment. First, I need to ask Grace a few questions. Have you ever lied, cheated, or stolen from anyone?"

She tipped her chin up in indignation. "No!"

"Would you ever lie, cheat, or steal from me or my family?"

"Of course not!" She stared at his aunt and mother to see if they understood what he was going on about. "You are the only ones who have shown me any kindness. I would never hurt any of you. I give thanks for your family every night in my prayers."

"We know, my dear," Mrs. Quinton said and turned to her son. "Why are you asking Grace these questions?"

"Because she is the reason I am back in London."

His tone sent a shiver up her spine. "Me? Why?"

And now his leopard gaze was on her again, but this time in a protective manner and not at all predatory. "Yes, you. However, I had no idea you were staying with my aunt. I meant to catch a solid night's sleep, then go looking for you. Seems you've saved me the need to hunt you down."

"Hunt me down? I was never in hiding."

Lady Miranda appeared to be as confused as she was. "I invited Grace to spend Christmas with us while she tries to sort through her family situation. Her mother is too overset to manage their affairs and relies on Grace for everything. Dear boy, kindly explain what is going on."

"Something very bad, Aunt Miranda." He ran a hand through the waves of his dark hair, almost a raven black, that seemed to enhance the predatory blue and amber swirls in his eyes.

Despite the winter's chill outside, Grace felt uncomfortably warm beside him.

The man exuded heat.

She tried not to look at him, but it was an impossible feat when he was standing so near and no one could overlook his presence, especially when he said, "You can forget about my sleeping on the library sofa. I am staying right here with Grace."

Grace erupted in a fit of coughs. "Are you mad? I have no idea what little jest you are playing at, but you most certainly will not get cozy with me. Lady Miranda…Mrs. Quinton…talk sense into your son. I am not sharing a bedchamber with him. And as for you, Mr. Quinton, rid your head immediately of any such notion."

He did not appear in the least bit moved by her demand. "If you think to keep me out, then *you* had better rid your head of any such notion. Consider me on assignment as of this moment. This is no jest, Grace. Your father and brother have made some powerful enemies."

"What has this to do with me? Well, I suppose we have all been tarred with their bad deeds. Those in the *ton* who were once my friends now toss jests behind my back and call me *Lady Disgrace*."

"Then they were never worthy to be your friends." He glanced around the hall, obviously preferring not to have more of an audience as he told them of the situation. "All of you, step back inside Grace's chamber. This is going to be a serious discussion."

His mother began to fret her lip. "Deklan, dear. You are giving us a fright."

"I'm sorry. It cannot be helped. I wish I could give you more encouraging news. Come in, and I will tell you why I am here."

"It isn't for our holiday celebrations?" his mother asked.

"No. Although I had hoped to find time for those. I've been away from home too long and dearly missed you all." He led them back into the bedchamber and shut the door. "A valuable heirloom was stolen from a foreign royal family shortly before the Montford family's activities were shut down by the Crown agents. Grace, the Home Office believes–"

"You mean the Duke of Wooton?" Lady Miranda said. "He runs the Home Office."

"Is he the one they call the Duke of Ice?" his mother asked.

"Yes to both your questions," he said with thinly veiled impatience. "Now will you let me finish? They believe Grace's brother, Richard Montford, is the one who planned the theft and the only one left alive who knows where this treasure is hidden."

Grace felt her legs go weak.

With shaking hands, she clutched the bedcovers as she took a seat on the bed and tried to absorb this latest infamy perpetrated by her brother. "Mr. Quinton, I thought your fellow agents managed to retrieve all the stolen artifacts. I was there when your own brother, Rafe, along with the Duke of Edgeware and a horde of the magistrate's men descended on our townhouse. They impounded everything and anything found in our home, in our art galleries, our warehouses, and anywhere else they knew to search."

"It wasn't enough. Some items have yet to be recovered. This one, a royal crown used for the ceremonial investiture of every reigning monarch since the existence of this foreign country, is among the few still unaccounted for. It is easily the most important item missing and not merely for the value of the jewels encrusted in the crown. It is the symbol of that foreign royal house, and without it, there is a good chance their monarchy will fall."

"Oh." Grace's stomach sank into her toes. "Which country?"

"I am not at liberty to tell you. It is highly sensitive information and must remain a secret. Needless to say, their royal family is enraged. Indeed, they are beyond enraged. Relations have always been fragile between our two countries, and this theft has made matters worse."

Lady Miranda pursed her lips. "Do they think our government is behind the theft?"

"They do not know what to think and no longer trust anything we say. Our diplomats are now in discussions with them at the highest levels, trying to assure them there was no government involvement. As a token of our good faith, we have turned over all the information we have on the Montfords and their activities, and have promised to do all in our power to find their crown and quietly return it. This is why I was sent home, to discover its whereabouts."

"What has Grace to do with this political intrigue?" his mother asked.

"Mr. Quinton, please believe I had nothing to do with any of it. But I will do all I can to help you," she assured. "However, I am confused. Why are you at all concerned with me when it is retrieving this royal heirloom that matters most?"

"Now that they know who committed this crime..."

Grace gave a short, bitter laugh. "How could they not? My family's downfall was front page news in every London paper."

"That's right, and you were mentioned in several of these articles. It was enough to draw their attention to you."

A shiver of foreboding tore through her. "To me?"

He nodded. "They are now out for blood and intend to take something precious from your family to hold hostage in exchange for return of their crown. They want *you*, Grace. They are demanding you be sent to them and held as their hostage."

"Is this why you are really here? To take me to them?" Her head began to spin, and she felt herself in danger of fainting, something she had never done in her life.

He reached over and took her hands in his. "Steady, Grace. It will be all right. I am here to make certain they do not take you."

"Oh, thank goodness," his mother whispered.

"But the best way to assure this does not happen is for us to find the crown and return it to its rightful owners. We have no more than one week to accomplish this task before their agents insist you be turned over to them. They have already arrived in London."

Lady Miranda stared at him. "Dear heaven…what can I do to help? What can any of us in the family do?"

"Nothing for the moment. Just let me handle it." He gave Grace's hands a light squeeze. "I am not going to let them take you, whether or not we ever find the crown."

She was suddenly glad this big man who moved with the stealth of a predator and seemed to have the soul of one, too, had declared himself to be her protector. What had her brother been thinking to steal a royal treasure?

"This is why I was assigned back to London," he continued, his touch warm and reassuring. "More is at stake than merely finding the stolen crown or protecting you, Grace. This incident could start a war between our two countries. If it does, there is no way I will allow you to be caught in the middle. No one is sending you from England if I have any say in the matter."

"But who will listen to you if their taking me might avert a war?"

He cast her that soft, lethally attractive grin of his. "It is more a question of whether I will listen to them."

She gasped. "No, you are talking nonsense. It is treason to go against the orders of our own royal family and our Home Office. I will never allow you to do this. Think of what it would do to your own family. Is it not enough mine is in ruins?"

He gave her cheek a light caress. "Grace, calm down. We are getting ahead of ourselves, are we not? Let's just concentrate on finding that crown. I'll need your full cooperation."

"Of course. You will have it. I will help in any way I can. But I promise you, I was not a part of any family schemes and would not even know where to begin hunting for this lost treasure."

"Do you think you can talk sense into your brother? He needs to tell you where it is hidden before the foreign agents get their hands on you."

She shook her head. "You think my brother cares what happens to me? He is my half-brother. We are born of different mothers. I assure you, he does not care a whit about anyone but himself. His only thought is for his survival. He will not even blink an eye if my father is hanged for this dirty business. No. If he is withholding this information, then he means for that precious crown to be his bargaining chip to gain his freedom."

"Is that so?" His expression turned hard.

He released her hands and began to pace across the elegant carpet that covered most of the wood floor. The carpet itself was of oriental design, an intricate pattern in shades of deep red, gold, and blue. The velvet drapes matched the blue of the carpet. Combined with the dark, mahogany red of the massive pieces of furniture, the room was decidedly masculine.

So was he.

He continued to pace.

This is why he reminded her of a jungle beast, the way he now quietly prowled back and forth, and that devastatingly sharp look in his eyes.

He paused a moment and turned to her. "He is mad if he believes he will escape retribution. The English government will not need to lift a finger against him. He will be done in by those foreign agents. However, by telling us where it is hidden, he can save you from abduction and England from possible war."

"Save your breath. He will only listen if you can offer him freedom as well as protection against those foreign agents." Grace wanted to fall back to sleep and pretend this was all a bad dream. But she knew it was merely a continuation of the living nightmare her father and brother had plunged them in when they turned to stealing precious artifacts. "Well, happy Christmas to me," she said with gallows humor. "Mr. Quinton, you will get nothing from my brother. Our only hope is to permit me to see my father. We have to start there."

He arched an eyebrow. "Do you think he knows anything?"

"I have no idea what to think anymore. But unlike my brother, I do not believe my father will lie to me. Nor do I believe he wishes to see his wife and children suffer. I know he was meant to be kept in isolation. But everything has changed now, hasn't it? I may be the only person able to get the truth out of him, assuming he knows anything. Truly, I have no idea if it will lead anywhere helpful. But my father loves me. I am the one who stands the best chance of convincing him to spill any secrets he may be holding back."

He nodded. "Let me clear this with the higher-ups in the Home Office."

"Do you think they will continue to deny me access to my father? They have to let me see him. I am not going to stand by and do nothing to help myself or England. What he and my brother have done is bad enough. I cannot allow their stupidity to start a war. As for myself, if I am to be abducted, then what choice do I have but to do all in my power to prevent it? We must start by questioning my father. Is there a reason we cannot go to him right now?"

"In the middle of the night?" He shook his head to express his dismissal of her suggestion. "We'll head to the Home Office first thing in the morning. All right?"

"No, it is not all right. But do I have a choice?"

He took her by the shoulders and gently turned her to face him. "I know waiting is hard, but we'll just get angry refusals if we start waking people now. However, I appreciate your willingness to cooperate. I think I am going to like being assigned to you, Grace."

She was already liking him more than was safe.

She watched him as he left her side and began to remove articles from his travel pouch.

Did he think to settle in here with her? "What are you doing?"

"You and I are going to be joined at the hip from now on."

Grace shook her head. "We assuredly will not. For starters,

you said we have a week before these foreign agents will ask for me to be handed over. Where is the need to share quarters now? We must discuss this. You—"

"No discussion. It is decided. I am not letting you out of my sight."

"Deklan!" Even his mother was aghast at the notion of their sharing quarters.

Grace clenched her hands at her sides. "Is this how we are to cooperate with each other? You making arbitrary rules and I am required to obey them?"

"Yes." He resumed unpacking the articles in his travel pouch.

"That is the most highhanded, insufferable thing I have ever heard." She gathered each item as he removed it and attempted to stuff them all back in the pouch.

"Grace, stop. I am exhausted, and you will not change my mind, so just let me prepare for bed."

"You are not sleeping in my bed."

Dear heaven.

The very idea.

Well, it was a delicious idea but one that would sink her further into ruin. "Even if these horrid men try to abduct me tomorrow, how can they break into Lady Miranda's house undetected while she has a full staff and the rafters packed with visiting family? *Your* family. Who in their right mind would dare take on the Brayden clan? So, I doubt anything is going to happen to me here."

He frowned at her. "That attitude will get you abducted for certain. Stop arguing and let me do my job. I did not gain my reputation by being an idiot. They will be sending their best agents to grab you."

"But—"

"Is this about my kissing you? Are you afraid I will do it again?"

His mother groaned. "You kissed Grace?"

Oh, heavens.

Why had she riled this man who was only trying to help her?

Was she not in desperate need of allies?

He shrugged. "Look at her. Who can resist? Besides, it seemed like the convenient thing to do. I was curious. I've never kissed a virgin before."

"Deklan!" His mother and aunt were once again scowling at him.

"And I've never kissed an idiot before," Grace shot back. "Especially one who paints the face of a snake on his backside."

"It is called a tattoo. It isn't paint. And I would not worry about the snake's face so much as I would about the snake's tail getting too close to you."

She had no idea what he meant by that.

However, his aunt and mother seemed to understand the remark. His aunt slapped him on the back of his head. "Behave yourself in my home. You had better keep that *tail* firmly inside your pants."

Grace finally understood.

Oh, mighty heaven.

This is the man she had to trust?

She blushed furiously. "How could you be so crass? You are abominable."

He seemed to find her distress amusing.

The wretch.

His eyes were gleaming. "And you, my lovely Grace, are delightfully innocent."

Was he flirting with her? Or did he always behave so recklessly in the face of peril? "Mr. Quinton, mock me again, and I shall punch you. My life is at risk if what you say is true. This is serious business."

"Do you think I am not taking it seriously?" He folded his arms across his massive chest, which was still open to her view since he hadn't the decency to button his shirt.

He followed her gaze to his chest. "Grace, you have only to turn away if you disapprove of the way I look. But I'll wager you are more intrigued than you are willing to let on. Do not fret about it. You think my liking you will prove a distraction? I assure you, it will not. I like lots of women. I am merely surprised to find you are not the wilting wallflower I expected you to be. But be assured, I have no plans to court you. Or touch you, for that matter. Virgins hold no appeal for me."

"Deklan!" His mother was once again scowling at him. "You will not speak to Grace in this insolent manner. I raised you to be a gentleman."

He cast Grace a glance.

She dared not show him any weakness…at least, no more than she already had done. "Rest assured, arrogant knaves hold no appeal for me. So do not worry that I might like you more than is proper. It is not going to happen. At the moment, I do not like you at all."

"I don't care. My assignment is to protect you, and this is what I am going to do."

"Protect me? Or use me to recover that crown?"

"Both. As for sleeping arrangements, I'll make a pallet for myself beside your bed tonight and that's an end to it. Mother and Aunt Miranda, kindly get out. This matter is not open for further discussion."

Grace gasped. "But–"

He emitted a soft, menacing growl. "Not another word, Grace."

His leopard gaze bore down on her again, and she knew there was no point to arguing. Nor were his mother and aunt offering more resistance.

She sighed in resignation. "Very well, Mr. Quinton. Set your pallet beneath the window since you seem to prefer the cold. The hearth fire burned out hours ago. You can toss on a few more logs and rekindle it if you wish."

"No, it will be too warm for me."

"As you wish. I should have realized your heart is made of ice. But if you dare creep so much as an inch closer to me–"

He gave a courtly bow, which under other circumstances, might have been viewed as polite, but here and now it was unpardonably insolent. "Miss Montford, I shall keep my distance."

"Good, and you had better keep your clothes on this time."

He rolled his eyes. "I give you my word of honor. I will not shed so much as a sock. Nor will I make any untoward advances. I do not need to beg a woman to share her bed."

She gasped. "You will not share my bed!"

"Is this not what I just said? Stop giving me orders, Grace. I know how to behave myself. But let's get one thing straight. From now on, I am the one in command. Not you." He turned to his aunt and mother. "Nor will I permit either of you to interfere."

Grace cleared her throat. "Were you always this insufferable? Even as a child?"

His tension eased, the stiffness flowing from his body like a ripple on the water. "Yes, Grace. Always been this way, as my mother will confirm it. She hasn't won an argument with me since I was the age of two."

Mrs. Quinton shook her head in obvious exasperation. "I love him because he is my son, but he has always been impossible to control. Fortunately, he is not a wicked boy and seems to have done quite a bit of good for our country."

His Aunt Miranda now spoke up. "My dear, under other circumstances, I would have my appallingly insufferable nephew tossed outdoors to sleep in the stables. But I've seen and heard enough of this nasty business going on with your family to be in dire fear for your safety. If the Home Office requested Deklan be brought back to England to guard you, then so it must be. He would not be here unless the threat was of the highest level."

She turned to her nephew. "However, I will crack you open like an egg if you dare break Grace's heart."

He cast Grace a wry smile. "Before you ladies make an omelet out of me, let me remind you that I have been at my job for years and know what I am doing. Do not meddle. Grace will be fine with me. Go back to your quarters. You have my word of honor she will come to no harm while under my guard."

Grace was calmed by the trust she saw in the eyes of the two ladies.

But it still troubled her greatly to have this man stay in her room.

And yet, what if those agents did somehow get in here and attempt to abduct her? This was far more dangerous than his unwanted presence in her room. Wasn't she ruined anyway because of her family's infamous behavior? No decent man would ever have her as his wife.

So, what was the point of sticking to her moral values?

She sank onto the bed and buried her face in her hands the moment his aunt and mother left.

He closed the door and locked it behind them, then came to her side and knelt beside her. "Oh, Grace," he said, his voice remarkably gentle as she struggled to hold back her tears. "All jesting aside, I am a man of honor. I've given you my word, and I shall not break it. You are safe with me."

"Your family obviously trusts you and so shall I. But this situation…I wasn't raised this way. I never imagined having a man sleep in my bedchamber outside of marriage. Your family might not say a word, but what about the servants?"

Her mind was in a jumbled whirl, and she felt quite helpless to control all that was happening. Strangers wanted to abduct her. Was she a prudish fool for fretting over a man sharing her quarters?

He sighed and rose. "The staff will keep quiet. They will not dare cross me, although I am sure they fear Aunt Miranda most of all. At times, even I am frightened of her," he said with a gentle humor no doubt meant to calm her. "Do not overset yourself, Grace. It is getting late, and we both need our sleep."

She nodded. "There is a spare blanket and pillow in the wardrobe."

He left her side and strode to it. "We'll talk further in the morning. Be strong, love. We're going to have busy days ahead of us."

Grace wiped her moist cheeks with the sleeve of her night-gown and watched as he removed the pillow and blanket from the wardrobe, then spread the blanket beneath the window. "Take the bed, Mr. Quinton. You obviously need the rest more than I do. I am better served by having you alert."

He shook his head. "I'll be fine right here. You take the bed and that's an order, Grace. I'm used to sleeping under far rougher conditions. You are not."

He smoothed the corner of his pallet and sighed as he glanced at her. "Are you going to fret and agonize all night?"

"I hope not. Give me a moment. You may think nothing of our sharing quarters, but it is still upsetting to me."

He approached her, staring down at her with his arms once again crossed over his broad chest. "Don't think of it that way."

"How can I not? What will the rest of your family say? I am sure they will realize it immediately. All they have to do is count the bedchambers to know something is amiss."

"If my mother and aunt are not up in arms about it, then the others won't say anything either. My cousins, Lorcan and Donal are active Crown agents. They were assigned to protect the ladies who are now their wives. I can assure you, that protection involved never letting them out of their sight day *and* night. None of them are going to say a word about our situation."

"But it is different. They married the women they were pro-tecting."

He glanced at the book that was now resting atop the night table. "Who is to say I will not marry you?"

"Marry me? No one in their right mind will come near me. I am worse than damaged goods. I am shunned and reviled by good society." She emitted a mirthless laugh. "Marriage to me? Why even mention such a thing?"

"Because of that book. Do you not understand what *The Book of Love* is?"

"Yes, I do. It is a guide to finding true love." She shook her head. "Something I may never encounter now. But there is no reason why you should not. It is very good reading. Actually, quite thoughtful in the way it explains what is important in a lasting and happy relationship. You ought to read it. I know you believe you know everything there is to know about love, but you are wrong. I don't think you understand the first thing about it."

He chuckled lightly. "Grace, insulting your protector is not a very clever thing to do. At least wait until the danger has passed before you berate me."

He uncrossed his arms and stepped away. "One more thing."

"Yes?" She watched him as he began to remove weapons off his person and set them out beside his pallet.

"Do not touch these. They are beside me in a precise order for a reason."

She climbed under her covers. "I have no intention of going anywhere near them or you. Sorry, I do not mean to sound so churlish. Mr. Quinton, I–"

"Call me Deklan. It is obvious Aunt Miranda already thinks of you as one of the family."

"She has asked me to stay on after the holidays and serve as her companion. I don't think I should remain beyond tonight. If what you say is true, am I not putting your entire family at risk? Do you think those in charge of this Home Office operation would permit me to return to my family's townhouse?"

"No, they won't allow it. I passed by it before coming here. The place has been ransacked, walls broken through in search of hidden loot. The servants are all gone. It is not feasible, Grace."

"But what if these agents harm your family?"

"They won't."

"How can you be so certain?"

"Because they are highly trained, and my family is not their target. Besides, they know I will hunt them down ruthlessly if they harm any of my kin. I am a man to be feared."

"Should I fear you?"

"No, Grace. I am going to protect you. And I agree, it is better you not remain here. We'll come up with a plan tomorrow."

"All right. I give you my promise, I will do everything in my power to see your family is unharmed."

He laughed lightly.

"Why are you laughing at me?"

"I'm laughing at myself."

"Why?"

"Because I think my nefarious brother and his matchmaking wife put *The Book of Love* in here on purpose."

"Rafe and Auggie? Why would they do such a thing? To what end?"

"Is it not obvious, Grace? It is their not so subtle way of telling me it is time I married." He emitted a low, throaty chuckle. "Would it not be the grandest jest if I were to marry you?"

CHAPTER THREE

"MARRY ME? YES, that is a hilarious notion. I suppose you think yourself quite the wit. I can see you holding your sides as you roll on the floor in stitches of laughter," Grace said, her wounded look unmistakable as she sat up in bed and stared at him with anguished eyes. "But I do not appreciate the jest at my expense. What makes you think I would ever consider marrying you? The very idea! It is idiotic. You are the last man I would ever marry."

"Is that so?" Deklan tried to keep the irritation out of his voice as he settled on his pallet, his hopes of a peaceful night's rest now dashed. He had not meant to belittle or insult her, and perhaps laughing heartily as he tossed the remark was in poor form. But he was merely commenting on his own reluctance to marry and his family's obvious schemes to bring his bachelor days to an end.

As for her, she was a beautiful girl. In time, once the Montford family scandal died down, some man would come forward and offer to marry her.

He had meant no harm by his comment, so why was she getting all worked up about it?

The last man she would ever marry? He was a catch. Women adored him.

Even she was attracted to him.

Oh, yes. The little innocent liked him even though she would never admit it to him or to herself.

He supposed he ought to let the matter drop since he was not in the market for a bride and was not about to propose to her, or anyone else, for that matter. He was here to find the crown and protect her while doing so, nothing more.

Was he not behaving like a gentleman and leaving her alone in that massive bed meant to be shared by two? So why was she so overset and kicking him in the teeth?

He was not trying to be cruel.

He liked her.

If ever he found himself ready to marry, she would be among his list of candidates. The girl was beautiful and sweet, even if she was tossing daggers at him at the moment.

But she was also tossing them at herself, beating herself down so badly it made his own heart hurt. He could not be angry with her because she had been through a rough few months since her family's downfall.

In truth, the ordeal would have worn down the hardiest souls.

Bollocks.

Knowing how she had suffered, he ought to have been more considerate with his words.

He gnashed his teeth as he tried to make amends. "Grace, do you see me rolling on the floor in gales of laughter? If anything, I was making fun of myself, not you. What is so terrible about marrying me? Most women consider me irresistible and would happily accept to be my wife."

She gave a dismissive snort.

"They would. And has it not crossed your mind that marriage to me would solve all your problems? Why are you so put off by it?"

She was still sitting up in bed, looking delectably prim and irresistible despite her scowl. "How can you ask such a question?"

Gad, those buttons at her throat were driving him insane. He wanted to open them one by one and slip his hand inside, but he was officially on duty now and could not act on any of his urges.

"What is wrong with such a plan? You would be marrying the Crown's top agent. No one would dare abduct you if you were my wife. I've worked hard to earn my reputation as England's most resourceful and feared weapon."

"Is this how you think of yourself? As a weapon?"

"Yes, and what is wrong with that? I am fierce, lethal, fearless. I protect England and its royal family. The job is dangerous, and I get it done."

She sighed. "I know you do. I do not mean to sound ungrateful. But you've given the idea of marriage no thought at all. It is obvious you have no desire to settle down. And to marry me? I suppose you are right, it is the most laughable thing imaginable."

"Don't say that, Grace. You dismiss your worth."

She gave another irreverent snort. "What worth? I have been stripped of all valuable possessions. I would bring nothing to the marriage but the clothes on my back."

"You would bring yourself and that is treasure enough for any man. I don't want to hear you belittling yourself again."

"I am only speaking the truth."

"No, you are merely repeating what the cruel gossips are saying. You've told me that you have done nothing wrong."

She nodded. "I would never cheat or hurt anyone."

"Then how are you not a treasure? If I were to propose to you, how would I be making a bad bargain? Should a man not want an honest, compassionate wife?"

"Are you mocking me again?"

"No, Grace. I haven't been mocking you at all." He had been lying on his pallet, propped up on his elbows while he studied the girl. He shifted position to sit up for a better look at her.

She now had her knees drawn up against her body. All he saw were her big, green eyes staring back at him.

Heaven help him, he really liked the look of this girl. "What about you, Grace? Would you not be interested in marrying into the Brayden clan? Anyone foolish enough to come after you would not only have to take me on but my entire family."

"Do stop. You are talking nonsense."

"Why is it nonsense? By marrying me, you would be better able to protect your mother and younger siblings. Does this not count for something?"

To his mind, those reasons were quite sensible and not idiotic at all. So why was she not making every attempt to persuade him to marry her?

"Go to sleep, Mr. Quinton."

"The name's Deklan."

She huffed again. "Go to sleep, Deklan."

"Why are you so resistant to marrying me?"

"Seriously?"

"Yes, seriously. Not that I am proposing, mind you. But it is not outside of the realm of possibility. I wouldn't have asked if I did not care to know the answer." He lay back on his pallet and propped his hands behind his head to stare at the ceiling. He could hear the light *whoosh* of her elegant sheets as she sank back and began to restlessly toss and turn in bed.

"First of all," she said softly, her voice achingly sweet, "marrying me would taint your family name. Deny it all you want, but it is the truth. I would never insult your loved ones in this fashion after they have been so kind to me. Second, I would rather remain a spinster than agree to a cold marriage. Oh, I know what you are thinking."

"You do? Pray tell, what is on my mind?" He was too peeved to bother to hide his sarcasm. He hadn't expected to be rebuffed and did not particularly enjoy the set down. Women fawned over him. They chased him. They offered themselves to him.

The threw themselves at him.

Why was Grace being so difficult?

"You are thinking that I would be so grateful to be rescued from my plight, I would say not a word when you went on with your life as it has always been. You would expect me to hold my tongue while you walked off to spend your nights cavorting with your lady friends."

"You think I would *cavort* after marriage?"

"Wouldn't you? After all, you would not be accepting to marry me out of love. It would be nothing more than an act of charity on your part. A convenient act of charity, because you could then disappear for days, months, years without a word, and not feel any remorse for leaving me behind."

"Why should you care? We hardly know each other."

"Precisely my point. You would come and go as it suits you without any thought for my feelings. What kind of life is that for me?"

"A safer life. I still do not see what is wrong with such a plan."

"Marriage is not a *plan*. Love is not something to be *bargained* over. To me, marriage is about love, commitment, and devotion. Did you think I am so beaten down that I would jump at the crumbs you offer?"

He emitted a soft growl. "Crumbs?"

"Yes. And now you must believe I am the most ungrateful girl you have ever met. But I cannot do it, Deklan. I cannot be in a marriage where love and companionship are an afterthought. I do not know where that leaves me." She gave a light, groaning laugh. "Probably in a terrible position. But it would truly break my heart if I found my husband with another woman. It would destroy me. I cannot help feeling this way."

"Grace, you are thinking too hard about this."

"And you are not thinking about it at all. You have grown used to answering to no one but your superiors in the Home Office, and I suspect you rarely answer to them. Would you ever agree to answer to me? Is this not what husbands and wives ought to do for each other?"

She sat up in bed once again and continued. "My heart can never be cold or detached. I may have fallen low, but I will not accept to be treated as a doormat."

He groaned.

This is why he avoided virgins.

"Grace, you are giving me a headache."

"I know. I am sorry."

"I would never marry you and simply abandon you."

"I know you are a good man and would never do it on purpose."

"My brother and mother would take you in and look after you whenever I am gone. They would have full access to my accounts to provide for all your needs."

"Exactly my point."

"Gad, you've lost me again. What is your point?"

"You will enlist your entire family in the cause…and give nothing of yourself."

"Enough, Grace. Well, that settles it. I'm glad I did not actually propose to you."

"So am I, Mr. Quinton."

"Deklan, damn it."

She sighed. "Deklan. I can feel the anger radiating off you. All the more reason why I could not marry you. You are used to getting your way…always. I can only imagine the stubborn child you must have been. Despite all these reasons, I'm sure you still think I am an idiot for refusing to consider you as a potential husband. Perhaps I am."

She sighed again. "My mother and siblings might resent me for not taking this obviously easy way out of our troubles. But it would not be easier for me. I am heartsick that love may be out of my reach now. However, I cannot give up hope. I want to find love. Even if that joy is never to be. I cannot give up yet. Perhaps I will come around in time and settle for less. I would just like something more than…more than a big, empty nothing."

He needed to read this book on love his brother had dumped atop his bureau.

Not that he wanted to be married. But…damnit…neither did he want Grace to reject him. Perhaps he was being peevish about it, but Grace was wrong.

He would make her a good husband.

She continued to chatter. "Let's concentrate on finding that crown and then go on with our separate lives. Do you think the Duke of Wooton might go easier on my mother and siblings if you did find it with my help? We don't need much. Perhaps a pleasant cottage in the countryside or by the sea. And a small allowance, enough for us to meet our basic needs."

How was he ever going to fall asleep now?

The girl had him completely in a roil.

He wanted to be angry with her for rejecting him—not that he had proposed to her—and yet he was proud of her for holding true to her convictions. Her decision was foolish and yet he did not think of her as foolish at all. If anything, he found her refreshing and endearing. Grace was the sort of girl who would take her marriage vows seriously.

It frustrated him to no end.

He did not know why it should.

He growled softly. "So, you would choose to live out your days as a struggling spinster rather than marry me?"

"Why are we still having this conversation? Have you decided to propose to me?"

"No, I am merely trying to figure you out."

"There is nothing complicated about me. You know my feelings on the matter." Grace blew out the candle and buried herself under the covers.

Deklan lay awake in the darkness, his eyes on her until the slivers of moonlight no longer illuminated her slender body.

The blasted girl was crying again and was lost in that big bed.

He wanted to climb in beside her and comfort her.

Lord, he ached to put his arms around her, swallow her up in his embrace.

Well, he wanted to do more than merely hold her. He would start with removing that fortress of a nightgown off her exquisite body.

Finally, after what seemed an eternity but could not have been more than twenty minutes, he heard her soft breaths.

Knowing she was safely asleep, he drifted off as well.

Morning came too soon.

The sun was not very strong in the winter except in the early hours immediately after dawn. The blasted golden orb now shone with an intense glare right in his eyes. Grace must have drawn aside the curtains.

She was that sunny sort of girl who probably woke up smiling and chirpy most mornings. Well, she might have done so in her happier days.

"It figures," he grumbled, blinking against the impossibly bright light as he sat up and stretched his aching muscles.

He slowly rolled to his feet.

Between the cold night air, the hard floor, and his tension in knowing Grace's bed was within arm's reach of him and he could not touch her, he was not about to greet the day in jolly humor.

Not that he was ever jolly.

"Good morning, Deklan," Grace said, her voice rippling through him like a soothing wave.

He turned, surprised to find her already washed and dressed.

She cast him a delicate smile. "I went next door to your mother's room to attend to myself. I did not want to disturb you."

Lord, this girl was even more beautiful by daylight.

Beautiful and elegant, even though her gown was simple and she wore little adornment. It was his habit to notice everything about a person, whether friend or enemy. Grace's gown was of dark green wool, the green of a pine forest, and it was another of those modest clothes that covered her from her throat to her toes. Her hair was done up in a braided twist at the nape of her neck, but it looked soft and golden on her. "What time is it?"

She blushed as she spoke to him. "Almost eight o'clock."

He glanced down at himself to make certain he was properly covered.

Yes, all clothes still on.

Although he needed to take a long piss. "Get out a moment, Grace. Please."

"Fresh chamber pot is under the bed," she said with an *eep* and scurried out. "I'll see you downstairs for breakfast."

He checked the wardrobe and was relieved to see most of the spare clothes he kept at Miranda's still neatly stowed inside. He hadn't bothered to look closer last night, just eager for the pillow and blanket so he could get to sleep. But this morning, he noticed Grace's gowns and dainty underclothes were in there along with his garments.

A warm feeling came over him.

He had never thought of sharing quarters with a woman before. In truth, he had not been thinking of it at all last night. No wonder Grace had kicked his arse soundly in their marriage discussions…all hypothetical, of course.

Only, it was beginning to feel quite real to him.

He liked that her clothes were beside his.

He'd thought she was beautiful last night and even more beautiful this morning.

He glanced at *The Book of Love* perched on the night table. It certainly was cutting a swath of destruction on the lives of every bachelor who came in contact with it. His brother, Rafe, had been the last to fall victim to its powers.

Perhaps he ought to read it tonight.

He liked to learn everything he could about an enemy, and this book was as much a threat to his freedom as any person, hostile country, or spy organization.

Someone knocked softly at his door. "Come in."

It was his Aunt Miranda. "You need a shave and a bath, dear boy. I've taken the liberty of assigning Tiswell as your personal valet. He's arranging for your bath to be brought up now. Do not worry about him. He is the soul of discretion. Been with me for decades. Come downstairs whenever you are ready."

"What about Grace?"

"What about her? She is downstairs with the family, her face in flames because she is so embarrassed about this situation. Your mother is there to calm her."

"I ought to be with her. I don't like the idea of her facing everyone alone. Even if my mother is with her, it isn't the same as if I were there."

Miranda's eyebrows shot up in surprise. "Since when are you so considerate of a woman's feelings?"

"Why does everyone think I am such an ogre? Grace is my responsibility now. Why would I not worry about her?"

"Worrying about keeping her alive is not the quite the same thing as caring for her feelings."

He moved aside as Tiswell rolled in the small copper tub and two footmen followed with laden water buckets.

"Well, I shall leave you to your grooming," Miranda said and strode out.

Deklan waited for the footmen to leave and shut the door behind them before he addressed the elderly butler who was to be his temporary valet. "What has my aunt told you, Tiswell?"

"She has confided that Miss Montford is in grave danger and you have been assigned to protect her. But I expect you are really asking about the fact you shared the same room last night."

"The men who are coming for her are highly trained professionals and are ruthless. I cannot leave her on her own for a moment, especially not after darkness falls. This is the time they are most likely to strike."

Tiswell poured water into the tub. "I understand, Mr. Quinton. Truly, I do. Miss Montford is a gently bred lady. A true lady in every sense. I speak for the entire staff. We can see how distraught she is about her family's scandal. And now this morning she…well, she came downstairs looking like a wounded kitten."

He nodded, for this was precisely how she had appeared to him last night. "Yes, she does have that soft look about her, doesn't she?"

"It is easy to see how humiliated she is by this arrangement."

"It will only be for the week."

"But it is Christmas week when all your family is around.

Half of them are already here and more will come tonight for Lady Miranda's dinner party. Miss Montford will be among you, pretending to be happy while she is desperately missing her family and ashamed to be living with a man in her bedchamber. At the end of the week, Lady Miranda will have everyone over again to decorate the house with boughs of holly, velvet ribbons, and mistletoe. This will only make the dear girl feel worse."

"I wish it could be otherwise," Deklan said. "And I hope the staff will keep their mouths shut. Will you let them know I will not tolerate any insolence toward her?"

He nodded. "No one will breathe a word."

They spoke no more about Grace as he quickly bathed, washed his hair, then shaved and dressed. He gave himself a final inspection while Tiswell finished adjusting his cravat, and then went downstairs to join Grace and his family.

He was delighted to find his young nephew at the breakfast table. "Uncle Deklan!"

He scooped the boy up in his arms and gave him a hug. "Sam, you've grown so big. And you're looking more like your father every day."

After greeting the boy, who quickly ran off to join the other children playing upstairs, he greeted the other members of his family. His cousin, Caleb Brayden, was down from Scarborough with his wife, Faith. "We intended to stay with Marcus and Lara," Caleb said, referring to his brother and his brother's wife, "but Aunt Miranda would not hear of it. So, we are settled here for the next few days."

"It is quite convenient since most of the festivities will take place right here," Faith chimed in. "I have only to walk upstairs to put the little ones to their naps. It is much nicer than having to drag them around in the cold."

It also felt good to see his cousins, Shayne, Donal, and Lorcan, all with their lovely wives. But he regarded Lorcan, puzzled as to why he was here. He and Cammy had their own townhouse in London. So why were they all packed in at Aunt Miranda's?

Lorcan emitted a hearty chuckle, understanding the direction of his thoughts. "We may be fierce enough to take down enemy agents, treasonous rebels, and vicious killers, but not one of us dares defy a summons from Aunt Miranda."

Shayne put his arm along the back of his wife's chair and nodded. "So here we all are. It's rather nice, actually. Just like old times, except the wildebeests are too big to toss into one room. We've taken over the entire house. Miranda's sons will be along later with their wives. So will James and Romulus with their wives, even Gabrielle," he said, referring to James and Romulus's sister, "will be arriving with her husband and their brood. They were originally going to spend the holidays with her husband's family in York, but Gabby could not pass up this touching family reunion."

Deklan ran a hand through his hair as he glanced at Grace.

"I know," Lorcan said quietly. "Dozens of Braydens, Quintons, and their wives and children here to celebrate while her family is in shambles. We tried to talk to Miranda about the situation. Cammy and I offered to take the visiting family into our home. Her own sons offered the same. We certainly are not short on family residences in London since most of us already live here. But she will not hear of it."

Deklan nodded. "Well, Grace cannot stay here. Her presence will put your wives and children at risk. Even though I think the risk is low, that it even exists is cause for concern. I plan to move Grace out of here tonight."

"But what of the family dinner? Miranda will have your hide if you do not attend."

"I'll move Grace out of here once it is over, or tomorrow at the latest."

His cousin, Donal, had been listening in and shook his head. "Leave her with us for now. Would she not be an easier target if you moved her away?"

"That will be my problem to figure out."

"If she is here, we can all protect her," Shayne remarked. "I expect the Christmas festivities will be hard on her considering her situation, but it cannot be worse than sitting through the holiday on her own. Just think about it, Deklan."

Deklan would have removed Grace already were he dealing with any family but his own. His cousins Shayne, Donal, and Lorcan were trained agents of the Crown. Shayne had since retired to become Taunton's magistrate, but he had not lost any of his abilities. As for his cousin Caleb, he was an army general and so was Caleb's brother, Marcus.

Miranda's sons, who would be joining them later, were just as fierce.

Lorcan cleared his throat. "Let me know if I can help in any way. I'm still the best tracker Wooton has in his service."

"I've thought of it," Deklan said with a nod. "We may need your talents. One week to discover the whereabouts of that stolen crown does not give us much time. Has Miranda told you the rest of it?"

He nodded. "Yes, she told us whatever you revealed to her. We won't let Grace come to harm."

Deklan said nothing.

While he trusted his family and was glad to have their support, he did not particularly wish to encourage their further involvement. Perhaps he would have to avail himself of Lorcan's tracking skills, but this was as far as he wanted to go. The situation could get ugly, and he would never forgive himself if any of his loved ones were injured.

He piled a plate high with kippers, bacon, boiled tomatoes, eggs, and two raisin scones, then took a seat beside Grace who looked like she just wanted to be blindfolded and led against the wall to be shot. "Have you had enough to eat?" he asked, shoveling eggs into his mouth.

"I wasn't very hungry."

He dropped one of his kippers onto her plate. "Here, eat this. We have a long few days ahead of us. You have to keep up your strength."

She did not look pleased but made no protest. Mostly she poked her food from side to side. She already considered him an overbearing ogre, so he did not force the issue. She was loathe to marry him, so why give her more reasons to refuse him should he ever offer for her?

Of course, if he did propose, it would be to protect her and nothing more. He'd made that clear, and she had been just as clear in rebuffing the suggestion.

Still, it irked him.

Why wasn't the girl leaping at the possibility of becoming his wife?

If he were in her position, he would not have hesitated to align himself with a powerful family. One of the advantages was their useful connections.

Donal had married the Duke of Wooton's daughter, Lucy. Wooton, top man at the Home Office and otherwise known as the Duke of Ice because of his cold and calculating manner, doted on his daughter.

Why would Grace not use this connection to her advantage?

Deklan was not surprised to see Wooton stride in a short while later. After greeting Miranda and the rest of the family, he nodded to Deklan and motioned him over. "I see you've met Grace Montford."

Deklan nodded. "You might have warned me she was here."

"I did not know it when I sent off your orders. In truth, I never considered that your Aunt Miranda would bring her under her own roof. The Montfords are pariahs in society. Leave it to your aunt to thumb her nose at public sentiment. When did you get back to London? Have you had the chance to speak to the girl?"

"I got in late last night. Yes, she'll do all she can to help us."

Wooton arched an eyebrow. "You trust her?"

"Yes, and I need her to speak to her father as soon as possible."

"Out of the question. I cannot allow her to pass along secret plans to him."

"Grace is not involved in their crimes and will do nothing of the sort. You'll see for yourself once you bother to get to know her." He glanced toward the buffet where she now stood looking fragile and achingly vulnerable. "I'll escort her into Miranda's study where the three of us can speak in private."

Wooton nodded. "Very well. You had better be right about her or I shall have your hide. The security of England is at stake."

Deklan dismissed the comment. "When have I ever been wrong?"

He crossed the room to where Grace stood and took the empty plate she was now holding out of her hands. He knew it was merely an avoidance tactic on her part since she hadn't eaten anything on her first plate and fooled no one by pretending to take another helping for herself. "Come along, Grace. This is your chance to persuade the Duke of Ice about the advantages of seeing your father."

He held out his arm, and she grabbed onto it as though it were a lifeline.

He led her into the study.

Wooton was pacing in front of the large desk in the center of the elegant, wood-paneled chamber. "Lady Miranda is quite fond of you," he said in a surly bark before Grace had taken her seat.

She tipped her head up to meet the old duke's stern gaze.

Deklan liked that bit of fire he saw in her eyes.

"I am fond of her as well." Grace tried to sound as surly as the duke but her voice was too sweet to pull it off. "She has been very kind to me. However, I gather I have enemies because of my brother's dealings. Richard is a vain and arrogant man. Thinks only of himself. I have no doubt you've noticed."

The duke nodded.

Grace spared a glance at Deklan before returning her attention to the duke. "I have explained the situation to Mr. Quinton. My brother will never tell me where to find this missing crown. There is no point in having me talk to him, at least not yet. But you must let me speak to my father."

Wooton frowned. "We've questioned him many times over on the matter. What makes you think he will reveal something useful to you?"

"He may not. But what have you got to lose by allowing me to try? My father has done a terrible thing, but he was influenced by my brother…my half-brother. Richard's mother was my father's first wife. Well, I suppose you know this. I expect you have made it a point to learn everything you can about each member of my family."

She took a breath and continued. "Truly, my father has done foolish things. Dishonest things. But he is not a cruel or evil man. I know he will want to make matters right. He may not even realize he knows something relevant about the crown's theft. Let him open up to me. Do I not have as much at stake in the outcome as anyone else?"

"All right," Wooton said with a curt nod. "However, Quinton stays with you and your father while you speak."

Deklan shook his head "No, Your Grace. He needs to be alone with his daughter."

Grace cast him an approving smile.

The duke was not yet persuaded. "The situation is enough of a mess. I don't need the Montfords planning an escape and using Miss Montford here as their go-between to pull it off."

"She has no intention of helping them out," Deklan said, not about to give in. "Aunt Miranda trusts her and that is good enough for me."

Grace smiled at him again. "Nor do I intend to be held prisoner by some foreign government. I don't even know which country suffered the loss of their royal crown."

"We cannot tell you that, Grace." Deklan cast her a warning glance. "All hell will break loose if word gets out to the newspapers. The matter is so sensitive, this foreign government will not even acknowledge the crown has been stolen."

"I see. Do you think my brother arranged for its theft because he was paid by an opposing faction hoping to bring down their reigning monarch? Should you not start by looking there for the missing crown?"

"We have done, Miss Montford," the duke said. "Mr. Quinton spent the last month infiltrating their operations abroad. We are fairly confident they do not have it since they have now sent agents here who are also desperately searching for it."

Grace turned to Deklan in alarm. "Then it isn't only the foreign government I ought to be worried about, but the opposition factions, too. What if those men come after me?"

Wooton exchanged a look with him.

No, he hadn't told her all of it.

Was it not bad enough a major foreign power wanted her as hostage? He did not need Grace falling apart when she learned the opposition parties also wanted to abduct her. Damn it. She was realizing it now and was not at all happy with him for withholding the information. "When were you going to tell me this? As they bound and gagged me?"

Well, he preferred seeing her angry rather than whimpering or cowering. "I was going to tell you today. I dared not say more last night. Too much was already being tossed at you. I knew about the danger and that was enough."

She was a soft thing, but looked ready to punch him. "I want to hear all of it now. What else have you not told me?"

"We've hit a wall at every turn. Do not toss daggers at me, Grace. There wasn't time to tell you all of it last night. What we do know, besides the opposition faction also wanting to get their hands on you, is there were two bidders for this crown and each made a hefty deposit into a secret account held by your father and brother. These two are powerful private gentlemen, wealthy as Croesus, who might have funded this sort of theft simply for the thrill of possessing something uniquely valuable."

She turned to regard the duke. "Your Grace, have you spoken to these gentlemen? Is it possible one of them received the crown?"

"They haven't, my dear. We know they are just as hungry to get their hands on it as we are. Nor do they have any idea where your brother might have hidden it. We've questioned them, searched their properties, and managed to recover a good quantity of stolen valuables."

"But not the crown?"

The duke grimaced. "Not this elusive crown. They are now being held under house arrest and I have several of my best men investigating their recent activities. In addition, I have planted reliable informants in their households. We take nothing for granted and are using all means possible to discover its whereabouts. Every precaution is being taken to intercept them should they discover its whereabouts before we do."

"And we have not dismissed the possibility they may also send men to abduct you," Deklan added. "For some reason, everyone involved in this blasted mess has gotten it into their heads that holding you hostage will gain them leverage over your father and brother."

Her eyes widened. "But it isn't so."

Deklan had not meant to add to her worries, but she wanted the truth and here it was. Best she know of all potential dangers. How else was she ever to trust him? "All the more reason why you need me to guard you."

"All the more reason why I must talk to my father right away. Will you allow me to talk to him, Your Grace?"

"Yes, Miss Montford," he said, obviously unhappy about his decision. "I suppose we have little choice but to trust you for now."

"And will I be allowed to speak to him alone?"

"Yes." The duke breathed a resigned sigh. "Only this one time. Mr. Quinton will remain with you at all other times. Understood? If you dare attempt to elude him, I will have you locked up."

Deklan did not like the rough manner with which the duke spoke to Grace, however, she seemed to handle the threat well enough. "I have no intention of escaping his company. In truth, I was thinking I ought to have more guards on me."

"No, Miss Montford. You are in safer hands with Mr. Quinton than you would be with an army of guards at your disposal. He is all the protection you will need and all you will get."

The duke borrowed stationery from Lady Miranda's desk, scribbled a quick note and marked it with his seal. He handed it to Deklan and then strolled out to join the family festivities.

Grace stared at the parchment now in Deklan's hand.

He nodded. "Yes, Grace. It is the order permitting you to see your father. I suggest we attend to this immediately. Bundle up and put on some sturdy walking boots. We're going to slip out the back way and keep to the mews and alleyways."

"How far are we walking?"

"Can't tell you that. We'll flag down a hackney once we are out of Mayfair. Taking a family carriage is out of the question. We would attract too much attention."

"Then you think Lady Miranda's house is already being watched?"

He gave a reluctant nod. "I know it is."

She surprised him by taking his hand. "I thought I could be brave about this. But I am officially scared. What are our chances of ever finding this crown?"

Slim to none, but he was not about to tell her that. "We are working every angle, Grace. Chances are very good."

"You needn't lie to me to spare my feelings."

"Come on. Gather your gloves, scarf, and hat."

He was not a religious man, nor was he ever one for wishing upon a star or believing in Christmas miracles.

This girl was so innocent.

He had been working in the dregs too long and forgotten that sweet, decent girls like Grace still existed.

He watched her fuss with her hat, tipping it at just the right angle before she pinned it to her hair. His gaze remained on her while she slipped her slender fingers into her gloves and then tucked a scarf about her throat. "I'm ready," she said and turned back to him with a fragile smile.

She devastated his senses.

"Stay close." He tucked her cloak about her shoulders, then took her hand and led her to the kitchen door used only by Miranda's servants.

"What now?" Grace asked when he nudged her slightly behind him.

"We wait for my cousins to create a distraction out front."

"Deklan, I'm sorry for being surly to you last night. I do appreciate everything you are doing for me."

Truly, he was not a praying man.

But every blackguard and potentate connected to this crown was after Grace. It would be a miracle if she came out of this nasty affair unharmed.

He glanced upward and made a silent plea.

Do you think you can spare a miracle for Grace?

CHAPTER FOUR

"How are you, Papa?" Grace's heart tore to shreds as she sat across from her father and noticed the dull resignation in his eyes.

"How can I be anything but disheartened? They treat me like a common criminal."

Grace wanted to point out that he was a common criminal but held her tongue. It would only anger him, and she was already worried about not gaining his cooperation. He had not greeted her warmly and had yet to ask about how she or others in the family were faring through the ordeal.

"Gracie, I have been treated abominably, and you must do something about it."

"I am trying, Papa. But would it not help if you were more cooperative?" She studied him, looking for signs of abuse but found none. He sounded surprisingly robust and appeared to be well treated. He was groomed and there were no obvious signs of his having been beaten, no bruises or marks on his wrists to indicate he had ever been restrained.

Thank goodness.

Grace cleared her throat. "Perhaps they would release you if–"

"I am not some ruffian off the streets. I am a viscount and should be extended the privileges of my rank."

She thought he had been suffering from remorse, but he

appeared to be suffering from nothing more than the annoyance of being caught.

He was not even feeling shame.

Not a trace of shame, just irritation.

Did he not see himself as a thief?

What may have started as complicity in assisting gentlemen of his station to secretly sell their valuable works of art had soon led him and her brother down a more sinister path. As much as she loved her father, she now knew he was not as honest as he should have been. Being born to privilege and having a taste for the finer things in life had skewed his perception of right and wrong.

He obviously felt entitled.

Somehow, being born into privilege made everything he did, whether hurtful or dishonest, all right.

Had he always felt this way?

How could she not have noticed this pettiness in his character?

"I am not well, my darling." He placed a hand over his heart, no doubt hoping to gain her sympathy. "You must find a way to get me out of my confinement."

"Have you asked for a doctor to see you?"

He shook his head. "No, why bother when I know they want me to suffer?"

"Papa, please tell me the truth. I am dealing with enough just now trying to protect Mama and the children. You haven't even asked about them. Are you merely griping or truly ill?"

He dropped his hand from his heart. "Very well, ignore my needs."

"I am not ignoring you. All I ask is the truth from you." She looked around the townhouse Deklan had brought her to in an unfamiliar part of London. Perhaps they were not even in London anymore.

They certainly were not within the walls of old London now.

No doubt another bit of misinformation about his whereabouts meant to confuse her and anyone else interested in finding her father.

Deklan had hailed a passing hackney as soon as they were out of Mayfair. Their progress was slow because the London streets were crowded, but even so, they had been in that carriage a very long time.

Well, they were here now and this house did not remotely resemble a prison. It was elegantly furnished and comfortably heated despite the wintery chill outdoors. She and her father were seated across the table from each other in what appeared to be a dining room.

Although small by society standards, it was more than adequate for their meeting. After all, they were not hosting a dinner party for the London *ton*. "Papa, answer me. Are you truly ill? You must tell me the truth."

"The truth? Who knows what it is anymore? Well, Gracie? Do I have your promise to help me?"

"I am trying my best, Papa. But you have to help me, too. What can you tell me about the theft of the royal crown?"

"That again?" He slammed his fist on the table. "Is this the only reason you have bothered to see me? Have they turned you against me? Told you terrible lies about me?"

She wanted to throttle her father. "Papa, please calm down. And do not insult me. I have been trying for weeks to see you, but they would not let me until now. I am finally here. Do not waste precious time by declaring your innocence when we both know the nature of the enterprise you and Richard were carrying on."

"Now, Gracie–"

"No, do not coddle me. You were complicit in the art thefts. Perhaps not the more serious ones pulled off by Richard, but you had to suspect something dangerous was going on. I will do all I can to help you, but you cannot lie to me. You have to give over that foreign crown or we shall all die. Do you understand me? You and Richard are not the only ones at risk. Mama, the children, and I will be harmed if it is not returned."

"Is this what the Duke of Ice has told you? Horrid man. He will stoop to any means, even frighten you, to get that information out of me."

"If he were that horrid, he would have beaten the truth out of you by now. But you appear to be doing just fine. And yes, I believe the Duke of Wooton when he tells me I am in danger. That foreign government now wants me as their hostage. They have sent agents to abduct me. So, what are you going to do, Papa? Continue to lie and stall? Or are you finally ready to admit the truth?"

He glared at her, but she stood her ground. "If you have no care for your family, then think of England. Our country might end up in a war because of that theft. Will you end your days as a traitor as well as a thief?"

He stood up in indignation. "Get out."

She stood as well, shocked by his response. "Is this all you have to say to me? I just told you I am to be taken hostage, held as a prisoner in some foreign land because of your crimes."

"You are in England. We are civilized here. Wooton is just trying to scare you. Believe me, Gracie. I know how that man operates."

"You are deluded if you believe any of us are safe." Grace had never spoken so harshly to her father before, but how else was she to make him understand the severe repercussions of his silence? "So that's it? You will now abandon all of us? Your wife? Your children? Your country? And for what? Riches you will never be free to enjoy? Papa, so help me, I will throttle you myself if you do not agree to help them recover it."

"Ungrateful child."

She gasped. "This is what you think I am? I am ready to do everything in my power to save you. But I am helpless unless you take this first step. Where is the crown?"

He shook his head and sank back in his seat. "I don't know, Gracie. That is the truth. It was all Richard's idea, and I could do nothing to stop him. You know how your brother gets when he wants something."

"I do know, but you are the parent and the one in charge." She shook her head and tried to ignore the pang to her heart. She could tell her father was lying. He was actually *lying* to her when he claimed he did not know of the crown's whereabouts. "Please, Papa. Do you not understand the danger? I have no idea what will happen to me if this royal family manages to abduct me. And what of Mama and the children? Who will look after them if I am not able to do it?"

Her father glanced around and then leaned forward to whisper in her ear. "Hold strong, child. Richard and I have a plan. Do not believe anything Wooton or his henchmen have told you."

"Henchmen?" She drew away, unable to hide her disgust. "They are loyal agents of the Crown."

"They are liars and thieves, no better than me or Richard. They merely operate under the protection of the English monarchy. Beware of Wooton. He is a master at manipulation. I can see he has succeeded in preying on your innocent and trusting nature."

"He has come to me for help in recovering the crown. I don't care if I am being used by him. It does not alter the fact that Richard stole this valuable item. It needs to be recovered before something worse happens. You have to help them, Papa. Whatever ploy you and Richard have devised will not work. You need to think of Mama and the rest of us. We have lost everything."

She motioned to the room they were in, noting the fire blazing in the hearth. "Look at you, residing in this fine residence and obviously given every comfort while we are forced to struggle. Will you do nothing for your family?"

"Do not threaten me, Gracie. I gave you all a good life."

"By stealing from others." She clenched her hands. She had never seen this petty side of her father before and truly detested it. "Mama is now destitute. Our homes have been ripped to pieces. She and the children are living amid the wreckage of our country manor. Why does this not sink into your head? You cannot save Richard, so why will you not help save us?"

"Your mother's family will take you all in."

"No, they won't. They refuse to have anything to do with us."

He frowned. "Why are you being so difficult?"

She returned his frown with one of her own. "Why are you?"

Had she thought to come face to face with a remorseful and cooperative father? She did not even recognize this man. She held back her anguish and tried once more to make him see reason. "The Duke of Wooton says there are two men who paid you and Richard for this crown. Papa, had you started a bidding war between them? I know you received their deposits. So, in addition to this angry foreign government, you now have two rich and powerful men furious with you for playing one against the other, and wanting revenge."

"They'll stay quiet until the matter blows over for fear of drawing attention to themselves."

She sighed. "You have a glib answer for everything, don't you? Those men are going nowhere for a very long time. They are now sitting under house arrest because other stolen articles were found in their homes. They have no access to their bank accounts and will not be able to help you bribe your way to freedom. Papa, please. End this misery for all of us. Tell me where Richard has hidden this treasure."

"Go home, Gracie. This discussion is getting us nowhere."

"Home? Have you not listened to a word I've said? I have no home anymore. I don't even recognize you, my own father."

He suddenly reached out and grabbed her hands. "Silly child, you are my own flesh and blood and I will always do my best to protect you. Trust me to know what I am doing. Do you not realize that crown is our only bargaining chip? We cannot give it up now."

"Even if it means I will be abducted? Perhaps enslaved or

murdered?"

"Do not get hysterical. You are not in any danger. Let me and Richard handle matters. Wooton must be getting desperate if he is using you to press me for information. That is very good. Have they encouraged you to speak to Richard?"

"No, they will not allow me to see him." Grace turned toward the door because she could no longer stomach her father's presence and wanted to leave. But she had not yet succeeded in her purpose, so she remained. "Wooton believes you will use me as a means of conveying information to Richard. I see he is right. This is all I am to you, a messenger. I doubt they will let me see you again. I'm sorry, Papa. I really thought you would recognize the error of your ways and agree to help."

"Enough, Gracie." He crossed his arms over his chest. "Just go. They have corrupted you, and you are now useless to me or Richard."

"Useless? I have been a devoted daughter to you all my life."

"Well, you are no daughter to me now."

He could not have hurt her worse if he'd physically struck her. "I'm sorry to have disappointed you, Papa. Ask those holding you to send word to me if you ever change your mind."

She walked out with her head held high.

The two guards standing just outside now entered the dining room and shut the door behind them, leaving her alone in the hall with Deklan.

He had been waiting for her, no doubt prowling up and down as she spoke to her father. "Oh, bloody hell. Grace, what happened?"

She took several shattered breaths before responding. "He never even asked how Mama and the children were doing. Not once. All he thought about was himself. I have two younger sisters and a younger brother, all of them under the age of ten. Oh, I suppose you know this."

He nodded. "Wooton's reports are always thorough."

"I told my father how badly they were struggling, and he did not even bat an eyelash. I thought he loved us."

He gave her cheek a light caress, running his thumb over it to wipe away a fallen tear. "I'm sure he does in his own way."

She laughed bitterly and shook her head. "Yes, in his own selfish and indulgent way. I thought Richard had inherited his bad traits from his mother, who was never known as a kind person. Truly, she had a horrid reputation. But I see she is not the only one to blame for the flaws in Richard's character."

"Did your father tell you anything helpful?"

"No. I'm so sorry, Deklan. I feel this meeting was a complete waste of time. If anything, he now believes he holds the upper hand and will never give over the information without large concessions from Wooton. I've hurt rather than helped."

"No, Grace. None of this is your fault." He placed an arm around her and led her down the hall. "Well, at least you got to see him."

She cast him a mirthless smile. "And had a rude awakening. How could I have been so blind to his faults?"

"He always showed you his best side."

"What do we do now? Would you allow me to see the Montford Gallery ledgers? I wasn't involved in running the business, but there may be something that strikes me as odd. Would you ever let me speak to Richard? I doubt he will give me any helpful information, but it cannot hurt to try."

"I don't think Wooton will allow it. He doesn't trust you yet and will believe your father gave you information to carry to your brother."

She wasn't surprised. "I see. Yes, of course. Do you believe I would do such a thing?"

He paused as they were about to walk downstairs and gave her cheek a light caress. "No, I know you wouldn't."

She emitted a ragged sigh. "My father suggested it, but I refused. In hindsight, that was stupid of me, wasn't it? He might have divulged something useful. But I was so angry with him, I wanted no part of his continued deceit. Oh, why did I not play along? Stupid. Stupid."

"Stop kicking yourself. None of this is your fault. Come on, love." He placed her arm in his and led her downstairs. "We'll figure out something else."

He called for their cloaks and gloves.

"Are you not angry? It is obvious I've made a muddle of this visit. Drat! Why did I not play along? So stupid of me."

"Stop that, Grace. You did your best, and that is all I can ask of you. You are not a practiced liar. I know how difficult it was for you to see your father and feel the weight of his betrayal upon your shoulders. It is not your burden to bear. You did your best under difficult circumstances."

"I allowed my feelings to get the better of me. I should have agreed to act as messenger between him and my brother. You know it was a big mistake on my part."

The guard returned with their belongings.

Deklan took her cloak and wrapped it around her shoulders. "He would have seen through your attempt," he said, his manner surprisingly gentle. "Never be ashamed because you have a lovely, honest heart."

She looked up at him in surprise. "Why are you being so nice to me? I've made things worse. And how can you be so sure about me? What if he did tell me and I am lying to you?"

He stared at her and then cast her a melting smile. "I am able to see into your soul, Grace Montford. It is a beautiful soul. Open. Honest. You can hide nothing from me."

"I bet you say that to all the girls," she said in a gentle jest.

"This is why I am so successful as an agent of the Crown, this ability to sense a person's character and know when I am being fed false information. Besides, you are the worst liar I have ever encountered."

She cast him a wry smile. "I suppose I am."

He gave her a light kiss on the cheek. "Don't ever change, Grace. And don't ever apologize to me or anyone else for being yourself. You are perfectly lovely just as you are."

He made certain she was properly bundled up, and then took her arm again to lead her out of the townhouse. They were met with a blast of icy wind. "Damn weather," he grumbled, hailing down a passing hackney. "Climb in. Quickly, Grace, before the snake tattoo freezes off my arse."

She tried not to laugh but could not help a giggle escaping her lips.

He settled in beside her, his grin irresistible.

She turned away before she made a moon-eyed fool of herself. This gorgeous man was too clever and quick, easily able to read her thoughts. She peered out the window and pretended to study their surroundings.

The window was smudged, and she could see very little through the blur. Sighing, she removed her handkerchief from her reticule and attempted to clean off the pane. But the dirt was on the outside.

Well, she supposed it mattered little since she had no idea where they were. Whatever she could make out was still unfamiliar to her.

She sat back as their conveyance rolled past rows of neatly maintained homes. Deklan had obviously taken her to a part of town she had never seen before, somewhere not in London proper but on the outskirts perhaps. She did not recognize any church spires or towers off in the distance. "Where are we?"

"Cannot tell you. Best you don't know." He turned to stare out of his smudged window. Perhaps these smudges were put there on purpose, not only to keep her from seeing out, but also to prevent anyone from seeing in and identifying the occupants inside.

Perhaps this passing hackney had not come along merely by chance.

Was the driver another agent of the Crown?

She asked Deklan.

He ignored the question, so she asked another. "Where are we going next? Can you tell me that?"

He shifted his big body closer. "Actually, I thought we would just ride around for a while and talk right here. But I could take you back to Aunt Miranda's if you prefer. It will be noisy, the house turned upside down with all the children running around and Miranda fussing over tonight's dinner party."

"Here is fine." In truth, they needed to talk. Their visit to her father had only raised more questions in her mind. "Do you have any more questions for me?"

He shook his head. "We are going to take another approach."

But he said nothing further, merely raised the seat on the opposite bench, withdrew a woolen blanket from its storage compartment, and tucked it neatly around her legs. "You looked cold. Does this help?"

She nodded. "Yes, but what did you mean when you said we are taking another approach? I'm ready. What do you wish to know?"

"Tell me about your brother."

"Richard? Well, he is the eldest of my father's children. He was eight years old when I was born. We did not see much of each other after he went off to Eton and then to university at Oxford. I've already told the Crown agents all this. I also spoke at length to your brother, Rafe, since he is the one who uncovered what my family was doing. He was investigating possible art thefts in Exeter, and the trail led him straight to my family's London art gallery."

"I've read the reports. It isn't the same as hearing the story firsthand from you. Would you mind repeating what you told Rafe and the other Crown investigators? You may have revealed something none of you realized was significant at the time."

She nodded. "Let's give it a try. Where would you like me to start? I don't know much about what went on in Exeter. I never accompanied him there. How far back in our lives do you wish me to go?"

"Let's start with just this past year."

"That is easy enough. My mother and the younger children

remained in the country most of the time while I joined Richard and my father in town. You see, I was preparing for my upcoming society debut and we had scheduled appointments with my modiste. Mama was supposed to join me, but the children got sick and then she got sick…nothing serious, but by the time they had all recovered, it was decided she should stay in the country."

"So, you remained here alone with your brother and father?"

"Yes, but I was kept quite busy taking lessons on the pianoforte and dance instruction, visiting friends. Constant visits to my modiste. What a silly waste of time it all was, and pointless now."

He took her gloved hand in his.

She glanced at him in surprise.

He cast her a wry smile. "I am not letting go of you, Grace. I want you to know we are in this together. Whatever happens, know that I will protect you."

Deklan was arrogant and annoyingly confident. She knew he had no use for women beyond having them as occasional bedmates, and doubted he had ever been in love, certainly not the deep, devoted kind, or ever seriously courted a young lady.

In all likelihood, he was terrible husband material.

She wanted to dislike him but simply couldn't.

He was being incredibly kind to her at the moment.

Her father would say he was manipulating her.

Perhaps he was.

After the ordeal of these past few months, she did not care.

She was starved for companionship and craved any morsel of affection. Not that he was being affectionate. He was merely being thoughtful and tossing her an occasional compliment.

At this low point in her life, the smallest kindness was precious to her.

However, she drew her hand away.

She wasn't trying to be rude, merely trying to save herself from growing too attached to him. Their acquaintance would not last longer than a week, for they would either find the crown and he would then move on to his next assignment…or they would not find the crown and she would be sent off as hostage to that foreign royal family.

Assuming someone else did not abduct her first.

He took her hand once more and gave it a light squeeze to regain her attention. "You are getting lost in your thoughts, Grace. What is on your mind?"

"Nothing worth discussing. Go ahead and ask the rest of your questions."

He arched an eyebrow but did not pursue the comment. "All right, next question. If your mother remained at the Montford country estate, then who served as your chaperone in London? Someone must have accompanied you whenever you went to the shops, and who sat in the room with you and your instructors when you had your lessons?"

"My maid, Agnes, was assigned the task. She remained by my side night and day. I took her with me wherever I went. She's gone now. Wooton scared all the servants off."

"No, I believe he intends to send some of them up to your country estate to assist your mother and siblings."

The comment caught her by surprise. "Truly? I hope Agnes is among them. She was quite devoted to the family. I hope so, for my mother's sake. Well, for the sake of Agnes as well. It cannot be easy to find employment without good references, and who would take her on if they knew she came from the Montford family?"

"So, you went around with just your maid as chaperone?"

"Not at all. My father also saw to it that I had two footmen accompany me on errands and social calls. I was guarded at all times."

"What about the evening entertainments?"

"I did not go out very much since I was not yet officially out in society. But my father served as my escort whenever I did."

"And not Richard?"

She cleared her throat. "No, he enjoyed...um, faster entertainments. My father would not allow me anywhere near him and his friends. They were gamblers and often spent evenings at the copper hells and less reputable clubs. Do you think he might have hidden the crown in one of those places?"

"No, Grace. It is unlikely. There is no honor among thieves. He could not trust something so valuable to anyone who worked in those places or any friend of his who frequented the hells along with him."

"I see. Well, my father was a member of several reputable clubs. Do you think it might be hidden in one of those?"

"Not there either. Too many people have access to those rooms. There is no privacy in a club. I'm thinking it is somewhere only Richard or your father would have access."

She pursed her lips in thought. "In London? But the Crown agents tore everything apart here. They even discovered several secret passageways and chambers in our home. I had no idea these hiding places existed. I'm sure you read about those in your reports."

"I did. So tell me about places outside of London. Did your father or Richard travel anywhere on a regular basis?"

"I've already been asked this question several times. All I can think of is our country estate. That has also been searched high and low. The house, barn, and stables. Your agents even discovered an abandoned well and searched it. We had no idea it ever existed."

At his urging, she listed every detail she could recall about their country home.

He then asked her about her father's daily routine in London.

"He never wavered from it," she said. "He rose promptly at seven each morning, washed and dressed, and then joined me in the breakfast room at eight o'clock. Mother, when she was in town, preferred to take her breakfast in her bedchamber. My father had eggs and coffee while reading the morning papers. When finished, he would have his carriage summoned and head to the art gallery. He arrived there promptly at nine. The driver would then return and take me on my calls for the day."

"How do you know your father did not stop elsewhere?"

"Oh, I suppose I don't. But the Crown agents questioned his driver, and this is what he told them. I don't think Crawford would lie about this, especially under their questioning."

"And what of your brother, Richard? Did he ride with your father?"

"No, he rarely came downstairs before noontime because he stayed out with his friends until all hours. But Papa did not mind his coming late to work because the art gallery rarely got busy before midday. Richard would show up by then and do whatever it was he did there. Truly, I have no idea what his function was at the gallery. I wasn't involved in the business, and my father was adamant no daughter of his would ever soil her dainty hands by working."

She shook her head. "I thought he was just behaving like an old fossil who thought women belonged in the home and their only role was to bear children. As it turns out, he simply did not want us interfering with what he and my brother were doing. By the way, my brother was not a wastrel when it came to work. Yes, he carried on with his unsavory friends in the evenings, but I never heard my father complain about him shirking his duties. I believe he oversaw the warehouse transports, and I know he was responsible for the many galas and soirees held at the gallery. Those were quite popular. Richard knew how to throw a good party."

Their carriage rolled past her former home.

"Did you have our driver pass by here on purpose?" In truth, she did not care if it was coincidence or planned. She wanted to go inside and look around.

She was pleased when Deklan agreed. "Something might jolt your memory." He rapped on the carriage roof. "Rivers, pull up here. Wait for us. We won't be long."

"How did you know the driver's name? He never told us." She shook her head and sighed. "He is one of the Crown agents, isn't he?"

"Wooton isn't leaving anything to chance. Not only the villains have their eyes on you. The good guys are watching as well." He hopped out, took a moment to look around, and then assisted her down from the carriage. "Stay close to me."

"I will. Does Wooton have more agents watching this place?"

"He might, but I doubt he will use an active field agent for this purpose now that there is nothing more to be found here. Perhaps he's assigned a clerk to keep an eye on whoever passes by." He placed a hand lightly to the small of her back to guide her inside.

His merest touch shot tingles through her, but she did not allow herself to be distracted by the warmth of his hand or gentleness of his touch.

"We are in broad daylight and the street is busy, so we ought to be safe enough. But take nothing for granted, Grace. The foreign agents who are after you are the best money can buy. I have no doubt a few are lurking close. The smallest lapse, and they will swoop in and carry you off. Do you understand?"

"Am I in danger even when we are inside the house?"

"Yes, even then."

She did not mind holding onto him or burrowing close to his side. Deklan was sleek as a leopard, his shoulders broad, and his build big and powerful. He scouted their surroundings with a predator's eye, absorbing every detail.

She could see his agile mind at work as he took in every detail with a sharp and critical precision.

There was no question this man was intelligent.

"The lock to the front door is smashed to bits," she noted with dismay, remaining close as they entered the house. She had seen the damage done by the Crown agents in those early days when the thefts were first being uncovered, but was unprepared for this utter devastation. "The walls have been demolished down to their studs. I knew they were going to search high and low, but this..."

"Wooton thought the crown might be hidden behind one of

the walls."

"Obviously, he found nothing."

He shook his head. "Oh, he found plenty. Just not the crown. He and his agents tore apart the art gallery and warehouse, too."

"And our country estate. My mother and siblings are still living amid the damage. Some kindly neighbors have helped restore a few of the rooms. People are much more charitable in the countryside than in London."

"I'll see what can be done to restore the rest of it. Sending over a few servants is not enough. Your mother and siblings should not be forced to live under those conditions," he said before returning the conversation to her brother. "Richard did quite a bit of traveling for the Montford art business, did he not?"

"Yes, and he alone did most of it this past year. My father used to travel quite a bit, but no longer. He has slowed down considerably and does not leave London unless it is to spend time at our country estate. And before you ask, he hasn't left London in almost a year."

"Tell me about Richard's travels. Would he have stopped anywhere of significance within the last six months?"

"Right after the crown was stolen? I'm not sure I understand what you mean."

He kept hold of her hand as they carefully made their way from room to room. "Think, Grace. In his travels, did he pass near properties familiar to you? For example, what of the estates owned by his mother's side of the family? He came into an inheritance recently from his maternal uncle, did he not?"

She nodded. "Yes, including a title. Richard is now the rightful baron and owner of several entailed properties. Oh, I see what you mean."

She paused at the foot of the staircase and glanced up. Not even the steps were safe since those had all been pulled apart as possible hiding places. "But those properties are up north, not far from the Scottish border. Richard has not been anywhere near them since the crown was stolen. I would have known had he taken any trips there."

"Then he has remained in the south of England all the while?"

"Yes, several trips to Exeter. Well, also trips to the Continent, and those must have been to plan and execute the theft of the crown along with legitimate business dealings as a cover for his intended crime." She followed him as he led her into the kitchen. "Why are we here?"

"It is the safest way to take you upstairs. Wooton tells me the servants' stairwell is not too badly damaged. Are you up for it, Grace?"

"Yes, although I doubt it will serve a purpose other than appeasing my curiosity." She noticed soot stains along the kitchen floor as they passed through the dank chamber to reach the back staircase. "Seems your agents searched each chimney as well."

He nodded. "We try to be thorough."

"Indeed, you are. Have you missed anything?"

"Obviously, we have. The crown has not been found."

"Oh, that's true."

He began to muse aloud as they climbed the stairs and strolled toward the bedchambers. "We have pretty much traced every moment of your brother's whereabouts since the theft, but we are clearly overlooking something. It is possible he never brought the stolen article to London but hid it somewhere between here and Dover. Tucked it away somewhere he thinks no one will ever look. An old, unused well. A mausoleum. A smuggler's tunnel. An ancient priest hiding hole."

"Have you not searched for such places on all our properties?"

"Yes, and found nothing. Which means there has to be someplace else of significance between here and Dover. Can you think of anywhere that might be? Something out of his childhood, or–"

She gasped.

They had just walked into her brother's bedchamber, and she saw the portrait of the dog he had owned as a child. It was still in its frame, undamaged, but left on the dusty floor. She picked it up and carried it over to the bed, ignoring the fact that the mattress had been ripped apart.

"Grace?"

"Could it be a dog's grave?"

"What?" He helped her to dust off the painting.

"He had a favorite dog when he was younger. This is her portrait."

Deklan's eyes seemed to bore into her soul. "Wooton searched the animal graves on your country estate. He found nothing."

"Because this grave is not on any of our properties." Her heart began to race. Why hadn't she thought of this before? Perhaps because everyone seemed convinced Richard had brought the crown to London or hid it somewhere on the family estate. "Vixen was the old girl's name. She was a sweet retriever with a beautiful golden coat. The two of them were inseparable."

"And?"

"We were on holiday, staying at a lovely manor house overlooking Pevensey Bay near Bexhill. My father had let the house for a month in the summer, wanting us all to enjoy the sea air. Richard and Vixen were playing by the shore one day, Richard tossing a stick and Vixen jumping into the water to retrieve it. The game was harmless, and the day had turned beautiful and calm after a morning rain, or so we thought. Vixen swam out too far and got caught in a riptide. She was not spry enough to escape its dangerous undertow. She drowned. Richard was devastated. He almost drowned himself trying to save her."

Deklan shook his head. "I'm truly sorry for that."

"We were all of us overset and searched for hours until we found her body. My parents did not know what to do. I suggested we hold a funeral for her, and it seemed to help. She had been in our family since before I was born." She paused and began to nibble her lip. "Richard changed after that incident. Not that he was ever the warmest soul, but at least he had the capacity to love his dog. Afterward, he never cared for a blessed thing but himself."

"Grace, you are brilliant. Bexhill, it is. I'll advise Wooton, and he'll send his best agents to–"

"No." She glanced around at all the destruction surrounding them. "They will not touch Vixen's grave. Let me be the one to do it."

"Now you are speaking out of sentiment. I cannot let you go to Bexhill."

"Why not? Are you not England's best agent and more than capable of protecting me?"

He cast her a wry grin. "I did not earn that accolade by indulging the wishes of those I am charged to protect…no matter how beautiful they might look when they plead with me or pout."

"I am not pouting. I am casting you a fierce scowl."

He laughed. "I am going to kiss you if you keep it up. You look delicious, not the least bit fierce."

She rolled her eyes. "You cannot dismiss me. My idea is a good one and will solve several problems. Recovering the crown, of course. But it will also get me out of your Aunt Miranda's home. She has a houseful of children residing there at the moment. I know you and your cousins are brawny and brave, but those children are not. I am a danger to all of them so long as I remain there. Is this not so?"

He gave a reluctant nod. "I had considered moving you out of there no later than tomorrow."

"I agree. It is the only solution. Never mind about finding a new place to hide me. You and I must sneak off to Bexhill. *Alone.*"

"Grace, I am not trying to be difficult, but getting you away from Aunt Miranda's residence is not the same thing as running off with you to the south of England. It is not a good idea."

"What is wrong with it?"

"Other than the fact we would be an unmarried couple traveling together?"

She dismissed the concern with an unladylike snort. "You are already sleeping in my bedchamber. My reputation is in tatters, and I am already considered ruined. Why are you suddenly behaving like a prim schoolmistress? Aren't you the one who told me you have no delicate sensibilities whatsoever?"

"I don't, but you do. More important, it is a dangerous plan and I don't like it. What if we are seen attempting to leave London by these foreign agents?"

"Wooton claims you can take down armies."

"I can, but this is different."

"How?"

"Because it involves you." He reached out and gave her cheek a light caress. He'd taken off his gloves, and the feel of his fingers upon her skin once again shot tingles through her. Perhaps it was the way he stroked her cheek with the rough pad of his thumb. It felt so intimate, as though he were stroking her in unmentionable spots on her body.

He wasn't, but this did not seem to stop her from responding in those unmentionable places.

Fortunately, he was too busy thinking of retrieving the crown to notice the heat building up inside of her.

"Grace, if something went wrong, it would leave us exposed and too far away for help to arrive in time. No, it is much better to keep you in London and maintain the pretense of a search while other Crown agents go to Bexhill."

"They won't know where to look."

He tweaked her chin. "They will if you draw us a map."

"No."

"Damn it, Grace. This isn't a game."

"Don't you think I know it? I was only seven years old that summer. How can I be sure my memory is correct? But I would know if I was there and could walk the property in question. Inform the Duke of Wooton where we are going, if you must."

He groaned lightly. "No, he will take it out of our hands if I do. I will tell Shayne and Caleb."

"Not Donal or Lorcan? Are they not still active agents of the Crown?"

"Yes, and this is precisely why I will not tell them. I dare not risk having them censured for failing to report the information to Wooton. Shayne and Caleb will know when the time is right to tell them where we have gone."

"So, we are agreed? You and I alone to Bexhill? With luck, we can make it there, retrieve the crown, and be back in London in time for Christmas dinner with your family. There is not a blessed thing wrong with this plan. Are you not the one who loves plans? You even think marriage can be planned."

"Ah, but it can be. One might also argue that a marriage based on mutually agreed terms is more reliable than one based on love. You are frowning at me. So be it. Just keep in mind that a solid arrangement is quite the sensible thing, unlike falling in love, which turns your guts inside out and your brain soft as pudding."

"Duly noted, but I am still going to marry for love."

"Why, Grace? It can only cause you unbearable pain."

She stared at him in surprise. "Why would you say such a thing? Have you been in love before, and did she break your heart? Oh, Deklan, I am so sorry. What happened? Could she not bear your long absences? Is this what destroyed all hope of love for the two of you?"

"Gad, how did we get on this subject?"

"You brought it up, and I'm glad you did. *The Book of Love* has an entire chapter on this very thing, expectations that cannot be met and will only lead to unhappiness in a marriage unless the couple can accept to compromise. But I think you were determined to give your all to protecting the royal family and were not about to sacrifice any of those responsibilities to be a dutiful husband. Do not be angry or resentful toward her for wanting more of you than you were willing to give. It–"

"Grace, how did we get on the topic of me? And who are you to give me advice on love when you are a complete and utter novice? You had never even been kissed before I kissed you last night."

"How is this my fault?"

"I am not saying it is your fault. Nor was I speaking of myself when I spoke of love's betrayal."

"Betrayal?"

"Loss, pain, betrayal…whatever. I was only thinking of you. I am not the only one who will not compromise."

"What do you mean?"

"Your lot and that of your siblings would be made much easier if you were willing to marry someone of solid circumstances. But you will only settle for love and nothing less. I am not condemning you for it, merely pointing out the difficulties you face in achieving it. Life would be much simpler for you if not for the requirements of your soft, trusting heart. Mine is not soft, and I do not trust anyone. Just don't be…" He ran a hand through his hair in apparent consternation. "Hell, just don't be…"

"What? Should I not be myself?"

He cast her a look hot enough to melt her bones. "Be yourself, just…hold back your heart a little, will you? I don't want to see you hurt."

She emitted a mirthless laugh. "I have already been hurt beyond repair. But I cannot lose hope, or I shall spend the rest of my days alone and crying. I have to believe in love. It is out there for me. *He* is out there for me. My dream man. My perfect hero. He has to be."

"You've done it again, turned me inside out," he muttered. "As for Bexhill, I–"

"Do you have a better idea?" She stuck out her hand. "What's it to be? You and I together? Are we in agreement on this? I am going there with or without you."

He glanced at her hand.

Ignored it.

Drew her into his arms instead. "All right. Agreed. Bexhill it is. But a handshake is no way to seal a bargain."

"It isn't? Then what is?"

"This," he said and kissed her breathless.

CHAPTER FIVE

"Y OU ARE A complete and utter hound," Grace muttered as Deklan led her down the servants' stairs after the scorching kiss he should never have given her. Of course, he had not regretted a moment of this kiss even though it should never have happened.

He loved the way her lips softly sank against his.

They were made to fit perfectly to his mouth.

Like a lid to a jar.

Creating a perfect seal.

Well, that description wasn't very romantic.

"Do you hear me?" She was still berating him as they walked through the front door toward their waiting carriage. "You are a hound."

"Never said I wasn't." His heart was still pounding, and it took him great effort to quell the bonfire raging inside him. "But I am still going to protect you with my life."

She took a deep breath and set a delicate, gloved hand across her flushed cheek. "Dear heaven, look what you've done. My face is in flames."

His smile was utterly wicked as he said, "It wasn't your face I was trying to light on fire."

He silently kicked himself for behaving like an arse. How could he have said such a thing to the sweet girl? She really did have him turned inside out.

He ought to apologize but doubted she would accept it.

Her eyes were ablaze.

Of course, they were ablaze with anger.

What was it about Grace he could not resist?

Well, one thing for certain, he was taking *The Book of Love* along with them on their journey.

He could not even catch his blasted breath.

This is how she left him, breathless and on fire.

She wasn't even trying to seduce him.

But those soft, sweet lips.

Her incredible eyes.

The delicate shape of her body.

This is what frustrated him most, because the more she buttoned up and bundled up, the more he wanted to peel those layers off her and discover what lay beneath.

In theory, he knew.

He had seen plenty of naked women.

But Grace would not be like the others.

She would be pink and soft, and when he touched her skin with his tongue, she would taste as sweet as newly ripened strawberries.

"You cannot kiss me whenever it is convenient for you," she said, trying to shake off his assistance as they neared the carriage.

But a flash of metal caught his attention.

He grabbed her by the waist and pushed her to the ground as shots resounded and scared the carriage horses.

"Ack! What–"

"Keep down!"

The carriage rocked back and forth wildly as the horses reared and bucked in panic. Rivers tried to control the team. At the same moment, two men converged on Deklan with weapons drawn.

He went on the attack, punching the first assailant in the throat and quickly disarming him. He grabbed the pistol the man was pointing at him and used it to shoot the other in the arm as he was about to plunge a knife into Deklan's neck.

The knife fell out of this man's hand, and he stumbled to the ground beside Grace.

Deklan kicked him to hold him down when he tried to reach for the knife, or perhaps he was hoping to grab Grace.

Deklan wasn't about to let him get either.

Two more charged at him from his left, both armed with pistols aimed at his chest.

He rolled forward to avoid the shots, grabbed the knife laying beside Grace, and threw it with lethal precision to fell one of them. He then shot the other.

Both of them fell dead too close to Grace.

"Time to go." He hauled Grace to her feet, hoisting her over his shoulder, and setting her none too gently in the carriage now that Rivers had managed to subdue the horses.

He hopped in after her. "Rivers! Get us out of here!"

The carriage took off with a hard jerk that tossed both of them across the bench and caused him to land atop her. Of course, he did his best to contort himself in order to minimize the impact of his big body falling atop her slight frame.

It must have worked, because she wasn't winded at all and immediately tried to wriggle out from under him.

"Stay down," he barked when she tried to sit up.

He eased off her and turned to peer out the window.

Grace squirmed beneath his palm which he'd kept splayed across her stomach to hold her down. "What is happening?"

"Stay put and stop fighting me." Those first two assailants were only now starting to get up. The first man had been easy to subdue, for he was big and ungainly, all brawn and no speed.

The second had been spryer, but still not fast enough to do Deklan any harm. He, too, was staggering to his feet. By the angry movement of his mouth, Deklan could tell he was cursing him and Rivers.

Well, the wretch could do little while clutching his bleeding arm.

The other man was still bent over and breathing hard, no doubt trying to regain the wind Deklan had knocked out of him.

Both were alive because Deklan had not intended to kill them.

But those last two he had killed.

They were not agents of the foreign government, but opposition faction men. He knew from his month of working undercover just how brutal and dangerous they were. He did not want to think of what they would have done to Grace if they'd ever gotten their hands on her.

He hoped there were agents of the Crown close by to haul those two survivors in for questioning. Well, this was Wooton's problem.

Grace was his assignment, and keeping her safe was all that mattered to him.

He allowed her to sit up the moment they turned the corner. "Are you all right?"

Rivers had regained firm control of the horses, and they were now heading back to Miranda's house at a steady pace, moving as quickly as the congested streets would allow.

"No thanks to you. First you presume to kiss me and then you shove me to the ground. How do you think I feel? I had no idea your hand was the size of a bear paw." She was not upright longer than a few seconds before she scampered over him to peer out the window. "Where are they? Are they following us?"

"Damn it, Grace." He drew her back. "Do not stick your head out and give some assailant a clear shot. Have you not had enough of an adventure? And kindly get off my lap unless you would like me to do something about it."

She darted off him and sank back against the squabs. "I have no idea what that means. What would you do to me if I sat on your lap?"

He arched an eyebrow. "That is a question asked by a young woman who has never had sex in a carriage."

Her mouth fell open, and she gaped at him. "I would hit you

senseless if I you hadn't just saved my life. You did save it, didn't you? Everything happened so fast, it was all a blur. I heard shots and grunts, and bodies seemed to be falling everywhere around me. But I dared not look up to see what was happening. So, you saved me?"

He nodded. "Yes."

"I am still angry with you for your boorish behavior. However, thank you. I mean it sincerely. Were there only four men? Or more of them trying to grab me?" Her face paled, no doubt as their narrow escape began to sink in, and she realized just how close she had come to being abducted. "I do not mean to make light of it. Four men? One would have been too many."

"Grace, it is all right. You are safe now."

She nodded.

Her hands began to tremble.

He could see his assurances were having no effect, so he hauled her onto his lap and wrapped his arms around her. "Just calm down."

"But I am on your lap!"

"Good grief, I am not going to have sex with you. Nor will I kiss you again…at least not yet, anyway. I'm sorry if I was too rough when tossing you to the ground. Seriously, did I hurt you?"

"No, just a little dirt on my gown. That's all. I am better now. You needn't hold me." She squirmed out of his grasp and settled on the seat across from him.

But he wasn't better.

For pity's sake, she was just an assignment.

So why was his heart still in a rampant roar?

One would think she mattered more to him than anything in the world. It was ridiculous. They had known each other less than a day.

Her eyes widened as she studied him. "Are you hurt? Forgive me, I did not think to ask you."

"I'm fine, Grace. They did not set a hand on me."

"But you threw some hard punches, did you not? You moved

so fast. I also saw you kick that man hard in the gut."

"There is no honor when someone is trying to kill you. He was reaching for his knife or perhaps he was reaching for you. He is fortunate I did not end his life then and there."

"I see."

"So now you know, I am no gentleman. One cannot afford to be in this line of work. A gentleman would not have saved your life just now."

"Was it in danger? I thought they only wanted to abduct me."

"Is this not frightening enough? Has it escaped your notice they were willing to kill me to accomplish it? Who do you think they were aiming at with their first shots?"

She reached out and ran a gloved hand gently across his forehead. "Thank goodness they missed you. Dear heaven, do you think I am admonishing you in any way? I am so sorry. Forgive me if I sound in any way unappreciative."

"Don't apologize to me. You've done nothing that requires it. I am the one who behaved like a boor toward you, just as you accused."

She cast him a wry smile. "Well, you were very honorable in saving me and restored yourself despite that shocking kiss."

"The kiss was tame…well, perhaps more ardent than I intended. I am not a saint, Grace."

"I've noticed. But you are a Crown agent and did your job magnificently."

He liked the idea of being honorable and magnificent for her. He had every intention of stepping up to protect her life and her reputation should it ever be required. Yes, her reputation. Only marriage would ever restore that. Not that he wanted to force her into an unwanted marriage, nor was he ready to be leg shackled to a girl he'd known for mere hours.

But he would do whatever was necessary to keep her safe.

He would at least give her situation more than a passing thought.

The little innocent had gone on earlier about expectations

and sacrifice, obviously spouting whatever was written in the book she'd found atop his bureau.

It was beginning to make sense to him.

Yes, he was uncompromising and wanted his way in all things.

But Grace made him...he did not know what was going on with his heart, only that he could not bear to see her hurt. Sacrificing his own desires to make her happy suddenly did not feel like a chore for him.

Those men had gotten too close to her.

"Oh, dear. My gown has a little tear. I'll sew it back up when we return to Lady Miranda's house."

He leaned forward. "Let me see."

"Not on your life," she said, her eyes glittering with mirth as she shrank back.

"Why not?"

He was glad she appeared amused rather than appalled. "It is too close to my bosom, and I will not have you staring there. You are already too much for me to handle. I am sure you are impossible for anyone to tame."

He folded his arms across his chest and eased back against the squabs. "I do not behave this way around other women."

"Then why do you take liberties with me? Because I am a Montford and already tainted?"

He hated the way the gossips had beaten her down. "Nothing of the sort. It is because I find you irresistible. Not that this is any excuse for my behavior. But I will claim no more than kisses from you. I am bound by honor to protect you and this I will do with my life. As for that tear to your gown, let me see it. I will be very careful not to touch you anywhere untoward."

"The damage is insignificant, and I am already undone every time you look at me with your leopard eyes."

"Stop referring to me as that animal. I am not going to eat you."

"Then stop looking at me as though you are."

Well, he did want to devour the luscious girl.

Peel the clothes off her body.

Not merely want to peel them off her, for that denoted delicacy and there was nothing delicate about his feelings for Grace.

He could hardly think straight for wanting her.

It was disconcerting how quickly the logical part of his brain seemed to shut down whenever he looked at her.

Raw, animal instinct simply took over.

Perhaps he was a leopard.

Mine.

Not sharing her with anyone.

Not giving her up to anyone.

Why was this happening to him?

She was completely the opposite of seductive, buttoned up to her throat and layers of linen and wool between them. He had yet to catch even a glimpse of soft, pink flesh peeking out from anywhere.

"Deklan, you may take these feelings lightly, but I cannot. Perhaps we ought to ask the Duke of Wooton to replace you with another of his top men."

He emitted a soft growl. "No one protects you but me."

How could she suggest such a thing?

Grace frowned at him. "Then tell me this, how do you protect me against you? Because you cannot keep kissing me as though I matter to you. I am terrified I will start to believe it and then you will break my heart."

He was glib when he wanted to be, but those easy words failed him now. "Grace, dear heaven. You do matter to me."

He often played the role of fawning gentleman when on assignment because women fell for it and gave up whatever secrets he was after.

But he was not playing any such games with her.

No, he was just the arrogant agent of the Crown who was ready to give his life for her. "You don't need protecting from me. Have I not vowed I will never hurt you?"

The carriage chose that moment to hit a rut, and she bounced directly into his arms.

He closed them around her like two iron bands.

She tried to wriggle out of his grasp, but he would not let her go.

More to the point, he could not let her go because she felt too good against him. Awareness surged through him, especially of the crush of her full, soft breasts against his chest.

Blessed saints.

He was going to expire from the pleasure of it.

This was a terrible turn of events.

He had only to tip his head to hers and all restraint would be lost the moment his lips met hers. She did not need to worry about her heart, for it was his at risk here.

How was it possible to lose his heart to a girl he hardly knew?

He released her and set her back on the opposite seat. "You don't get to replace me, Grace. I am with you to the end."

"And then what?"

"Let's find the crown first and then we'll figure out the rest of it." He rapped on the roof and asked Rivers to speed their return to Miranda's residence.

Upon arrival, he hurried her inside.

Just getting her safely through the front door was a battle plan, for there were several strangers watching the house.

But he managed it without further incident.

A footman came forward to take their cloaks, gloves, and scarves.

"Wait, let me take off my hat as well," she said when Deklan tried to take her upstairs. She quickly removed the jaunty thing and added it to the pile in the footman's arms. She spared only a glance in the hall mirror to brush back a few stray curls with her fingers before turning to him. "Were we watched as you hurried me inside?"

"Yes, Grace."

"But I did not see anyone. Not that I doubt you after what

just happened. You've taken your predator's stance again."

"My what?"

"That leopard stance. You know, your body becomes taut and you stand ready to spring into action at the enemy's slightest move. Why are you still on edge?"

"Because that attack means you are in imminent danger. No one is giving us a week to find that crown. They are coming for you now."

"And they are right outside our door?"

He nodded.

"Where are they hiding?"

"Come upstairs with me, and I'll show you." He took her hand. It was a simple touch, their fingers lacing together perfectly.

The perfection of it jolted him.

Deklan had never felt anything like this before.

She surely belonged to him.

Did it work both ways?

Belonging to each other?

This was bad.

They reached the staircase landing, and he paused beside a window shaped in an octagon. "Stand back a little, Grace. Don't let them see you."

He positioned her out of their line of sight and then pointed to a bench beside a hedgerow in the garden square around which the houses on this street were built. "See those two men seated on the bench facing us? Those are agents of the foreign royal house."

He then pointed to the neighbor's wall. "Two more are be-hind that stone wall. Those men are hired by the opposition faction."

She looked up at him, her eyes big and questioning. "How can you see through a stone wall? Anyway, wouldn't they be noticed by the neighbor's footmen and chased off?"

"I noticed them this morning and again when our carriage

drew up in front of Miranda's house. To answer your question, I cannot see through walls. And yes, they would be noticed by the neighbor's staff." He continued to peer out the window as he spoke, keeping his arm loosely around her waist in a gesture that was possessive as much as it was protective. "But Miranda's neighbors are not at home for Christmas. Lord and Lady Barrett left yesterday morning to spend the month in Oxford with their children and have closed up the house."

"All their servants are gone?"

He nodded. "Those not taken with them have been given the month off, all but an old, doddering butler left here as caretaker. Ineffectual, obviously. His eyesight is failing, and he can hardly see beyond his nose. His hearing is poor as well."

"How do you know this?"

"It is my job to know all that is going on around us."

His gaze remained on the men outside. There had to be more than four of them. Likely more were positioned by the rear of the house. He needed to scout the area as soon as darkness fell, which it did rather early at this time of year.

"Deklan, how do you know which side these agents represent?"

"As I said, it is my business to assess these things. It is not hard to do once you know what to look for. Their clothes alone often give away who hired them. The expressions on their faces are another hint. Their boldness or lack of it."

He drew her slightly behind him.

"Is there something else going on out there? Why are you peering out so intently? And you just nudged me behind you."

"No obvious threat, Grace. I'm just trying to plan our escape without any of the villains noticing. Since you insist on our going to Bexhill instead of letting the Crown's men attend to it, it falls on me to safely get you away from here."

She sighed. "You are peeved."

"Not with you. None of this is your fault, and you are doing your best to help us find that stolen crown." His gaze fixed on her lovely mouth now pursed while she was lost in thought. "I've seen all I need to see."

He drew her away from the window, but they had taken only a few steps down the hall before she stopped him.

"Wait, I have another question to ask you. Why are the men behind the hedgerows and the men behind the stone wall not going after each other? Would they not want to get each other out of the way before they come for me?"

"They will once the time is right."

"And when is that?"

"When they manage to separate you from me. Four of them tried it unsuccessfully a short while ago, and more will attempt to grab you again tonight. I'm just sorry Wooton did not have our own agents positioned at your home to bring those two surviving louts in for questioning."

"Should we have held them there until Crown agents arrived?"

"No, getting you to safety was the priority. They are mere underlings and would not have given us much information of use. I can guess most of it, anyway."

"You killed two and left two surviving. Was there a reason? Were they not all coming at you with weapons drawn?"

"Yes, but the first two agents were working for the foreign monarchy and they have orders to deliver you safely to their king who will hold you in his protection. The other two agents were working for the opposition faction, and I do not know what they would have done to you if ever they abducted you. They are ruthless and brutal."

"Oh, I see. They would have killed me after I had outlived my usefulness."

Or worse, used her in other ways he dared not mention to her. "I'm fairly certain the two factions have formed an unholy alliance for the purpose of abducting you. They think they'll stand a better chance of defeating me if they work together. Now, it is a matter of waiting for another opportunity to present itself."

"Under cover of darkness? You said this is when they are most likely to strike."

"They can wait all they want, but none of them will ever get their hands on you. I am not giving you up under any circumstances."

He realized he'd frightened her.

While he wanted her to understand the dangers, he had not meant to terrify her.

He cast her a wry smile and caressed her check. "You have the prettiest eyes. Has anyone ever told you that? Come on, let's return to our bedchamber and plot our escape."

She blushed. "It is not *our* bedchamber. Please, don't call it that."

"All right. Too intimate for you?"

She blushed again.

"Grace, you need to get used to me and my blunt manner. We cannot be arguing while on the run. I may say things that upset your delicate sensibilities...I will say things, but you must take them in stride."

"About me and my family?"

"Not about you. Can you not see that you are someone special to me? I am not as immune to your charms as I ought to be. It irritates me, and I seem to be taking it out on you by goading you."

"Do you really find me charming?"

He cast her a wry smile. "Yes, Grace. Unfortunately, I do. Liking you is not a good thing. It makes my assignment harder. I lose the advantage if feelings slip into the equation. Keeping you safe requires cold calculation and nothing had better interfere with that."

"I have a solution." She returned his smile with an impish one of her own. "I'll make myself as irritating to you as possible."

He laughed. "I'm afraid it isn't going to work. I was not kissing you earlier because I am a brash arse and simply felt like it. Well, I certainly am an arse."

"Brash, too."

He nodded. "But I really do like you, Grace."

She reached up on tiptoes and kissed him lightly on the cheek. "I'm glad someone does."

"Hellfire, are you going to cry now? Don't you dare." He had no weapon to defend himself against her tears.

Why did she have to feel so perfect for him?

"I won't shed a single tear, for I have none left in me. I've felt so low and awful ever since my family's downfall, I've forgotten how to feel good about myself."

She made his head spin.

He would be lost if she ever actually attempted to seduce him.

Fortunately, she was too prim to ever try.

She thought too little of herself to ever try.

"Perhaps you are only being kind to me to encourage my cooperation," she said, her lips once more puckered in thought. "You needn't bother. I have every intention of helping you recover the crown."

"Do I strike you as the sort to flatter a woman if I do not mean it?"

"Yes."

He gave a laughing groan. "The correct answer is no."

"Oh, are you sure? Because what do I know about men? You could be deceiving me and yet appear so convincing, I would believe every word. Wooton must deploy you in this fashion. You are too handsome not to be used to flatter and seduce."

"On occasion, but I am under no such orders with you."

"I suppose it doesn't matter. I could do with a good dose of adoration at the moment. It is nice to pretend that I fascinate you, a welcome change from the sneers and derision heaped on me by my society friends."

He took her hand to lead her back to their bedchamber.

Of course, she refused to think of it as *theirs*.

He could think of nothing else.

He liked that her belongings were in with his.

He did not mind sharing the wardrobe and bureau drawers with her.

It was also possible he would not mind sharing a lifetime with her.

Lord, what was happening to him?

Was it all to blame on that blasted book?

CHAPTER SIX

"I AM GETTING you out of here tonight, Grace." Deklan shut the door to their shared bedchamber, hoping to keep his cousins out while he formulated their escape. But Rivers was now going to report the attack to Donal or Lorcan, and it would only be a matter of minutes before they were at his door, asking questions.

"Before or after Lady Miranda's dinner party?"

"I don't know. This is what we are going to work out now. However, our escape must be tonight."

She seemed intrigued rather than scared, for her eyes were big and sparkling. "All right, do you have a plan in mind? I was thinking of taking supper in my room so I am not in the way of your family reunion."

"You are not in the way at all. Why would you think so?" He frowned. "You just wish to hide, is this not so?"

She sighed. "Is it not for the best? I am not a part of your family."

"You are family in Miranda's eyes and that is good enough for all of us. I have already told you I find you charming. If you have ensorcelled me," he said, ignoring her snort of laughter at the remark, "then I can assure you, the rest of my family adores you. I am thick as a brick and often the hardest to convince."

She shook her head and laughed as she held up her hands in mock surrender. "You have made your point. No moping or wallowing for me this evening. All right?"

"Good," he said with a nod. "Besides, you need to remain close to me throughout the evening for this plan to work. As I said, supper tonight when the wildebeests will be present."

She looked up at him again. "Who are the wildebeests?"

"This is what Aunt Miranda used to call the boys in the family. We were all close in age, big men now, but utter beasts when growing up. We played hard, usually three or four of us winding up with bloody noses or assorted minor injuries on any given day, and we needed to be fed constantly. Miranda would toss slabs of meat at us and shut the door as we scrambled for our share of the kill."

Grace clapped her hands and cast him a smile that reached into her lovely eyes. "I knew you were an animal. The others may be wildebeests but you are a leopard."

He chuckled. "That again. All right. I shall be your leopard. However, to get back to the plan...tonight's supper is to be a welcome party for Caleb, Faith, and my family since none of them have been to London in a while."

"Nor have you."

He shrugged. "I'm here more often than they realize, but usually on assignment and do not make my presence known. This celebration dinner is not to be mistaken for the Christmas supper to be held in a week's time, also to be held at Aunt Miranda's and certain to be a crush since friends as well as family will be in attendance."

"Your aunt really hates an empty house. I think this is why she invited me to stay on. She adores having family around her and will miss all of you terribly once you are gone. I think I am a poor substitute, but my bad reputation should cause quite the stir and provide a little bit of entertainment for her."

"Grace, that is awful. You are not a grotesque to be ogled at a side show. I'll have to speak to Miranda about this later. For now, slipping away tonight is our top priority."

"How are we to accomplish it with those agents watching our

every move?"

"We'll have to create a distraction."

She nodded. "All right, but how?"

"Fireworks. I'll have to act quickly to get my hands on as many as can be found on short notice. Setting them off after dark should do the trick. I'll enlist Rafe, Caleb, and Shayne in the planning. Miranda's going to meddle, too. It is her house, after all. She loves this sort of intrigue."

Grace sat at the foot of the bed and watched him as he paced like a penned animal.

Perhaps she was right and he did have a bit of the jungle beast in him. Leopards were solitary creatures, and did this not define him? Until Grace came along, he could not imagine himself with any woman.

Indeed, the moment one got too close, he would feel trapped and flee.

But he did not feel trapped around Grace.

Quite the opposite, he could not seem to get enough of her.

He did not even care that he was shut in here with her, a young woman who insisted on marrying only for love.

Love also meant commitment, sacrifice, compromise. Devotion.

Grace would demand all these things and yet, the possibility of marrying her did not frighten him. Perhaps he had been on his own too long and was ready for this change. The thought of pledging himself to her sent not a single shudder through him.

He laughed silently, knowing this might be a sign he was finally growing up. He had been an unmitigated brat as a child and much the same as an adult. Well, he needed to be unmanageable in order to succeed in his job. He was proud of his work, those hard, dirty assignments vital to the safety of England and her royal family.

Having spent years up to his eyeballs in intrigue and deceit, was he now ready to move on and give more of himself to marriage and family?

Was he having these feelings only because of Grace?

He had faced this decision once before.

What a time to think of Lady Genevieve.

He dismissed the thought and returned his attention to Grace and their escape to Bexhill.

She had her big eyes trained on him and appeared to be hanging upon his every word. He cleared his throat and continued. "I'll ask Rafe and Shayne to acquire the fireworks for us. I'm sure they can do it."

"Because they have made friends at the highest levels while participating in taking down my family?"

His heart tightened. "Grace…"

"It is all right. I know mine was in the wrong. Yours has every reason to shun me and yet, they have gone out of their way to be kind."

He knelt beside her and took her hands in his. "Do you feel you are betraying your father by staying here?"

She nodded. "A little. Sometimes. Mostly, I feel humiliation for what he has done."

"And I do not help by treating you in my oafish manner."

"No, Deklan. Not at all. For the most part, you are decent to me. All my other friends treat me as though I no longer exist."

"It is their loss. And I hope you find me more than just decent toward you." He sighed. "But let's get back to our escape plan."

She cast him a delicate smile. "You do love your plans."

"A good agent must always be prepared," he said with a laugh and resumed his pacing. This was a habit of his whenever he needed to think. "Caleb and I will arrange for horses to be at the ready."

"Where will they be? The foreign agents must be keeping an eye on the mews behind Miranda's house. Would we not be seen riding off?"

"We'll have to leave them elsewhere. I'll figure that out with Caleb shortly."

"But we'd still need to slip away unseen or all is lost."

"This is why we need to confide the plan to Miranda and others in the family. We cannot do this on our own. As I said, Rafe and Shayne to obtain the fireworks while Caleb and I deal with the horses and other details."

"What can I do in the meanwhile?"

"Nothing other than staying safe. I'll have to leave you for a while. You need to be careful while I'm gone. Remain downstairs with the women. Or invite them up here, I don't care which. I know Auggie, Willow, and Faith will help out," he said, referring to the wives of his brother and cousins. "Their husbands are going to confide in them anyway, so I might as well include them in our planning."

"This is how it ought to be between husbands and wives. Couples do not keep secrets from each other in a love marriage."

"Neither should you ever keep secrets from me, Grace." He leaned over without thinking and kissed her on the forehead. "Don't yell at me. I know we are not a couple and I have no intention of speaking of love, but you are mine to protect and I will not shirk my duty."

But it was more than mere duty that bound him to Grace.

She had an exquisite softness about her.

He could not look at her without wanting to hold her in his arms.

In truth, he wanted more.

These feelings she roused in him were intense and utterly confounding.

He was experienced.

She was naive.

How did she gain such power over him?

He shook his head and proceeded to relate the rest of his plan. "What do you think?" he asked when he finished.

She was not looking at him, but had her slender fingers wrapped around the bedpost and was nibbling her luscious lower lip.

"Grace?"

Her eyes were rounded in dismay.

He knelt beside her. "Is there something about the plan you do not like? The fireworks? They are a necessity. We need the noise and bright bursts of light to distract everyone."

"No, it is brilliant. A marvelous idea."

"I hoped it would dazzle you," he teased, casting her a warm smile to mask his concern. She needed to be ready to participate wholeheartedly or their escape would fail.

A light blush stained her cheeks.

"Is it the masks? The gowns? We are all to wear masks as part of the festivities and you ladies need to wear similar gowns. This is meant to have you blend in and make it harder for those agents to distinguish you from the other blondes."

"I know. In truth, I find it ironic. We spend fortunes at our modistes in order not to look alike. We pride ourselves on standing out."

"Yes, well…not tonight. We need to confuse those who are watching us. The gowns do not have to match exactly, just try to wear the same colors. Masks, matching gowns, fireworks, and some of those rockets will be purposely aimed at the foreign agents."

"That is clever. Do you think it will work?"

"Let's hope so. They'll be forced to dive for cover. That's when you and I make a run for the mews and our waiting horses. The travel pouches will already be attached to the saddles."

"It all sounds good, Deklan."

"We'll have to ride fast out of London. We need to get as far away from here as possible before our game is found out."

"I can do it. I happen to be an accomplished rider."

"I know."

"You do? Was it in one of your reports?"

"No, I noticed your riding habits in the wardrobe earlier. A dark emerald velvet and a sapphire blue. You obviously take pride in your equestrienne abilities. But do not bother to bring those outfits along to Bexhill. Everyone will remember you if look like a princess. You need to look like a scullery maid. Drab gowns. Plain, dull colors, but make sure they are warm because we are going to be traveling in the cold for hours."

She nodded. "Drab. Scullery."

He tweaked her chin. "But I doubt anyone will ever believe you are a scullery maid. Those poor women have miserably hard lives and their careworn faces make them look eighty years old by the time they are thirty. You are far too pretty. Nor will your hands ever pass for those of a worker. Not a trace of redness or raw blisters on them."

He reached for her hands again and took them in his. "Perhaps a soldier's wife. This is what we shall be, a captain and his wife traveling home for the holidays. What do you think, army or navy?"

"Does it make a difference?"

"No, not really. But I think navy since we'll be headed toward the sea. I'll have to borrow a uniform from Romulus or Ronan since I have don't happen to have one here. I am about their size, so I won't have to worry about the fit."

"You are all the size of gladiators," she muttered.

"Yes, we do run big in this family. Are you ready for the journey, Grace? Once we are safely out of London, we'll be able to slow our pace. But we'll be traveling as husband and wife, sharing quarters there and back."

Of course.

This is what had her so distracted. "This troubles you, doesn't it? It cannot be helped. This is the only way we can avoid suspicion in our travels."

"I understand." She nodded. "I should not be this sensitive about it since we are already sharing a bedchamber and it is enough of a humiliation. In truth, our escape will be a relief to no longer be under the watchful eye of your family. They have all been wonderfully kind, but we are unmarried. Everyone knows it. I cannot hide from it. The shame destroys me."

He cupped her face in his hands. "You are a lady through and through. None of this will change a thing."

"You are wrong. We may outwit these foreign agents to-night, but what if we are recognized along the way? Our families are well known. It is not inconceivable. If so much as a whisper of our traveling together gets out, I'll be labeled a…I cannot even say the word aloud."

"We'll address this problem if it comes up. Nothing to be done about it now…unless you wish to change your mind and let Crown agents go in our place."

"No, we have to do this ourselves. I am not making it up when I say I am not certain where to look. I need to see the grounds of that manor house in Bexhill."

"All right. Give me a moment to talk to Shayne, Caleb, and Rafe, then I'll return to pack. In the meanwhile, I want you to set out whatever clothes you'll need. Remember, warm and serviceable. Nothing to draw the attention of strangers. Also keep in mind we have to travel light. One pouch for each of us, but you can add some of your things to mine if you haven't the room in yours."

She watched with surprise as he took *The Book of Love* and tucked it in his pouch. "We're taking it?"

"Yes."

"Why?"

"Because I want to read it."

She cast him an impish smirk.

"Go ahead, Grace. Enjoy your moment of gloating," he said, responding with a gentle smile. The girl was so tender at heart, he ached for her. "I know you are eager to do so."

"I am not gloating," she said, but her eyes remained glittering in amusement. "If you must know, I am delighted you wish to read the book. Not for my sake, but for yours. Do not be put off by that first chapter. I found it rather shocking, but quite informative."

He laughed. "Now, I must read it without delay."

"I think falling in love is a gift always to be cherished. You must have been in love before, even though you insist on denying it. I won't pry. You'll just tell me it is none of my business."

"Because it is none of your business."

"I had a suitor, did you know?"

He nodded. "I know almost everything there is to know about you. The Duke of Lockbridge was sniffing around you, isn't it so?"

"Ugh, there you go again. You really are an animal, I am convinced of it. He wasn't sniffing me, but he did express interest in me." She looked up at him with big, sad eyes. "He dropped me so fast, my head is still in a spin over it. He won't even acknowledge me now. The last time we happened to cross paths, he gave me the cut direct. He did it with such flair, all his friends congratulated him on how perfectly he'd pulled it off."

"Bastard," Deklan muttered. "Pardon my language, but the man is an utter arse. You are better off without him. Besides, he could not possibly love you."

"I know," she said, emitting a ragged breath. "How can anyone now?"

He hated to see the shadows of pain in her glorious eyes. "You misunderstand me, Grace. You are beautiful beyond belief. I kissed you within a few minutes of our first meeting and still ache to kiss you every time I see you. My point is, if he knew you for months and never made any untoward advances, then he obviously cared for your dowry more than he ever cared for you."

"How do you know? Not all men behave as you do...or rather, misbehave as you do."

"This is where you are wrong. Men are not civilized by nature. We see a pretty thing and want to claim it. We fight like dogs if someone comes along and tries to take it from us. You are that pretty thing and if I were not on assignment, I would be kissing you into Sunday at this very moment. I would not be kissing your dowry. I would be kissing you."

"This is what the book suggests. Well, what the book makes

clear. It is hard for me to admit Lockbridge was an oaf who intended to use me as a business proposition. I suppose he wanted to acquire a share of my father's wealth or some bit of Montford land abutting his own. Hah! He had a rude awakening, didn't he?"

"Consider yourself fortunate Lockbridge did not stand by you. He would have made you very unhappy. You had a lucky escape from a doomed marriage. Now I am decidedly eager to read that book."

"I need to read it again, too. Especially the chapters about the warning signs of a doomed courtship. I've had no experience. It is very hard for me to tell what is real and what is not, especially when the beaus are glib and quite convincing in their flattery. Well, the matter is not urgent. No one will have me now, and perhaps not ever, because of the Montford name."

"We've gotten off the topic of our escape again."

She nodded. "Oh, yes. Sorry."

"Decide on the clothes you want to bring along. Don't bother with elegant slippers. Take only your sturdiest walking boots. I'll send Willow, Faith, and Auggie up to you shortly to keep you company. I don't want you alone at any time. Remember this, Grace. You are safest in a crowd. I'll be back as soon as possible."

He strode to the door and paused by it. "Grace..."

"Yes?"

"You were right."

"About what?"

"There was a girl once, but I hurt her badly because she wanted me to settle down and I was not ready to do it."

"I see. I thought there had to be. You are too handsome not to have had someone...well, you could have had any woman you wanted. What happened to her?"

"I don't know."

"But wasn't she someone special to you? How could you not know? You make it a point to know everything."

"Yes, everything about my assignments. But I did not want to complicate my life. She wasn't an assignment. She wanted a commitment and all I wanted to do was run."

"And now?"

"I don't know. We'll see what happens once we find the crown and you are out of danger."

"Deklan…"

His hand tightened on the door's knob. "Yes, Grace?"

"Will you forget me when this assignment is over?"

CHAPTER SEVEN

DEKLAN WALKED AWAY without responding to Grace's question, but the answer to it was no.

He would always remember her.

She was unforgettable.

But he was not about to have this discussion with her when they had not known each other longer than a day. He set her out of his mind while he gathered his brother and a few cousins in Miranda's study for a quick family meeting. They were easily unnoticed while the servants scurried about polishing silver, moving furniture, setting out the best table linens, and rolling up carpets in preparation for tonight's dinner party.

Miranda, always the perfectionist, could be heard in the hallway issuing orders as she bustled from one room to another, making certain all was proceeding smoothly.

The children had been outdoors playing in the snow most of the morning, their parents close by and ever vigilant considering Grace's situation and the strangers watching the door to Miranda's townhouse.

The littlest ones were now up in the nursery taking their naps. He had no idea what the older children were doing now that they were all back in the house, but the women in the family were ever watchful, so he doubted those imps would get up to much mischief.

"You needn't ask Ronan or Romulus for a uniform," Deklan's

cousin Caleb said. "I'll let you borrow one of mine."

Deklan's brother, Rafe, and their cousin, Shayne, had joined them. The four of them were now comfortably seated in the study while going over his escape plans.

Rafe leaned forward with a grunt. "But you are an army general, Caleb. The point is not to attract notice. Everyone will remember an army general staying at their inn. No, a captain is just the right rank. It will get Deklan into the decent inns without much notice."

"Shouldn't he avoid them? This is the first place the enemy agents will look for him and Grace."

"We'll be well ahead of them," Deklan said. "I'm not having Grace stay in some foul inn that is infested by all manner of crawling creatures. If all goes according to plan, no one will realize we are gone until tomorrow. With luck, our absence might not be noticed for days."

Caleb nodded. "Fine, I'll head over to Ronan's right now. I'm sure he has a uniform to spare. And a pair of fine horses for your travels."

Shayne rose along with Caleb. "I'll leave word for Miranda to dig out masks for all of us to wear. She must have a chest full of them packed away somewhere in this house. The children will be delighted. In truth, so will Willow. She and her sisters enjoy this sort of thing. My stoic brother," he said, referring to Lorcan, "saw Cammy dressed up as a masked fairy on Midsummer's Eve and his tongue rolled to the ground. I don't think he has ever recovered."

The two cousins strode out and left Deklan with his brother. "Rafe, do you think you can get the fireworks?"

He nodded. "Leave it to me. I'll enlist the other wildebeests if I have to."

"No, just you and Shayne. I've already involved too many of you. Lorcan and Donal especially must stay out of it. They came knocking at my door after Rivers told them of the incident, so I had to put them off. They are reporting it to Wooton right now, and likely deciding where I ought to hide Grace."

"All the more reason you should let them in on your escape plan."

"No. They are still agents of the Crown and I dare not risk a problem if they have countermanding orders from Wooton. It is enough Wooton will skin me alive when he knows I've run off with her. I do not want to be fighting them as well over this plan. It is a good one and I am not changing it. Give me a few hours head start and then you can tell them of our whereabouts. I would not mind having their assistance once we retrieve the crown from Bexhill. I would prefer to hand it off to Donal and Lorcan, then just hide out with Grace far from London until the incident is put to rest."

He ran a hand through his hair in consternation. "Grace is not used to this sort of adventure. I tried to convince her we ought to stay put and let others retrieve the blasted crown, but she won't hear of it."

"She is sentimental, and you like that softness about her. And now, you are already too involved to keep your heart out of the decisions you need to make."

"No." He sighed. "Maybe. It's all your fault. Whatever possessed you to plant that stupid book in my bedchamber?"

Rafe laughed as he patted Deklan on the back. "Stop grumbling, baby brother. You were bound to fall in love someday. Auggie and I just helped you along."

"I am not in love."

"Fine."

"Who falls in love in the span of a day?"

"I had better get going."

"I am not in love with Grace."

Rafe shook his head and laughed again. "Stop talking about her. I'm trying to get your fireworks. Not that you need any since she seems to have you going off like those rockets. You always were the dramatic one in the family."

Deklan walked out with his brother to attend to the final

details.

He could not use Miranda's stables since those would be watched, and Caleb's idea of using Ronan's horses was a good one.

He and Grace would have to slip out and run fast. He worried about her ability, but Ronan's house was not too far from here. If she could not make it the entire distance, he would carry her over his shoulder.

Once at his cousin's stable, they would grab the waiting horses and ride off.

He knew Grace was an excellent rider.

However, this meant their travel pouches would have to be sent on in advance and reliably secured to the saddles. This should not be hard to accomplish since all manner of delivery men were coming and going from Miranda's home. Butcher, baker, milkman, fishmonger.

More carts were pulling up by the servants' entrance to deliver cases of wine and a dazzling array of flowers. Miranda was holding nothing back for this party.

It would be the easiest task to sneak whatever they needed in and out, including delivering their travel pouches to Ronan. The mews behind his townhouse was well-sheltered and the foreign agents would not know to look for them there.

By early evening, his plan was underway.

Not all of his ideas worked as perfectly as this one did.

The children went wild over the prospect of wearing masks and later viewing the fireworks. The ladies all found gowns to wear in matching colors and wore their hair in matching styles so that even he had trouble distinguishing one honey-blonde from another at first glance.

But he recognized Grace fairly quickly because he was familiar with the shape of her body despite her constantly wearing thick layers. There was no mistaking the way she moved. Her hips had a distinctively light sway to them he found most appealing.

He came up behind her as the moment neared. "All right, Grace. Take my hand. We are going to run as soon as the next round of fireworks goes off."

"I'm ready."

In the next moment, chaos erupted. The night sky above Miranda's garden filled with massive bursts of light. The children roared with excitement as sparkles and smoke filled the air and a few purposely aimed rockets whizzed toward the foreign agents. The spectacle lasted no more than a few minutes, but it was all the time Deklan needed to have them slip away unnoticed.

Grace was prepared, having worn boots instead of delicate slippers, and she did an admirable job of keeping stride with him.

Ronan's friend, Captain Robbie MacLauren, was waiting for them at Ronan's stable. "Are ye sure ye dinna need me along for protection?"

Deklan laughed as he helped Grace onto her saddle. "Sure, a brash Scot the size of a bull moose? No one will notice you. Thanks for the offer but I'll pass."

"All right. I'll no' take offense this time. Grace, ye are in good hands with this lout. Dinna question his orders. Even a moment's delay can be fatal."

She nodded.

And then they were off, masks handed to Robbie, and cloaks securely wrapped around their shoulders as they tore through the London streets to put as much distance between them and Mayfair as quickly as possible.

Deklan thought he would have to slow his pace for Grace's sake, but Grace was an even better rider than he realized, and she had no intention of holding back. He found himself in the unusual position of having to keep pace with her.

It eased his mind to know she could outrace an enemy if the need ever arose.

They slowed their mounts outside of London since the roads were not as well lit. Fewer torches now guided their way, forcing them to ride carefully through these less populated areas. In their favor, the moon was a big, silver ball shining brightly in the sky and shedding just enough light to illuminate the snowy ground.

The night was crisp and clear, completely unmarred by clouds, which was also in their favor. However, this was winter and a particularly cold night. There would be patches of ice on the ground, particularly treacherous for their horses. They had to slow almost to a crawl in spots to prevent the nervous beasts from slipping.

The frigid breeze grew stronger as the evening progressed.

Deklan realized they would have to seek shelter if the biting wind did not ease up. If it cut through his bones like a sharply honed saw, then it had to be worse for Grace.

"How are you doing, love?" Perhaps he should not have used the endearment, but they were riding in rough conditions and she was holding up admirably. He was proud of her resilience and surprised she had not begged him to find an inn where they could stop for the night.

Well, she had a lot at stake.

But these were harsh conditions, more than most trained agents cared to endure.

"I am doing just fine. You needn't worry about me. I'll keep up with you."

"Don't try, Grace. You haven't my endurance and must not be brave for my sake. No one is following us. We can stop at any point. The greater danger is frostbite. You must tell me at once if you start to lose feeling in your fingers and toes."

"I will, but I am well bundled. Let's keep going."

"Promise me. There is no point in making a martyr of your-self."

"All right, I promise."

But not long afterward, he tugged on his reins and asked if she wished to stop.

Grace drew up on her reins as well. "Would you be stopping now if you were on your own? The truth, Deklan."

Their horses were snorting vapor through their noses, he was cold, and knew that Grace had to be much worse off and likely on the verge of frostbite. "We are hours south of London and the weather is treacherous. Yes, I would stop now. There's an inn I have in mind not far from here."

"I have the feeling you are doing this for my sake," she muttered. "Women are hardier than you give us credit for."

"I have no wish to put it to the proof." He spurred his mount and trotted ahead, always making sure Grace was either beside him or close behind.

The horses were spent and he was worried about having pushed Grace beyond reason. Soon enough, they reached the turnoff for the inn. "Not much longer now," he said.

She was a proud, little thing. But it was not wise to stay proud under these harsh conditions. "I will admit, I am ready to stop. My horse is tiring and so am I. My fingers and toes are beginning to numb."

"So are mine."

She patted her mare's neck. "There, girl. You'll be warm and well fed soon."

He liked Grace's determination.

Yes, she was gently bred and quite sentimental. Probably too compassionate for her own good. However, he knew better than to mistake those qualities for lack of strength or spirit.

Grace seemed to have a deep well of both in reserve.

In truth, she was proving herself to be as capable as any experienced agent. He thought it was entirely possible she would find the stolen crown and with it save England, her mother and siblings, and herself.

He stifled a grin.

He had thought their chances of success quite slim at first.

Not anymore.

Knowing Grace – and he was slowly getting to know her better – she would not stop at merely saving the day and averting war. She would press on until she saved her father and that decidedly unworthy brother of hers.

Well, he doubted the brother could be saved.

But if anyone could manage that miracle, it would be Grace.

He dismounted and led his tiring horse on foot the rest of the distance.

The Blue Moon Inn was an old and rambling stone manor nestled off the beaten path amid the hills of the North Downs. Deklan noticed a torchlight in the distance and recognized it as a marker to guide travelers toward the inn. "Here we go. The inn is at the end of this lane, Grace."

Their progress was slow because the path was steep and winding. They had to make their way in darkness because the trees hid much of the moonlight even though their branches were devoid of leaves.

If not for the glimmers of torchlight in the distance, it would have been impossible to tell where they were or how far they still had to go to reach their shelter.

Grace was shivering noticeably by the time they arrived. Deklan quickly rang the bell hanging frozen and dripping with icicles beside the large door.

The inn's occupants would have retired some time ago since the hour was well past midnight judging by the position of the moon. He helped Grace dismount, but kept his arms around her after wrapping her in his cloak. He held her against his body to warm her while they waited for the innkeeper to open the door.

"I'll be all right," she insisted, her words belied by her chattering teeth. "Let's see to the horses first."

"No, you are my priority. I'll take care of them after I see you safely inside."

"But–"

"You first, Grace. You are too cold. I'm sorry, love. I pushed you too hard."

"No, our journey is important. This coaching inn is so far off the main road, I'm sure we'll be safe here."

"It only feels far because we had to pick our way so cautiously to it. What took us twenty minutes in the dark would not have taken more than a minute or two in daylight. But, yes. We will be safe here. No one is going to find us this far outside of London."

A visible trail of vapor blew from his lips as he sighed. "I should have taken it easier on you and stopped sooner. Those foreign agents won't realize we are missing for hours yet. Perhaps it will take them days to realize we are gone."

"But once they do, what then?"

"Nothing. They won't know where to begin searching for us." He rang the bell again, giving it a solid clang. "You'll like The Blue Moon Inn. It is quite cozy, assuming we ever get inside."

"You've stayed here before?"

"Yes."

"With other women?"

He arched an eyebrow. "No. You are the first I've brought here. The first and only who will share my bed."

She gasped. "We are going to share a bed?"

"Yes, quite likely. They'll grow suspicious if they notice my pallet on the floor. We cannot risk it. By the way, they happen to know me here as Captain Adam Driscoll."

"I see. How convenient."

"It is, fortunately for us. Promise not to flinch when I sign us in as husband and wife. We are newlyweds. They'll probably make a fuss because until now, they've only known me as a bachelor. But you and I are married and there is no negotiation on this point."

"Understood."

"And another thing, look away while I speak to the innkeeper. You are the worst liar on the face of this earth. I do not need them kicking us out because you cannot keep a straight face or keep our names straight in your head. They like me, but it is a reputable establishment and they will not accommodate us if the innkeeper's wife believes you are a…how shall I phrase it politely? If she is convinced I have brought you along merely for a night of…paid pleasure."

"The gall! They'll know at once I am respectable. First of all, I would have to be incredibly stupid or desperate to agree to be led to this isolated location on a night like this. It would take a king's ransom to entice me."

"You would be surprised just how desperate some women are. But we are off the point I am trying to make which is that we need to convince everyone we are married. No jest. This is important. Remember the name Driscoll. Adam Driscoll. Captain in the Royal Navy. Don't botch the plan."

"Your confidence in me is heartwarming."

"And your lack of attention is worrisome. I know you are exhausted, but try to concentrate. Who am I?"

She sighed. "Even if they suspect we are not married, I'm sure you can talk them into giving us a room. You are quite persuasive when you want to be. Or we can ask for separate quarters."

"No, you stay with me at all times. Just try not to give us away, all right?" He rubbed his hands up and down her arms. "Come on, Grace. Who am I?"

"Captain Lambert…I mean, Collins. No, Driscoll."

"Grace!"

"It is a jest. I remember what you told me. Captain Adam Driscoll."

"You are going to give me an attack of the heart. Don't play games. You are not a practiced liar. You are already terrible at it and it is very easy to make a mistake."

"Yes, George. I mean, Deklan. I mean, Adam."

"Stop playing games, Grace. Remember we are on an important mission. This is why I always like to work alone. Then I never have to deal with smart-mouthed chits like you."

"Oh, I am a *chit* now, am I?"

"I am going to spank you if you keep it up." He rang the bell once more.

"Will I like it? Your spanking me, I mean."

He groaned. "Gad, behave yourself. I hear footsteps. Someone's coming."

"Sorry, I have never done anything like this before."

"I know. You are obviously tense and poking fun seems a harmless way to relieve it. But you are tired and have let down your guard. This is when mistakes are always made. By the way, I would never hit you. That includes spanking. I will never raise a hand to you."

"I did not think you ever would."

The breeze blustered around them and their horses pawed the hard ground impatiently as they waited for the inn's door to finally open. "Hold on," an elderly sounding fellow called through the solid wood door. "Let me fetch a lantern."

"No, Mr. Harcourt! Open up!" Deklan pounded on the door, but to no avail.

He heard the innkeeper's footsteps lumbering away.

"Blast it, he's grown deaf as a post." Deklan put his arms around Grace once again because she was still cold and shivering. "Remember, I'll be signing us in as Captain and Mrs. Adam Driscoll."

"What about my given name?"

"You shall be Grace, just as always."

Finally, the door groaned open. "Forgive us for the late arrival, Mr. Harcourt."

The old man held up his lantern. "Why, if it isn't Captain Driscoll. What brings ye here at this late hour…and with this lovely lass?"

"She is lovely, isn't she?" He kept Grace wrapped in his arms. "This is my wife. We are married all of two weeks now."

He made quick introductions.

"Newly wed, are ye? Oh, Mrs. Harcourt will be fussing over ye, that's for certain. And what a pretty lass ye've found for yerself. Come in, come in. Give me a moment to wake the old ball and chain, and my son to care for yer horses. Are ye hungry? No doubt ye're frozen. I'll have her heat up some soup for ye both. But what are ye doing out here at this hour? And on a wicked night like this?"

"It wasn't intentional. We ran into a spot of trouble with our carriage coming up from Dover."

"It is all my fault," Grace said, ignoring his warning to keep quiet. Lord help them if she got them caught in a lie. "We should have remained in Tunbridge Wells along with the carriage, but I was eager to reach London and introduce Captain Driscoll to the rest of my family."

"Ah, heading north are ye?"

"Yes," she replied, sparing a glance and a triumphant smirk at Deklan.

Yes, clever of her to mislead the innkeeper as to their destination. But any agent picking up their tracks would not be fooled for a moment since they had just come from London and would know they were heading anywhere but back there.

He still had an arm around Grace and gave her shoulder a little squeeze. She needed to keep quiet now and not give more away. "How could I deny my wife's wishes? I am usually very good about distances and thought we could make it here by early evening. I ride like the wind, but my wife is not as able a rider. By the time I realized my mistake," he continued, ignoring Grace's subtle kick, "we were already committed to stopping here."

"And here we are," Grace added brightly.

Fortunately, she said no more as the innkeeper left them to wake his wife.

Deklan settled Grace at a table in the small common room. Since he was familiar with the place, he knew where to find a lantern and matches. After lighting the lantern, he moved to the hearth. The hearth fire had burned itself out hours ago. "Oh, don't light it just for me," Grace said.

"Aren't you cold?"

She nodded. "Yes, but we'll only be down here a short while and then it will have to be put out again. I'd rather the fire be lit in our chamber."

He cast her a rakish grin. "No fire needed there, my love. I'll keep you warm enough tonight."

The innkeeper's wife emitted a shriek. "I knew ye'd find

yerself the loveliest lass! And it is a love match, too. Did ye hear what the naughty man just said? Warm enough? You devil. And she's such a sweet thing. Aw, Mr. Harcourt, just look at the way they smile at each other. Lovebirds, for certain."

She left them a moment to bring in their soup. "I hope you like it. Nothing fancy, just a potato pottage with some greens and pork mixed in. The bread is a day old and not as fresh as I'd hoped, but it is good for dunking."

Grace smiled at her. "It is the best meal I have tasted in an age, Mrs. Harcourt."

"Why, thank ye Mrs. Driscoll."

Deklan could see that Grace was dead on her feet, so he led her upstairs as soon as she finished her soup. The Harcourt's son had tended to their horses in the meanwhile and now brought in their pouches.

Deklan took them from him and bade all the Harcourts a good evening.

Grace fell onto the bed with a breathy sigh the moment they were alone in their chamber. "I was fine until about half way through my soup and then exhaustion set in."

"I know the feeling. It is like a wall suddenly rising up in front of you and you slam straight into it. You did magnificently, Grace. I'm very proud of you. But we both need a solid night's sleep or we'll collapse again before midday tomorrow. Let me help you out of your gown. Did you bring any nightclothes?"

She nodded. "Of course."

He chuckled. "Bundle yourself up in them. I'll keep my back turned as you undress."

"It would be better if you stepped out of the room."

"No, we are married."

She sat up and stared at the bed. "How are we going to share this? It doesn't look very big."

He arched an eyebrow. "We will simply have to manage. I am not sleeping on that icy floor. However, I will keep my trousers on for the sake of your delicate sensibilities. I don't need you to panic. You'll be safe enough with me."

"We'll see just how safe."

"No, Grace. I would not harm you for the world." He assisted her with the ties of her gown then turned away to light their hearth fire while she slipped everything off, including her chemise.

His ears were attuned to the sound of material sliding down her skin. The gown first, the woolen fabric then neatly set upon the bed, and soon followed by her light breaths as she worked the front ties of her corset and set it atop her gown.

Last, the chemise came off. He knew the exact moment when she stood naked because she made a little shivering sound and quickly tossed on her sturdy nightclothes.

Blessed saints.

Had he been cold before?

He was burning up now and it had nothing to do with the blaze he had started in the fireplace.

It felt like an eternity before he heard her slide between the sheets. "Are you done?"

"Yes. Oh, my. The sheets are cold. We should have asked for a warming brick."

"Our body heat will warm us up soon enough." He removed all but his trousers and slid in beside her.

The bed had a fine, plump mattress and the bed linens were clean.

He also had the most beautiful woman in all of England beside him, her hair appearing more amber than gold under the glow of firelight, and her body exquisitely soft.

She was once again buttoned up to her throat, having gone to bed not only with her fortress of a nightgown but also a thick, woolen robe for an added layer of protection. He drew her into his arms so that she rested her head against his chest. "You need warming, Grace," he said when she tried to pull away. "This is a necessity, not a seduction. Frostbite is no jest."

She eyed him warily, but ultimately complied.

He liked the feel of her in his arms, but almost shot out of his skin a few minutes later when she lightly began to trace her finger across his chest, seemingly fascinated by the dusting of hair on it.

She then traced that same finger along the contours of his arm, obviously curious about the sculpture of his muscles. "Stop that, Grace."

"You are hot all over. Does the cold not affect you?"

"No, I do not mind the cold."

"Does nothing affect you?"

"Some things do."

Her touch.

Her scent.

The womanly curves of her body.

If he were any hotter, he'd be a walking torch and burn down the inn. "Go to sleep, Grace. I'd like to get an early start in the morning."

She snuggled against him. "Good night, Deklan."

"Sweet dreams, love."

"Why do you call me that?"

"What? Love? It is a harmless endearment. Would you rather I didn't?"

"No, it is nice. I don't mind it at all."

She fell asleep in less than a minute.

He stayed awake and listened to the wind whistle and howl outside their window. The logs he had earlier tossed on the hearth now sparked and crackled as they burned. Their sheets had a light, lavender scent to them.

Grace was peacefully curled against him.

He breathed in her strawberry scent, knowing it would linger on the sheets and on his skin.

Heaven would be like this, he decided.

It had to be.

Sleep eluded him for a while longer.

Grace was the reason.

He had come close to marrying several years ago, a *ton* beauty by the name of Lady Genevieve de Clare. She was a few years older than Grace and some men would consider her more beautiful, but he did not.

Perhaps because Genevieve did not have Grace's endearing warmth.

It was ironic that he, a man who was the definition of cool reserve, should be so attracted to someone as earnest and compassionate as Grace.

As for Genevieve, she was considered a diamond of the first water, for her features were classical perfection. A fine, straight nose. Lovely blue eyes. Pale blonde hair. She was tall and slender, and knew how to move with elegance.

She was also witty and sophisticated.

And yet, he had run from her.

Perhaps the reason was nothing more than a question of poor timing.

How would he respond if they met now? Would he still be averse to marrying her?

He dismissed the idle musings.

He had not thought of Genevieve in a long while and had no intention of reviving that connection.

His thoughts at present were on Grace alone.

Once this assignment was over, would he run from Grace?

CHAPTER EIGHT

GRACE'S HEART BEAT faster as she watched a shirtless Deklan, his body sleek and perfect, draw aside the drapes and frown. "Blessed saints, of all the bad luck."

She had just woken up from a delicious sleep, unable to believe she had spent the entire night cradled in his arms.

She tossed off the bedcovers and scrambled to his side. "Did they find us?"

"No, Grace. There isn't a chance of that happening now. We are caught in a blizzard." He drew her up so that her back leaned against his chest, and then closed his arms around her as though it was the most natural thing in the world.

"Look," he said, continuing to hold her against the heat of his body while they peered out the window together.

The wind was stiff and whipping the snow into swirls.

She drew back when a particularly fierce gust struck the frosted window panes and rattled them with such force, she feared they might break.

Deklan laughed. "Don't fret. The inn is as sturdy as a fortress."

"It will need to be in this storm. The snow is blinding and piled so high, I cannot even make out the stable. It is completely buried. But I think this place will look beautiful once the snow stops and the air turns gentle."

"Hmm," he said and rested his chin atop her head with the

comfortable familiarity of an old, married couple.

She turned ever so slightly to peek up at him before returning her gaze to the storm. "I've seen snowfalls at our country estate, heaps of snow piled high enough to block our doors. But afterward, the sun comes out and the sky turns the deepest blue. Icicles form on tree branches and everything is covered in a shimmering blanket of white. The deer and other wildlife start to come out, and you can see their colors so clearly against the white snow. I love the countryside in winter, it is a land of fairies."

"And it is best viewed from inside with a warming fire blazing in the hearth," he added with a rumble of laughter. "Well, we are in the middle of it now. I don't think it will stop for hours yet, which means we are not going anywhere today."

She glanced up once more, her heart racing as she stood beside this stunning man and tried to keep her mind from turning to pudding. "That will put us behind schedule and those men–"

"Will never find us here, Grace. If they are stupid enough to ride out today to search for us, they will likely die in this winter storm. Not even I would venture out in this weather and I am tough as nails."

"Then what are we going to do?"

"We are newlyweds," he said, and she could hear the amusement in his voice, "so I could make mad, passionate love to you for the next few hours. I know how insatiably you crave my body."

She giggled.

"What? Not tempted by your manly stallion?"

"Oh, good heavens. Has anyone ever called you that?" A bubble of laughter escaped her lips. "Wait, do not answer me. I really do not want to know."

He chuckled. "All right. Let me suggest another plan. We can sit together and read."

She inhaled lightly. *The Book of Love?*"

He turned her to face him and cast her a boyishly appealing

grin. "I must be losing my touch. It appears we are going to do nothing but read. So be it. I can see you are eager to lecture me about love."

"I am no expert and do not claim to be. The closest I came to courtship was the Duke of Lockbridge and he did not like me very much after all." She sighed in frustration. "And yet, I know I must hold out for love. You may be able to fall into bed with just anyone, but I cannot do this. There will only be one man for me and I will love him until the day I die."

He glanced heavenward and groaned. "We have not even had our breakfast yet and you are already twisting me inside out."

"Why? I am not suggesting you are my love. I hope you are not, because it would be awful if I did love you and you did not love me back."

"There you go again."

"And you are just too dense to admit there is beauty in love. I need my husband to be faithful. I think any woman you marry would be very unhappy if you were unfaithful to her."

"You are wrong, Grace. Most would not say a word about it."

"That is completely untrue. I certainly would open my mouth about it."

He caressed her cheek. "I know you would."

"And what is wrong with that? Any woman who truly loves you would do the same. But I suppose if they did not love you, then you would be free to do whatever you wished without a care. But why would you marry someone like that? Do you really want a woman who values your wealth more than she values you? Of course, this assumes you are wealthy. I expect you are since everyone knows Lady Miranda's son, Finn, takes care of the Brayden family assets. Even though you are a leopard, you are still one of the family."

"Grace, I am not a leopard. Good grief, will you get that out of your head? But Finn does take care of my investments."

"I am a little acquainted with his wife, Belle. She and her sister run the Farthingale soap company. Their scented soaps are marvelous. I use them all the time. My favorite is–"

"Strawberry," he said with a chuckle. "I know." To prove his point, he lightly nuzzled her neck. "It is delicious on your skin. The sweetest nectar."

"Dear heaven," she said in a ragged whisper, "I thought you were going to behave yourself."

"I am trying my best. You are far too tempting. No woman should look as pretty as you in the morning."

She groaned, but made no move to draw away. "Are you going to put on your shirt or will you prance about our bedchamber half-dressed all day?"

He gave her chin a playful tweak. "It does not count as prancing unless one is completely naked. Happy to oblige if you are interested."

The man was simply appalling. "I do not wish to see your horrid snake smiling back at me on your dimpled arse. Kindly stay fully clothed."

He laughed. "All right, Grace. You win. I'll order our breakfast brought up and then we can start reading the book. How's that for a plan?"

She shook her head and smiled. "Yes, it is a very good one."

But he did not toss on his shirt right away or leave for the common room. Instead, he stood there staring at her for the longest moment. "You truly are the prettiest thing in the morning," he said, his voice deep and mingled with a soft growl. "Your eyes have a sleepy, starlight sparkle to them, and your hair is a wild tumble down your back. I don't think I have ever seen anyone as lovely as you."

She swallowed hard.

What was his point?

Was he going to kiss her again?

Her heart was already in palpitations from the delightful neck-nuzzling he had just given her.

"Do you think the book will explain why I find you so appealing even though you are buried under all those layers of wool and linen? I cannot stop staring at you."

"In fact, it will. I know exactly why you cannot take your eyes off me."

He appeared genuinely surprised. "You do? Tell me."

"It is a rather long explanation."

"Go ahead," he said with a shrug, taking gentle hold of her shoulders as he regarded her with his soul-searing eyes. They were the anchors to a manly face, rugged in appearance since he had yet to shave the light stubble of beard that had grown on his chin overnight. "I have nowhere else to be."

"Shouldn't you order our breakfast first?"

"No, answer this first. I am utterly stymied."

"All right. But you mustn't laugh because what I am about to tell you is based on serious scientific observation."

His lips twitched. "Go on."

She took a deep breath. "Well, as you will find out when you read the first chapter, men have two brains."

"We do?" He cast her a rakish smile…well, he may not have been trying to look rakish. But he was naturally irreverent and too handsome for words even in his unkempt state. It was obvious he'd merely run his fingers through his hair when first waking instead of properly combing it. But even those wayward curls looked wonderful, some of them swirling behind his ears and giving him a boyish appearance.

But he was all man, and she dared not forget it.

"Two brains, Grace?"

"Yes, but it is not because you are smarter than women. Quite the opposite. You need two brains because one of them is very stupid and will often lead you into trouble."

He shook his head and emitted a genuine laugh. "Sorry, do go on. This is fascinating."

"You could read the book for a better explanation."

"No, I want to hear it from you." He glanced toward the bed. "Shall we sit?"

"Not on your life. You'll get ideas."

"I already have them when it comes to you. You may think I am brash and too forward, but I have been holding myself back. You have no idea how much of a struggle it has been to keep myself on a very tight leash. I spent last night in agony because I could not peel those layers off you."

She gasped. "How could you?"

"What kind of a question is that? Obviously, I could not. Nor did I touch you because I gave you my word of honor and will keep to it. However, do not goad me. I am quite adept at the game and could seduce you into willingly taking those layers off all by yourself. I could, you know."

"You could not."

"Do not test me, Grace. I am too experienced and you are a novice. You will lose your clothes and your virtue."

"That is a horrible thing to say."

"Why? It is true. But the question remains. Why am I so fascinated by you?"

"Because this is your low brain at work, as our conversation obviously points out. You also have a high brain, but that is something I shall talk about later since you are still trapped in your low brain and cannot seem to get past it."

"Is that bad?"

"Depends on how trapped you remain. Your low brain is the instinctive brain that propels you to…um…mate with as many desirable females as cross your path. Desirable is defined in the book as women who appear fertile to you. You are grinning again."

"I promise you, I am not. Pray, continue."

"This is why men are so fascinated by a woman's *breasts*," she said in a whisper, as though whispering would make the word less shocking. "Probably because they are the source of nourishment for their young."

"We like them for other reasons, too."

"Your eyes are gleaming wickedly. Stop it. My point is, any man will look *there* first, then move on to regard the shape of her body in general, especially her hips. He needs to know they are wide enough to safely bear his children. Afterward, his gaze will move upward to look at her face. All this will occur within a matter of seconds. It is instinctive and most men will not even realize they do this."

She thought he would toss a smug remark at this point, but he was now surprisingly serious. "It all happens on instinct," she said, hoping to sound authoritative, "and the man has ruled out hundreds of women in those few seconds, but he has also kept hundreds ruled in. Here is where he faces a dilemma. He cannot possibly protect all of them along with the offspring they will produce after a successful mating."

"So what does he do?"

"He must settle on one. She is the one who will bear his children and she is the one he will protect, along with their children, of course. If he abandons them to fend for themselves, they will be left vulnerable and likely be eaten by wolves. Well, we are no longer out in the wild and in danger of being eaten by actual animals. But hunger, poverty, sickness, these are the wolves at her door."

"Serious concerns," he said with a nod.

"Yes, this is why she needs the man to stay close, especially during periods when she cannot defend herself or their little ones. He has a vested interest in remaining by their side in order to ensure his children will survive."

"Take a step back, Grace. I understand about the necessity of picking my battles and selecting only the one woman to defend. But I still do not understand my response to you. Why does your body in particular fascinate me?"

"I am getting to that next. It is precisely because I am bundled up from head to toe that you cannot stop looking at me. Your low brain has selected me as a possible mate, but you have not managed a close enough look at my body, especially my...um..." She glanced at her breasts. "You get the point. You are frustrated because your assessment of me is incomplete and you cannot make a final determination."

He arched an eyebrow. "How do I complete it without undressing you and looking my fill?"

"Eventually, your eyes will decide they have seen enough."

"Doubtful."

She ignored the comment. "They will naturally complete their evaluation of what my body looks like by filling in the missing information through logic and experience."

"What would happen if you were to disrobe and show me your body? I am asking scientifically. Don't bludgeon me, Grace. I've seen plenty of naked women. I know what your body ought to look like. In fact, I'm pretty sure I know exactly how it looks."

"Obviously, you don't or you would not still be looking. Your eyes have not yet satisfied themselves. That's too bad because I am not going to undress for you."

He emitted a light chuckle. "I have another question for you. There are plenty of attractive women crossing my path every day, fully clothed, but I do not dwell on them in this same way. What makes you different? Is it because you are my assignment?"

"Perhaps. But it may also be that I am among the few women who remain a potential partner for you. Even though you are stuck in your low brain assessment of me, a little of your high brain is also at work and has not yet ruled me out."

"So, what happens next? If I must narrow my choice down to one, then how do I choose?"

She left his side to take out the book and place it beside her as she sat at the foot of the bed. "This is when your high brain takes over, the brain with the capacity to love. Do you want to know how this higher brain deciphers all the clues to select the right mate for you?"

He cast her a wry smile and followed her to the bed, stretching his large frame atop it. He clasped his hands behind his head and studied her with a feral gaze. "Yes, Grace. I do."

She opened the book and pretended to study one of the chapters, but mostly she was trying to avoid looking at him.

He was so handsome.

"Um…this is where the five senses take over. Sight, touch, taste, hearing, and scent. I am no expert in this by any means, but as the book explains, the person who is right for you must appeal to all your senses."

"This seems obvious enough. If I could not stand the sound of your voice, or your scent, or the look of you, and so on, then I would reject you."

"That's right."

"Well, that was easy. All I need to do is find a woman who is pleasing to all my senses and marry her."

"Ugh, no." She rolled her eyes. "Are you saying this merely to goad me? There is so much more to finding love with the right person. It is a delicate matter. Even if–"

She stopped upon hearing a knock at their door.

Deklan rolled to his feet, moving with his usual grace and blur of speed. He nudged her behind him when she followed, and did not seem to mind when she lightly clutched his shoulder. He was not wearing his shirt, so she could clearly see his shoulders were broad and muscled. In truth, deceptively so. His sleek appearance belied his impressive strength.

She could also clearly see the scars on his back. There were several, but one in particular was long and puckered. Without thinking, she put her lips to it. "Oh, heavens. I did not mean to kiss your wound. I'm sorry."

He chuckled. "I'm not. It is healed, Grace. It no longer hurts me. Stay back."

"Do you think those agents have found us?" She was still holding onto him and loving the warmth of his skin.

"Not a chance." He opened the door the littlest bit. "Ah, Mrs. Harcourt. Good morning."

"I thought ye two lovebirds might want breakfast."

"An excellent idea. I was just coming down to order it sent to our room."

Grace eased back while he peered down the hall and must

have seen nothing alarming for he relaxed his stance and addressed Mrs. Harcourt. "Let me make myself presentable and I will walk with you to the common room. I'll help you carry the tray back to our room."

"Ye needn't worry about that, Captain Driscoll. I'll manage on my own. But select whatever ye like and I'll fix ye up something nice."

"Very kind of you." He quickly tossed on his shirt and boots. "Sweetheart, would you prefer cocoa or tea?"

She tried not to blush, but his endearment had caught her off guard. "Cocoa, please."

"I'll be right back." He took a moment to kiss her on the forehead before striding out with a giggling Mrs. Harcourt who was clearly a romantic.

Deklan was playing the role of doting husband to perfection and giving the older woman a thrill.

Sighing, Grace closed the door behind him.

This was the perfect opportunity to attend to her necessaries. She had just finished by the time Deklan returned, his manner all business and none of the doting husband.

"The inn is full, Grace. I think we had better take all our meals in here. I don't want you to be seen in the common room."

"What about you? The other guests have noticed you now."

"Yes, some have." He nodded as he closed the door.

"And? Do you think any of them are a threat?"

He seemed not at all concerned as he stretched back on the bed, his head casually propped on his hands. "No threats, just ordinary travelers passing through. Mrs. Harcourt will be along in a few minutes. She's finishing up in the common room and will bring something for us when she has a moment. Seems you are a particular favorite of hers, not that I am surprised."

"I am certain you are the one she admires. She adores the sweet way you behave around me. You can be very convincing in your role, as though you are a man in love. Very well done. Truly."

He shrugged. "While we are on the topic, where did we leave off in our love lessons?"

"We were about to discuss the stupid mistakes you should avoid when choosing your mate."

He grinned. "Me specifically? Or men in general? But I think my attitude about marriage has you peeved. So I expect I am the idiot you fear will make a stupid mistake. Go ahead, Grace. Tell me why I am wrong."

"It isn't a question of right or wrong. Your problem is that you are not using your five senses properly when it comes to women. In other respects, I think your senses are more finely honed than anyone else's. You use them every moment of every day for your survival and have been quite successful. However, I think this success has given you false confidence. You think you know what you are doing. But when it comes to finding the perfect wife, you deliberately ignore the very senses that have served you so well."

"I disagree, Grace. I do use them and know what pleases me and what doesn't. It isn't something I can turn on and off. So what else is there besides the five senses I am misapplying?"

She gave thought to what he was saying before responding. She really was no expert and could not claim better knowledge simply from reading that book just the once. "The point you miss is that merely finding a woman who pleases all your senses is not the final step on the road to a happy marriage."

She picked up the book again and opened it to the chapter on expectations. "You ought to read it yourself."

"I will, but I want to hear your thoughts first."

"Why? The book addresses these issues so much better than I ever could." What could he gain from her inexperience?

"But you have definite opinions and I want to hear them."

"Oh, all right, I'll try my best." She took a deep breath and continued. "There are many reasons why two good people who like each other and find each other pleasing to all their senses will still end up unhappy if they marry. Expectation. Bonds of connection. Flaws we can or cannot tolerate in each other. They do not even have to be major flaws such as excessive drinking or gambling. Or womanizing."

She glanced at him and was surprised to find him regarding her with a contemplative expression on his face.

She had seen him toss rakish smiles and thought him handsome then.

He was also handsome when standing taut and alert in furtherance of his agent of the Crown duties.

But she thought him utterly devastating to her heart as he looked just now, serious in thought and demeanor.

She ignored the butterflies now fluttering in her belly. "Let me start with the chapter on expectations. Success or failure has to do with the expectations a wife and husband have when going into the marriage. Take us, for example. And I only make mention of us for this scientific purpose. Do not make more of it than it is. I am not suggesting we are a couple."

"All right," he said, now casting her a lazy smile that shot tingles through her. "Tell me what is wrong with us?"

"You mustn't approach this as a question of who is to blame. There is no party at fault, just differences we can or cannot accept in each other. You know I want a husband who will love me and make me an important part of his life. You want a wife who will leave you alone to do whatever you have always done. Do you see how this can become a problem?"

He nodded. "Yes, for one of us."

"For both of us," she insisted.

"But I think it is a bigger problem for you. Mine is solved if I married someone who will not mind spending large stretches of time apart from me."

She wanted to hit him over the head with the book.

Was he purposely riling her?

"Why would you want to marry someone whose goal in life is to avoid you? You are taking on a wife, not a housekeeper. Do you not want a woman who will care for you? Who will be a loving partner to you? A confidante and friend? Do you really want to have children with a woman who will be little more than a stranger to you? Who will only come to you when she wants her household allowance increased?"

"I am guessing by your tone that my answer should be no."

"Is it not obvious? Truly, I am going to hit you over the head with this book if you persist in being dense as a log. Your children need a mother who will love them with all her heart. Do you think she will love them if she does not love you?"

"Yes, Grace. She likely will. A mother's love is a separate thing from love between a husband and wife. Why will you not see it from my perspective? My work is dangerous and my life is always at risk. What if I died tomorrow? How would a loving wife feel? I'll tell you, a sweet wife like you would be shattered. And what of our children? I could not bear knowing how badly my loss would devastate them."

"So you would rather seek someone who does not care if you live or die? That is ridiculous. You are wrong to think that way. Your loving wife and children would be grateful for every precious moment they had with you. A week. A month. A decade. A lifetime. They would grab whatever they could and not regret it or trade a moment of that time with you for all the riches of ancient Rome." She plunked the book down on his stomach. "Read it. Talking to you about love just upsets me."

He set the book aside and sat up. "You are making my head split in two. Why must you take everything so deeply to heart? Not everyone feels the way you do. Most people do not wish to marry for love. They are quite content to settle for an advantageous union, one that will put a roof over their head and keep their belly full."

"I understand this, but why cannot I have a full belly, a roof over my head *and* love?"

"Gad, why do you do this to me?"

"What? Drag you down from your safe perch high in a tree and make you think with your heart?"

"Obviously, I am not good at it." He cast her a wry smile. "And stop comparing me to a leopard hiding in a tree."

"I cannot help it because this is what you are. Will you deny you keep yourself apart from others? Watch your prey from up in your safe branches. Always content to hunt on your own. Preferring to live life on your own terms and sharing nothing of yourself with others."

"And your fanciful notions about love have been indulged by your parents. Rest assured, had Lockbridge gone to your father asking for your hand in marriage, your father would have leapt across his desk and held out his hand to consent to it. He would not have cared if you were unhappy over the match. That alliance would have made you a duchess and elevated the standing of your entire family. Whether or not you loved the duke would have been inconsequential to him."

As little as a few days ago, she would have denied it vehemently. But she no longer recognized the man her father had become. The Viscount Montford she had seen yesterday would have forced her to the altar with Lockbridge just as Deklan had declared. He would have ignored her even if she had crawled on her knees begging him not to accept the offer.

"You are right." She could hardly speak for the ache in her heart. "I know."

Deklan emitted an anguished groan. "I worry for you, Grace. Love will not shelter you from the storms of life. You need to grow a tougher hide."

She rose and walked to the window, not wanting him to see her struggle with her sadness. Was she the only fool who still believed in love?

He came to her side and turned her to face him. "You have me in knots."

"Why? I am not your concern beyond recovering the stolen crown."

He placed his hands on either side of the window to trap her against it. "You will have a world of hurt if you believe the sun will always shine, birds will always chirp, and the man of your dreams will magically appear. What if he never does?"

But he had.

And he was standing inches from her.

Who else was she ever going to love but Deklan?

Perhaps she felt this way because he was protecting her and they had been thrown together every moment since their first meeting. But it was more than that, for she felt as though she had known him all of her life.

Was there such a thing as hearts recognizing each other?

Dear heaven, had it only been two days?

Love could not possibly flourish so quickly.

Weren't these rash feelings exactly what *The Book of Love* was warning its readers to avoid?

"You may think I am a ninny, Deklan. But I do know how precarious life can be. These past few months have taught me quite the lesson."

"And still, you want love?"

"More than ever."

He leaned his forehead against hers. "Oh, Grace. What am I going to do with you?"

She could think of many things, but they mostly involved kissing and giving their bodies to each other, which was a terribly dangerous idea. "You could teach me something useful. I am adept at dancing, having spent years under the guidance of a dance instructor. Music. Painting. Archery. But what good are these accomplishments to me now? I am just another genteel, young lady of moderate talent who has fallen upon hard times and must now learn to make her way in the world."

"This will not be your lot in life. I am not going to let anything bad happen to you."

"Then will you teach me something useful? I can embroider, but cannot sew a gown for myself. Nor can I boil water or bake a pie or tend crops."

"We are going to talk about this later. Blessed saints, you are giving me fits." She thought he was going to kiss her, but he suddenly moved away. "Mrs. Harcourt is making her way down the hall."

"You can hear her?"

"Yes."

She thought he was making it up as an excuse to move away from her, but he crossed the room to open the door and there she was. "Why, Captain Driscoll. What a coincidence. I was about to knock."

He stepped aside to allow her in. "Smells delicious, Mrs. Harcourt. Here, let me take the tray out of your hands. You've loaded it with delights and it must be heavy."

"Well, I'm used to lugging things about. Ye just let me know if ye need anything else." She turned to smile at Grace. "Mrs. Driscoll, ye seem a little overset. Are ye feeling all right?"

Grace nodded. "Yes, perfectly well."

"Are ye certain?"

Grace nodded again.

Deklan must have considered her response unconvincing, so he added, "She is disappointed because the storm will delay us from reaching her family."

"Oh, of course. Poor lamb, ye must be missing them something dreadful. But ye'll see them soon enough. The last of the snow will pass through by this afternoon. Of course, ye'd better wait for tomorrow before ye leave here. It'll be too dangerous to travel today."

She smiled at the woman. "Thank you, Mrs. Harcourt. You are perfectly right. And there is no lovelier place to be than snowed in with my husband at this lovely inn."

Deklan set down the breakfast tray on the small table nestled against the fireplace wall and cast the old woman a wink followed by a rakish smile. "And I intend to take full advantage."

The woman bustled out giggling.

Deklan closed the door after her, then began to set out their meal. The scent of cocoa, coffee, and warm bread tickled Grace's nostrils. "Let me help you with that."

She came to his side, but he had already done most of the work.

"Sit down, love. Can we call a truce to our discussion?"

"Yes, please. Let's talk of anything else. Or we can simply eat in silence. I would not mind that either."

"No, I want to get to know you better."

"What do wish to know about me?" She took a sip of her cocoa, loving the way it warmed her insides. "I should think my entire life is contained in your very thorough agent reports."

He grinned as he drew out his chair, sat back, and drank his coffee. "Those reports did not tell me how beautiful you are. Or reveal you had taken up lodgings in my aunt's home."

"In the bedchamber usually reserved for you."

His smile was tender as he said, "It was a delightful surprise."

She laughed and dug into her plate of eggs. "Shocking, humiliating, appalling. I would hardly call our meeting delightful. Speaking of which, what am I to say if Mrs. Harcourt asks how the two of us first met?"

He set down his cup. "Keep it as simple as possible. We met at an assembly ball in Bath over the summer and instantly fell in love. How's that?"

"I have never been to Bath."

"Neither has Mrs. Harcourt. Just keep your descriptions vague and she will never know the difference. An elderly aunt of yours wanted to take the waters and brought you along. The pump rooms were a crush. You toured the ancient Roman baths and found them to be a marvel. Mention your enjoyment of the assembly balls and nightly musicales."

She nodded and tried her hand at embellishing the story. "I was in raptures when you asked me for the honor of a dance. Um, do you dance?"

"Of course, it is all part of our agent of the Crown training. We must be adept at moving in all circles. Come, I'll show you." He surprised her by taking her hand to lift her to her feet, and then he began to spin her slowly about the room. "We danced a waltz…just like this," he said, his voice soft and deep as he drew her into his arms. "I held you close."

"As you are doing now?"

"Yes, love. The world and everyone in it melted away for us. No one existed but you and me."

She smiled, quite swept away and knowing she would have fallen in love with him had they ever really shared a dance. "You were quite dashing in your naval uniform. My heart was yours by the time we completed our first turn about the room. But Deklan, how were we allowed to share a waltz?"

"The rules in Bath are less rigid than in London. Your elderly aunt did not hesitate to give me permission. She knew of my sterling reputation. See?" He still held her, guiding her as they continued to slowly twirl.

"You make it sound so easy."

"Because it is."

Perhaps it would be for someone as experienced in the art of seduction as he obviously was. Were agents really given instruction on how to woo and seduce young ladies? If so, he would have gotten top marks. He was looking at her in such a way she could have sworn he was falling madly in love with her. "Did we speak to each other as we waltzed?"

"Yes, of course. I would not have wasted the opportunity to get to know you better."

"What would you have said to me?"

"It is in my nature to get right to the point. I would have said something like…" His smile faded, his expression no longer wry but suddenly serious. "I am in love with you, Miss Montford."

Grace was caught by surprise and missed a step. "Oh."

He quickly guided her back into their graceful turn about the room. "Too forward? Perhaps I would have said nothing, just put my hand to the small of your back and waited for a more appropriate moment to tell you how I felt."

"So we danced in silence?"

"Yes, with me in fiery torment as I led you onto the terrace to complete the dance beneath the silver moon and sparkling stars. Others had done the same because it was a warm, clear night. A light breeze carried the scent of jasmine from the nearby gardens. We twirled in our own orbit, you as radiant as the sun and I your servant moon, forever your heart's captive. I wanted to get on bended knee and propose to you as soon as the waltz ended."

"Did you?" Grace held her breath.

He grinned. "No, this definitely would have been too forward of me. I called upon you at your residence the following day, a pleasant townhouse let by your aunt in the Royal Crescent. I did the same on the day after that, and as often as permitted afterward until, with agonizing restraint, I proposed to you a full month later."

"It must have been very difficult for you," she teased.

"It was. Excruciating, actually. I asked for your hand in marriage on the day you were to leave Bath and return to London. You were wildly, madly, breathlessly in love with me by then and immediately accepted. Tears of happiness flowed down your cheeks."

"A veritable puddle of tears?"

"An entire stream of them," he said with a light laugh. "You could not believe your good fortune in landing the best man in all of Bath. No, all of England."

She laughed heartily. "Modest fellow, aren't you?"

"What? Too over the top? How about, we shared a waltz and spoke only of tame subjects such as the weather and who we might know in common? But I called upon you the following day...and the day after that. Before the week was out, I made it clear I was courting you. As I said, I proposed to you at the end of the month, on the morning you were to return to London."

She stifled her disappointment when he led her back to her chair to resume eating her breakfast. "What if she asks more questions?"

He took his seat beside her, this magnificent man who made

her heart flutter and also ache because their time together would soon come to an end. "You ignore them and steer the conversation to a safer topic. You are an accomplished rider. It is no different than guiding your horse down a particular path with a slight tug of the reins. You keep control of the conversation by directing it wherever you wish it to go."

"Oh, I see."

He took a bite of the scone he had slathered in marmalade and followed it with a sip of his coffee. "Now, I shall take charge of our conversation."

"What do you wish to know?"

"Everything I can about you."

She set aside her fork. "I am as easy to read as an open book. You probably know me better than anyone else does, no matter that we have only been together two days. Goodness, it feels so much longer."

"Because we've already been through so much together."

"Yes, that is true. Well, about me...I can read and write and am very good with sums. I enjoy history, music, and art. But my greatest enjoyment," she said with an impish smile, "is plaguing brilliant agents of the Crown about matters of love."

His laughter was genuine, the smile on his lips reaching into his magnificent eyes.

Grace often had to stop herself from gawking at him like a little fool. "Perhaps we shall soften each other's edges by the time this week is through. You shall have me thinking more logically and I shall have you saving kittens caught up a tree."

His smile was quite tender as he said, "Yes, I should like that."

It suddenly struck her this might be one way they would be good for each other. For the most part, she appreciated his logic and cold calculation. Those traits were important to who he was and she did not wish to change him. But he needed to realize decisions on love required him to listen to his heart and not only to his calculating brain.

"Grace, let's talk about your family."

"Must we?"

He nodded. "I would like to know more about them, too. Not merely your father and Richard. I've had my fill of them, but I'm curious about your mother and younger siblings."

She sighed. "I miss them so much."

"I know." He regarded her solemnly, their humor of only moments ago now faded.

"We have never been apart at Christmas. I wish we could be together now, but it is hopeless. You and I won't even make it back to London in time for Miranda's festivities if the weather continues like this."

"I'm sure it will improve."

"Perhaps, because your family will be terribly disappointed if you miss Christmas with them. As for me, there isn't the slightest chance I'll make it to my family's country estate in time to join my mother and siblings for Christmas supper. Even if it were possible, I don't think Wooton will allow me to go."

He placed a hand over hers. "The timing is tight for both of us. Would it be so bad if you and I spent Christmas together?"

The possibility had never crossed her mind, for she was too lost in her family's troubles to think about anything else. These past months had been spent trying to secure whatever provisions she could for her distraught mother and siblings who were still too young to protect themselves.

All she owned was now gone, the few pieces of jewelry belonging to her and not confiscated had been sold to put food on their table and pay for a cook and maid. Fortunately, costs were lower in the countryside. The meager funds she supplied were enough to last her family to the end of this month. It would have lasted barely a week had they been in London. But even in the countryside, their budget was bare bones and not enough for the extravagance of purchasing a goose for their Christmas table.

Her mother would be so disappointed.

So would her siblings, James, Serenity, and Hope.

But what more could she do right now?

Some of her savings had also gone toward trying to clear her father's name. What a waste of time and precious resources. Every door had slammed in her face because, as it turned out, he really was guilty of those accusations.

Amid all this, she had found the man of her dreams.

They were now on their way to Bexhill and she held out hope of saving the innocent members of her family if only they could find this elusive crown.

Would she mind spending Christmas alone with him?

Dear heaven.

"Deklan, I would not mind at all."

CHAPTER NINE

DEKLAN KNEW HE was in trouble.

He had never lost his heart to anyone before.

But Grace had tumbled into his life and changed all that from the moment he'd almost crushed her when falling into bed that first night. Ever since then, his nuisance of a heart would not stop calling out her name. Not merely calling it out, but screaming it and declaring him an idiot if he ever let her go.

"Shut up," he muttered to himself, knowing he could not afford to be distracted from his assignment or the danger constantly nipping at their heels.

Grace looked angelic standing beside the window, circled in light while watching snowflakes fall and lost in her thoughts. She turned to him with a shake of her head. "Sorry, were you talking to me? I missed what you said."

"Just muttering to myself."

Since they were finished with breakfast, he gathered the plates, cups, and jam pots, then left her a moment to bring the tray downstairs because he was going to do something stupid if he stayed closed in that room with her a moment longer.

"Captain Driscoll," the innkeeper called out, rushing toward him with arms waving. "Ye needn't have gone to the trouble. One of the boys would have picked up the tray. Ye should have left it by yer door."

"I didn't mind. I was hoping one of your maids might assist

my wife."

"Of course." He turned to a young girl who was toting fresh table linens in her arms. "Suzie, set those aside and go help Mrs. Driscoll."

"Yes'um, Mr. Harcourt." She handed the linens to another maid and scurried off.

Deklan remained in the common room to chat with the innkeeper and his wife. It was not in his nature to be amiable, but he wanted to give Grace time alone to dress and attend to whatever else women attended to in their morning routine.

As for him, he considered it a waste of time for Grace to dress since they had nowhere to go and he did not want her leaving their room. But she needed to pile on the layers, needed to lace herself up and button herself up from throat to toes in order to put a protective wall between his big hands and her delectable body.

Not that he would ever take Grace against her will.

His years of training and solid discipline would never allow it.

But Grace was not averse to his advances. She was sweet, innocent, and completely vulnerable at the moment. It would take nothing to have her surrender willingly.

But what then?

Best to avoid any complications.

Concentrate on protecting her.

He noted a surly-looking couple in their mid-thirties lingering over their coffee in a corner of the common room. Neither of them looked happy. The woman was rather sharp-eyed and looked familiar but he could not quite place her. He made a silent note to keep Grace away from that one. She'd sniff out their lie within a minute of talking to her.

The only other occupants of the common room were two gentlemen who appeared to be father and son by the look of them.

They seemed cheerful and rather easygoing.

Still, it was safest to keep Grace away from all of them.

Inns of this quality often had libraries filled with books, decks of cards, and other games available for their guests to borrow. He took his time and browsed through the shelves to select a few books. He also selected a pack of cards and several games he thought might interest Grace.

The sharp-eyed woman still had her gaze on him.

Did she know his family?

Had she recognized him?

He returned to his guest quarters before she could approach him. The maid was just coming out of his chamber with an empty ewer in hand when he arrived. He dug into his pocket and withdrew a few coins for her. "Here, Suzie. Thank you for assisting my wife."

She bobbed a curtsy. "Yer welcome, Captain Driscoll. Mighty generous of ye."

Since he had encountered the maid walking out, he assumed Grace must have finished dressing. "Grace, I–"

His heart stopped.

She was wearing nothing but a thin chemise and her hair was a wild, golden tumble spilling wet over her shoulders and clinging to the sheer undergarment which hid nothing of her exquisite curves.

What in blazes?

Is this how she had spent her time? Washing her hair?

His eyeballs bounced like pebbles hurtling down a cliff because he could not take his eyes off her scantily clad body, and yet knew he must…and yet, he could not.

What had she said about the male eyes needing to see their fill?

Oh, he was looking.

Gawking, to be precise.

His organs exploded when he caught an eyeful of the dusky peaks of her breasts. Droplets of water had fallen onto her chemise and dampened the fabric around her bosom to reveal two stiff, rosy buds.

Sweet Lord in heaven.

"Why aren't you dressed?"

She grabbed her robe and began to fumble with it. "I did not realize you would return so soon. Suzie went to refill our ewer with fresh water."

"I saw her as I walked in."

Grace licked her lips, a gesture meant to calm her nerves, but it had the opposite effect on him, inflaming his already heightened senses.

He needed to dive out the window and bury himself in an icy bank of snow.

Roll around in it.

Pack it on his privates.

She was still grappling with her robe. "We were not going anywhere today and since you did not want me leaving the room, I thought…"

Her voice died out as he tossed the books and games onto the small table where they'd just shared breakfast, then strode to the door to close and latch it firmly. "Don't cover yourself up, Grace."

Was this his voice? Raspy and ragged.

He took a step toward her. "Let me see you."

Her face was on fire, but she slowly lowered the robe and placed it on the bed. "Now you know what I look like under all the layers. I don't suppose my chemise hides anything of me." Her voice was barely above a whisper. She trembled as he approached. "This ought to satisfy you and you won't need to look anymore."

"It doesn't work that way. I don't think I will ever be satisfied now."

"What do you mean?" The chemise slid off one shoulder, and both of them glanced at it. Deklan realized she was too frightened tug it back up.

Her eyes were wide and she dared not move a muscle.

"You are beautiful, Grace," he said, nudging the sleeve back into place and doing his best to ignore the molten ripples of desire coursing like volcanic waves through his body.

The chemise would have been off her in a trice had he not been bound by his oath of honor.

If only he were a cad and had it in him to break his word.

No, he could never hurt this innocent girl.

Grace had the softest, most trusting eyes.

And the sweetest body.

He took a deep breath and inhaled the moist nectar of her skin.

Her hair fell damp and loose about her shoulders. Unable to resist, he brushed back those wet curls and put his lips to the pulse at the base of her slender neck. That pulse throbbed wildly the moment he placed a soft kiss to the spot.

Then he licked his tongue along the apple of her throat and kissed her lightly there.

She shuddered as he drew away. "Why did you kiss me like that?"

"Why do you think?"

"I don't know…to taste me?"

He nodded. "Did you like it?"

"You know I did." Her breaths quickened, drawing his attention to the rise and fall of her chest. "Deklan…"

"Yes, Grace?"

"What will happen if I let you do it again?"

"You cannot encourage me. It is too dangerous." His chuckle more closely resembled a groan. "I shall have that chemise off you, be kissing and tasting your breasts, and probably expire from the ecstasy of it."

She glanced away, and closed her eyes a moment to steady her breath. "So will I."

Had she really just said that?

Was she inviting him to–

A knock at their door shook both of them back to their senses.

Grace's face turned to flames again. "Oh, my heavens! What am I saying?"

She reached for her robe and began to fumble with it once more. "You must think I am the lowliest wanton."

"Stop, Grace. You have the garment upside down." He took it from her hands and helped her put her arms through the sleeves. "And you are the sweetest girl in existence. Do not be ashamed of the feelings we have for each other. Liking my kisses does not make you a woman of loose morals."

"It doesn't?"

He laughed. "No, love. Far from it."

He kissed her on the forehead. "I am going to open the door and let Suzie in now. Let her help you with whatever else you need to do. I'll turn away whenever necessary. I give you my oath on it. But I am not leaving this room again. All right?"

She nodded.

He unlatched the door and allowed the maid in. "Ah, fresh water. Thank you, Suzie."

The girl giggled. "Shall I help you to dress, Mrs. Driscoll?"

"Yes, please. That would be lovely."

Deklan picked up *The Book of Love* while Grace and her maid continued with whatever they had been doing.

It took him a while to calm down and begin to read. He ignored their chatter and now tried to concentrate on the first page and its opening sentences. *Love does not come from the heart but from the brain. It is the brain that sends signals throughout the body, telling you what to feel.*

Well, how about that?

Grace had been going on about his heart when all along these feelings of love started with the brain. But he understood the deep connection that could develop between two hearts.

He glanced out of the corner of his eye and noticed Grace had now donned one of her plain gowns, a woolen one the color of dark chocolate. The girl could wear a burlap sack and still look stunning.

He read on, sailing through the first chapter on the man's two brains since Grace had lectured him on it enough that he was familiar with its elements. Low brain was the sexual brain, the unthinking, need-to-mate brain. Blessed saints! Had he not exhibited every possible low brain urge to mate with Grace just now?

Body on fire, organs in spasms. The *tail* of his snake tattoo ready and willing to perform its happy dance inside of her?

He rubbed a hand across the nape of his neck and groaned.

Grace cast him a worried look.

"I'm fine," he lied. "Just realized I forgot something."

"What did you forget?"

"It isn't important." He returned to the book and pretended to read. It took him a moment to calm before he could actually resume reading next about the male's high brain. This was the selective brain, the one that would lead him to choose his right partner.

Grace.

Who else would it ever be for him?

The five senses came next, and he took a little time reading those chapters because he wanted to think about how this inexperienced innocent had managed to devastate each and every one of his finely honed senses.

Grace came to sit beside him at the table once Suzie had finished assisting her and left to return to her duties. "Where have you gotten to?"

"I've just finished the chapters on the five senses."

She leaned closer to read along with him, sending him into spasms again with the warm, fruity scent of her skin. "I think the most important thing I learned about using the senses," she said, unaware of her effect on him, "is not to lie to myself about what they reveal."

"What do you mean, Grace?"

"Well, sometimes we want a thing so badly, we ignore the warning signs. You know, the dangerous rocks ahead. Do not sail in these waters. Yet, we sail ahead and crash straight into them only to leave our heart in splinters. I think this often happens with young women because we are pushed toward making a match from an early age. We are given lessons on charm, grace, etiquette, and then tossed onto the marriage mart after having been sheltered all our lives and having no idea what to expect. We are told to keep smiling until we land a duke or other suitable title."

She cast him a wistful glance and continued. "We put on a cheerful face and I suppose the bachelors do the same. But what is real and what is feigned? Lockbridge did not think twice before jilting me, but did I see the warning signs in our earlier encounters? Toward others, he was all the things one expects in a duke, pompous, arrogant. Haughty. Did I make note of those qualities and put them down as danger signals? No, I did not."

"And he hurt you," Deklan said, aching for her because that cur had truly smashed her against the rocks with his disdain.

"I was embarrassed, confused. Caught unprepared, although I should have been ready for the worst having seen his treatment of those beneath his station. He was all sweetness and charm to me until then."

"It isn't your fault, Grace. How were you to know? It was impossible for you to see the real man when he hid so much of his true nature from you. He was your first beau and waging a campaign to win your heart."

"Had I read this book, I might have been better prepared. How would you have responded toward me after my family's downfall if you were Lockbridge, Deklan?"

He arched an eyebrow. "If I were courting you when your family scandal exploded onto the front pages of every newspaper in London?"

She winced. "It does sound awful, doesn't it? Perhaps I should not be so hard on him. After all, he is a duke and no doubt also pushed by his family to make an advantageous match. He is probably still mopping his brow and giving thanks for his lucky escape."

"Perhaps. But what would I have done? It would depend on how deeply I cared for you. Had I wanted to marry you, I might have put a halt to our courtship until I gathered all the facts. Yet, whatever my decision about marriage, I would never have ridiculed you in front of my friends. If you were innocent and as much a victim of your family's wrongdoing as anyone else, I would have stood by you and been a friend to you for as long as you needed me."

"And earned the scorn of your own friends?"

"If anyone of them turned their back on me, then he was never a true friend of mine. But as for me, I would have helped you because it is the right thing to do. I would not care what the *ton* gossips think. Offering to find a place for you and your family, perhaps helping to pay for it, is what I would have done. When the dust cleared and I knew you were not involved in any of your family's wrongdoing, it is likely I would have married you."

"Even if it made you a social outcast forever?" In the next moment, she laughed and shook her head. "Silly me. You would not care a whit for what anyone else thinks."

"To be fair, I am not a duke and do not have an ancient title to uphold. Therefore, I am at liberty to do as I please." He raked a hand through his hair and studied her. "Not that duty to his title excuses Lockbridge's behavior toward you in any way. Unfortunately, you learned a hard lesson, that holding a title does not make one noble in character."

"It is one I will never forget."

"They are no better than any of us. In fact, they are likely worse. Most of these noblemen gained their wealth and power by unsavory means. Wars, political alliances, chopping heads and killing those whose mere existence might weaken their stranglehold on power. This included killing women and children."

"It is obvious Lockbridge saw me as a mere alliance and had no qualms about ending it when he saw no profit in it. But Deklan, what do you see when you look at me?"

He smiled. "Is this a test of my senses?"

"No, it is more of a test of mine. I have read the book and gained some knowledge from it, but there is much I still do not know. You are a leopard so your sense of sight is quite keen, as are all your other senses. Keen hearing. Keen sense of smell. I'm not sure how to explain touch and taste, but you obviously satisfied those senses when you caught me after I had just washed my hair." Her cheeks were now a bright pink as she blushed. "I am still reeling from that encounter."

"In a nice way, I hope."

She nodded.

"Me, too. I mean it, Grace. I am better at hiding my feelings than you are, but I do have them, especially when it comes to you."

He glanced at the book and then back at her. "Getting the sense of a person does not mean merely taking in their appearance, or the sound of their voice, their scent, and so on. I think this book does not place sufficient importance on something I would call a sixth sense."

She regarded him, intrigued. "What is that?"

"I would call it the sense of character. The author does talk about it, but not until well into the book and jumbled in with talk of expectations and compromise. But there should be no compromise on character. I think discussion of it deserves to be up front."

She was smiling as she listened to him.

"Let's use me as an example, Grace. Knowing someone's face and body is but one small aspect of what my brain takes in. Yes, the five senses are important, but there are still many women who will pass this hurdle and please all my senses. So how do I narrow my choice down further?"

Her eyes widened as she waited for his explanation.

She had the prettiest eyes.

One could easily drown in their green depths.

"When I look at someone," he continued, "I must analyze not

only their appearance but their nature. Do they have strength of character? Or do they lack it? What does their stance reveal? Are they open and relaxed? Or tense and closed in? Do their eyes constantly dart about? What do their facial expressions reveal, especially when they think no one is paying attention to them?"

"But you are sensitive to these clues because you are trained to look beyond someone's facade."

"It is more a question of awareness than training. Certainly someone as smart and compassionate as you would pick up on this immediately. Do you ever look at a person and watch how they respond to others? Or to a particular situation? This is how I decipher a person's character, and it is something I rank higher in importance than a pleasing countenance. Are they petty? Selfish? Cruel? Inconsiderate of others? Dishonest? Reckless? Indecisive? Lazy?"

He rocked back in his chair and grinned. "Do you still want me to tell you what I see when I look at you?"

She nodded. "More than ever. I prefer your interpretation because it goes to the heart of who a person truly is. Do they go through their day cheerful and smiling? Or do they wake up surly and looking for reasons to complain?"

"Yes, this is it. Will their essential character bring sunshine into your life or perpetual dark clouds? I think even the most cynical of us would avoid someone who brings dark clouds to the marriage."

"And you? What do you want?"

He chuckled. "I may look at the world with a cynical eye, but why would I want my wife to be like me? I think most men want a woman who can bring sunshine into their lives. To a man, his home is his sanctuary. We have enough battles to fight while out in the world. Who wants to be battling at home, too?"

"I wish I was as discerning as you."

"You will be in time. Well, these are just my opinions. But I have also learned an important lesson, and that is not to overly value the five senses."

"Well, they are important. Just not all that matters."

"While you may not have been aware of what goes into making a decision about a person, you were closer to the mark than I was about finding the right spouse. You say you will only marry for love, but I think this means you are looking to marry someone who will make you happy, who will support you and be strong in the ways you need him to be. I would also add one more element to that. The right person will also bring out the strengths in you."

She cast him an endearing smile. "Oh, please go on. I am finding our discussion fascinating and I'm learning so much. Deklan, what do you see as failings in me? It is important for me to know. How am I to improve myself if I remain unaware of them?"

"Your failings?" He remained quiet a long moment. "The truth," he said softly, shaking his head and emitting a snort of laughter. "Do not fret, Grace. I am laughing at myself, not you."

"Why are you laughing at all?"

"Because I am looking at you...really looking. Taking in every aspect of you, and you are perfect. I am stating it as fact, not trying to flatter you. If I had to make a list of all the things I liked about you and disliked about you, I could not think of a blessed thing to put in the dislike column."

"But you think I am too soft-hearted and walk with my head in the clouds when it comes to holding out for love."

"You are those things, but I do not dislike them in you. Actually, it makes me like you more because you believe in yourself and have the strength of character to hold to your convictions."

"Even if you do not agree with them?"

He nodded. "Yes, even so. I would think much less of you if you had no thoughts of your own and merely parroted mine, or if you allowed others to easily change your mind on matters that are important to you."

"But you are a man who likes to be in control."

"On my assignments, yes. These involve dangerous situations

and I need to control those as much as possible." He arched an eyebrow in amusement. "Well, perhaps I like to control my own life and not have others tell me what I should and should not do."

"Hence your wanting an unobtrusive wife who does not care about you and will not shed a tear if you end up dead face down in a pit of mud."

"Oh, Grace. Grace. You have the sweetest way of kicking my arse." He cast her a tender smile. "I may be softening my position on that."

"Really?"

"Let's just say I am giving it more thought. Much more thought. Here's something else I took from the writings in this book, that the perfect match for me is not going to be the same as the perfect match for someone else. Think of it as pieces of a puzzle set out on a table. We come in all shapes and sizes. Only one of those pieces will perfectly fit mine."

"But the question remains, is that matching piece perfect for you because you can easily control her? What if she does not wish to be controlled?"

"Gad, I am not an ogre. I do not meddle in the lives of friends or family. Of course, I would speak up if I thought one of my loved ones was in danger. But otherwise, it is not my place to insert my opinion. The same goes for the woman I take to be my wife. Who am I to squelch her hopes and dreams? Ridicule her ideas? I do not want to marry a mindless idiot. Perhaps I would be in my own head much of the time, but I would never dismiss her thoughts and opinions."

She rested her elbows on the table and propped her chin on her hands as she studied him. "Do you wish to know what I think of you?"

He gave a mock groan. "Dare I say yes? Be kind. I have a delicate heart and it bruises easily."

She gasped with laughter. "You are the most indelicate man of my acquaintance. I could drop a hammer on your head and you would hardly notice. You are confident to the point of irritating. You are handsome to the point of irritating, too."

"How is that irritating?"

"It just is. You haven't a single flaw. Even when you are unshaven, you still look like some magnificent Olympian god. It is completely exasperating."

"Gad, why do your compliments feel like insults?"

"I don't mean them to be. But you completely overwhelm me. You are smart. Honorable. Brave. You know the world and have experienced everything. You are always right about everything except love. And now, I think you will be right about this, too."

"Well, as it applies to most women." He caressed her cheek. "But as for you, I think I must get to know you better because you think more deeply about love and marriage than other women do. So, we must now speak of *your* heart."

"I would rather we didn't. It is quite battered at the moment. I'm not sure it can take more bruising."

"How many times must I tell you? I would never hurt you, Grace."

She edged forward and planted a soft kiss on his cheek. "Never on purpose. Finish reading that book. I enjoyed our conversation very much and thought your analysis was very clever. I'll be here when you are done since I have no place else to be."

She moved to stand beside the window and study the falling snow.

Blessed saints, the girl was spectacular.

He forced himself to concentrate on the book and flipped the page to the next chapter which spoke about expectations in a marriage. He made quick work of it since Grace had already clobbered him over the head with that one. She expected love in her marriage. Commitment. Friendship. A life built together.

She would be disappointed if he offered her anything less.

He was about to turn to the next chapter, when Grace suddenly gasped and moved away from the window. "Riders are approaching."

He was on his feet in a trice and had his pistol drawn. "Stay behind me."

The snow had slowed and clouds were breaking up to reveal patches of blue sky, but it was too soon for regular travelers to be braving the aftermath of the blizzard.

He noticed only two men, but there could be more. He scanned beyond the lane to the forest of trees on either side, all of which were devoid of their leaves and would provide no coverage for anyone trying to hide.

No one else in sight.

Grace stood close, her hand pressed to his back as though needing that touch for security. "What do you see?"

"Just the two riders. Obviously, the only ones foolish enough to be out there. I'm going downstairs for a better look at them. They're too bundled up to clearly see their faces."

"No, Deklan!"

"I won't be gone more than a few minutes. I am not going to engage them in a brawl. They could be ordinary businessmen on their way to London for an important meeting."

"What if they are the villains come after us?"

"Then I will get you safely away from here." He handed her a full coin purse and a small blade withdrawn from the lip of his boot.

"What are these for?"

"You might need them. Bolt that door behind me and do not allow anyone in but me. I'll be back in a trice."

"What if you don't return?"

He kissed her softly on the lips. "I will always return for you."

"So you say, but what are the coins and knife for then? Is this one of your contingency plans? I know how you love your plans."

He strode across the room toward the door, then paused and turned to face her. "On the slim chance I don't return...and I do mean a slim to nonexistent possibility, I want you to sneak out of here and ride like hell to Bexhill. Rafe knows where we are headed and will have told Lorcan and Donal by now. In truth, it is likely my cousins are these two riders. However, I did not recognize their horses."

"They may have needed to leave theirs behind just as we did. Those agents must be watching the mews behind Miranda's house."

"Yes, quite so. But if these men are foreign agents and not my cousins…mark you, the chances of this are almost nil. But on the unlikely chance I am wrong and they kill or injure me, you need to get out of here and dig up the crown on your own. As I said, Lorcan and Donal will find you in Bexhill and get you safely back to London."

"Wait! Deklan, this is probably a terrible time to discuss your strategy. But my running off without you will not work. Please, do not confront those men."

"Blessed saints, do not tell me how to do my job."

"I'm not, but you are placing too much faith in me."

"No, Grace. It is the other way around. You are placing too little faith in yourself."

"Oh, dear heaven. You are going to hate me for this, but you must believe me when I say my running away will not work. How long do you think it will take these villains to find our room, break down the door, and grab me? Even if I did manage to elude them, what then? How can I ride off? A young woman alone with no idea which road to take other than a general southerly direction? I would be robbed or abducted within an hour of my riding out of here."

He could have put an end to their conversation and been downstairs already if he really thought there was a threat. But Grace was working herself into a state and he blamed himself. They should have discussed alternative plans in the event he was injured or killed.

It was his fault they hadn't.

Instead of reading *The Book of Love*, he should have been training her on survival tactics. His stupid fault, but he had not thought it necessary. She hadn't the heart of a killer and he could not see her plunging a knife into a man's neck.

If speaking of love overset her, what would speaking of death have done to her?

"So, are we agreed? Deklan, I will never leave you behind if you are wounded. Did you not tell me we are in this together to the end?"

"Grace–"

"So this is what we must be. Together to the end. This is not negotiable. If the villains injure you, then I will do my best to save your life by trading information. Of course, I will never reveal the location of the stolen crown but merely offer to lead them to where it is buried…well, hopefully buried. This will buy us time to plan an escape. It will certainly provide more time for Lorcan and Donal to rescue us."

"Are you done telling me what to do?"

"I would not presume to tell you how to go about your business. To be precise, I am trying to give you a realistic account of what I am capable of doing. Is it not important for you to know the limits of my abilities? There are some things I cannot or will not do."

"Such as leaving me behind?"

She nodded. "I thought you ought to know my thoughts since it will impact how you carry out your assignment."

He wanted to be angry with her, but somehow could not summon so much as a kernel of rage. "Anything else? May I leave now?"

"If you were truly worried about those new arrivals, you would have been out of here long before this. Well, I do have a few more thoughts. The timing is awful, I know. Sorry. I'll pack our belongings and be ready to flee, but never without you. Just to be clear on the matter. We are in this together…to the end. So you had better be careful and stay unharmed."

He had every intention of doing so.

Besides, two travelers, even if they turned out to be enemy

agents, were hardly a threat to him. He could easily dispatch them.

She folded her arms across her chest. "Are we in agreement?"

"Gad, you're a bossy thing. Now you are sounding just like me."

She managed a wry smile. "Loyal and resourceful?"

"No, Grace. Highhanded. Insubordinate. Utterly irritating."

"Thank you. I shall take that as a compliment."

CHAPTER TEN

THE BLUE MOON Inn, being a coaching inn, was usually quiet in the late morning. On an ordinary day, most guests would have left shortly after break of day and the place would not fill up again until the coaches stopped here to discharge their passengers for a midday meal and secure a change of horses.

However, due to the storm, all regular schedules were completely tossed to the wind. No travelers had left the inn and most were now seated in the common room, bored and restless as they drank ale and chatted with other guests for lack of anything better to do.

Deklan quietly made his way downstairs and slipped into the little-used library to peer out its window which provided a clear view of all who came or left the inn.

He laughed and hurried out to greet the newest arrivals who had just emerged from the stable and were now standing outside the inn's door dusting snow off their cloaks and hats, and stomping snow off their boots. "I ought to have known you two would be the only idiots reckless enough to ride out in this blizzard."

Deklan was never happier to see his cousins, Lorcan and Donal. "How in heaven's name did you find us so quickly?"

"It was easy," Donal said, "once Rafe told us where you were headed. Why did you hide the truth from us? Wooton is livid and has threatened to string you up by your privates if you dare show your face in London again."

Deklan shrugged. "An idle threat. He won't lay a hand on me. I am his best man, and right now he needs me to avert a war. How could I tell him my plan? He would have tried to overrule me, and I was not going to obey his orders anyway."

Lorcan chuckled. "I thought I was insolent and arrogant. I am an obedient servant compared to you."

Donal clapped Deklan on the back. "We've missed you. Glad you're back with us, even if you are on assignment. Speaking of which, where is your…ahem, lovely assignment."

"Grace? Fretting upstairs. I had better go tell her we are safe." He glanced around. "That is, I hope we are. Any chance you were followed?"

Lorcan shot him a scowl. "No one follows me unless I intend them to see my trail. We slipped away as cleverly as you did. No one will realize we are gone for at least another day. Miranda's house is a zoo and all the family has been summoned to add to the confusion. Those agents have no idea who is coming or going. The wives and our rambunctious children are doing their best to maintain the confusion."

"All part of our duties in protecting the Crown," Donal added with a grin.

"Well, I am grateful. By the way, I am here as Captain Adam Driscoll, Royal Navy. I'm traveling with my wife, Grace. We are newly wed and on our way to London so she can introduce me to her family."

Lorcan shook his head. "London?"

"Don't ask. Grace was trying to be helpful and thought she was cleverly throwing everyone off our scent. Who are you two supposed to be and how do I know you?"

"Old schoolmates of yours from Eton. But we are going to keep our true identities. We are not known here, so there's no need for disguise. Besides, we want those agents to pick up our trail eventually and think we are shadowing you."

"But you are shadowing me."

"No, we're here to divert them from you."

"Ah, purposely misdirect them. That is a good plan for now. But we'll need to pass the crown off to you at some point after we recover it. You are the ones with the best chance of getting it safely into Wooton's hands. Grace is too conspicuous."

Donal nodded. "We'll discuss it later. First, let us get settled in."

Mr. Harcourt came over to them, spouting apologies. "We'll have a few departures within the hour. You shall have those rooms. Just give my maids a little time to prepare them for you, gentlemen. In the meantime, our common room is open and serving meals."

Lorcan tossed a few extra coins onto the registration desk. "Our appreciation for your services. We've traveled quite a way and I am starved."

Deklan waited for the innkeeper to rush off before resuming the conversation. "Rafe knew we were headed to Bexhill, but he did not know Grace and I would be at this inn. How did you find us? And do not tell me you easily picked up my trail because I know it is not so. I was careful."

"It was a hunch," Lorcan said. "Only three suitably elegant inns along this main route, this one having the best food, the best accommodations, and also farthest off the path. A foreign agent would have to know of its existence to even begin to find it."

Donal gave Deklan a poke in the ribs. "Who is that wasp-eyed woman staring at us?"

"She's trouble. I've seen her before but cannot place her. She might have recognized me or perhaps she somehow caught a glimpse of Grace and thought she looked familiar. I'm trying to keep them apart. Grace and I are having all our meals sent up to our quarters. Speaking of which, I really had better let her know you are here." He shook his head and grinned. "Grace may look demure, but she is now holding my knife and intends to use it on anyone who tries to hurt me."

Lorcan laughed. "She's protecting you?"

Deklan raked a hand through his hair. "Early on, I told her we were in this together to the very end because I wanted to calm her down. Of course, I am in it to the end with her. Wooton cannot take me off this assignment. But she has interpreted my words to mean we are responsible for each other. She will not leave my side while there is still breath in me."

Lorcan gave him a playful punch on the shoulder. "Then you had better die fast. If it is any consolation, Cammy would do the same for me."

"So would Lucy for me," Donal said. "This is what comes of a love marriage."

Deklan groaned. "Do not bring up that word again."

"Love? Or marriage?" Donal asked.

"Both. And you can stop grinning at me. I had better get back to her. Come by our chamber after your supper tonight. We need to coordinate a plan of action once Grace and I find the crown."

He returned to his room and knocked on the door, softly calling her name.

She threw it open and pulled him in. "What happened? Who were those men? Are we safe? Are you safe?"

He took the knife out of her hands and then untied her cloak to set it back on a peg beside the hearth.

He also noticed their packed travel pouches and was glad to see she had been prepared to run. "The riders were Lorcan and Donal."

"Oh, thank heaven." She sat on the bed and emitted a sigh of relief.

He shut their door and then crossed to the bed to sit beside her. "They'll come by later to discuss what to do once we find the crown."

"Assuming we find it."

He nodded. "We will."

"I'm sorry I put up such a fuss before."

He took her hand. "Don't be. I should have gone over escape strategies with you earlier. It was my fault. I did not feel the urgency. In truth, I doubt those agents will ever pick up our trail until we are back in London. But they'll be waiting for us the moment we show our faces there and will descend on us like a pack of jackals, unless…"

"Unless what?"

"Grace, I'm thinking once we hand off the crown to Donal and Lorcan, I ought to keep you in hiding in the south of England rather than try to sneak you back into London."

"Why the sudden concern?"

"Wooton may decide to keep quiet about the crown's recovery until it is safely returned to that foreign government."

"In the meantime, those agents will still be after me?"

"Yes. Now, it may be that Wooton puts the word out right away. He hasn't told me or either of my cousins what he will do. Even if he means to report it immediately, it may take several weeks for the interested parties to get word of its discovery and rescind their orders about taking you hostage. This is why I am thinking to keep you out of London until we are certain the crisis has passed."

"I see. Was this your plan all along?"

"No, I truly considered getting you back in time for Christmas. But I'm having serious second thoughts about it, and not only because Wooton is furious with me at the moment."

She nodded. "That was my doing, wasn't it? You did not tell him you were running off with me."

"I wasn't going to risk his interference with our plans. You know he was not going to allow you to go to Bexhill."

"I know. He meant to keep me close in order to turn me over to that foreign government if the crown was not recovered. You did this for me. It is all my fault."

"No, Grace. The blame is squarely on me. I could have refused you, but I did not. Nor will I let anyone take you from me. Your idea is sensible, and bringing you to Bexhill is our best chance of success. And now I think keeping you away from London is our best chance of assuring you are not sent over to that foreign government along with their crown."

"But why would they want me if they had the crown back?"

"They probably wouldn't, but one never knows what can happen during these fragile negotiations. It is best to keep you out of everyone's sight. Wooton cannot agree to turn over what he does not have."

"Dear heaven."

He tucked a finger under her chin, noting she looked forlorn. "Not happy to be spending Christmas alone with me?"

She cast him a gentle smile. "As between you and being shipped off to a foreign government? I think I can suffer through the Yuletide season with you. But it isn't that, Deklan. I am worried about my mother and siblings."

"One problem at a time, Grace. Much will fall into place once we find the crown, especially a solution to your family's situation."

"But in the meantime, they do not have enough to buy a Christmas goose. I was hoping to send them one as soon as we returned to London. It seems they'll have to do without. It angers me because I know my father will not even think of pleading with Wooton to loosen the purse strings for this purpose. It saddens me, too. He has completely abandoned us."

"Grace, I'm sorry. Let me talk to Donal and Lorcan. There must be something we can do."

"I would be so grateful. I haven't very much of my own left to sell, but I will pay them back for the goose. Do you think they can get one to our country estate in time? I will understand if they cannot. They have their own obligations. I would not want to ruin their Christmas plans just to deliver a goose to my family."

He gave her cheek a light caress. "Do not agonize over a holiday meal. It is a small thing in comparison to the current threat you are facing. This threat is something we must talk about because we cannot leave things the way they are."

"What do you mean?"

"We'll be parting ways with Lorcan and Donal tomorrow.

You and I will be on our own again for the next few days. I am assigned to protect you. It does not work the other way around. You have to toughen up and be ready to leave me behind if the situation requires it."

She regarded him aghast. "After all you've done for me, I am to abandon you?"

"You are not abandoning me. What you are doing is saving England and your family. You can and must be prepared for this, Grace. If not for me, then think of your mother and siblings. They need you. They are the ones you cannot abandon. You need to find the crown with or without me."

"Assuming it is with Vixen."

"It has to be."

He drew her onto his lap, grinning when she eyed him with suspicion. "Yes, I've taken you onto my lap again. But we are not in a carriage and this is not an improper advance. This is me taking you in my arms because…well, I don't quite know what this is. Perhaps it is my way of telling you to dig into the well of strength I know exists inside of you."

She placed her arms around his neck, but she was frowning at him. "Teach me to fight instead of run. Show me how I can protect you."

"Absolutely not, you obstinate little baggage. First of all, you do not have the instincts of a fighter. Could you stab someone? Land a killing blow when they are already on the ground and bleeding?"

He did not await her response before continuing. "No, you could not. So I need you to do as I ask and keep out of my way. I am safest when working alone. The last thing I need is to worry about you because you've come out of hiding to attack agents who are ruthless and experienced. There is no negotiation on this. If they take me down, then you run to Bexhill like the devil is on your tail because they are devils. Dig up that crown and hand it off to Donal and Lorcan. One of them will stay behind to protect you while the other rides to London."

He took her hand and wrapped it in his. "Promise me, Grace."

He saw frustration, irritation, and then he saw the most heartbroken expression he had ever seen in anyone's eyes.

She was in utter anguish.

But this was Grace, too softhearted for her own good, and precisely the reason he was not going to teach her how to fight.

She could not hurt a butterfly.

"All right," she said, hardly able to catch her breath. "I promise. I'll run."

He kissed her on the forehead. "Thank you, love."

"Do not thank me. It is a terrible thing I've just agreed to." She closed her eyes to avoid his gaze and rested her head against his chest.

He heard a trembling sigh and thought she might be on the verge of tears. "Sweetheart, you are agonizing over something that is not likely to happen. The possibility is remote."

"Then why insist upon it?"

"Because if it does happen, you need to save yourself and not die along with me." He stroked her hair as he spoke. Those beautiful golden curls were now dry after their morning washing and were silky to the touch.

He buried his hand in her hair and tipped her head so that her lips met his. He needed to kiss this girl. Ached to kiss her.

Blessed saints, he was in love with her.

But he could not tell her now. She would never leave him behind if she thought he loved her.

She would break her promise to him for this…for love.

Would he not do the same for her?

Love changed everything.

He'd break every rule to save Grace.

Indeed, he was breaking rules now by ignoring Wooton and running off with Grace against his orders.

He nudged her lips apart and dipped his tongue inside the warm velvet of her mouth. She yielded to him immediately, her soft lips molding to the contours of his, and her tongue darting forward to mingle with his.

The words wanted to pour out of him.

Marry me.

I love you, Grace.

I'll love you always.

Could she feel his words?

Could she feel his love?

He ended the kiss, perhaps too abruptly, because he was going to bed her if they did not stop. She ravaged his senses, his thoughts, and restraint. She was perfection in his arms, seeming to fit every part of him as though created just for him.

He wanted her.

Mine.

Forever.

But only as his wife.

Commitment. Sacrifice. Faithfulness.

She deserved better than a casual tumble between the sheets.

Not that his feelings for her were ever casual.

They said little else to each other for the remaining hours before supper.

He finished reading the book and tucked it back in his pouch. She spent most of the time lost in her thoughts while seated beside the hearth fire. "Grace, I know you are not happy about the promise I extracted from you. Are you angry with me?"

She turned to him, surprised. "No, I thought you were angry with me."

"No, love. I know I am placing demands on you when you are already carrying a heavy burden on your shoulders. But I will not have you risking your life for me." He walked over to her and knelt beside her. "Running instead of fighting by my side does not make you a coward. Quite the opposite, it is a brave and difficult thing to do. But you must do it for my sake, otherwise you will impair my ability to carry out my assignment."

She nodded, but he saw the frustration in her eyes.

"You cannot throw me off, Grace. I need to be the leopard you are convinced I am. Working on my own. Stalking my prey. Slipping through the trees unnoticed."

"Yes, I've given you my word."

They said no more to each other as Mrs. Harcourt delivered their supper to the room, a hearty venison stew with sweet turnips, onions, and potatoes also tossed in. On the side was a freshly baked loaf of bread and two generous slices of apple pie sprinkled with cinnamon.

Grace drank tea with her meal while he had ale.

Soon after, his cousins joined them.

"Blessed saints," Lorcan said, settling in one of the chairs beside the table. "Did you taste the stew? Have you ever had anything better in your life?"

Deklan laughed. "I licked that plate clean and then stole half of Grace's meal."

"I had plenty to fill me," she assured. "I hope we don't have to run tonight because the best I can do is waddle."

Donal took the other chair, groaning as he settled into it. "All right, now that we are all gathered here, what's the plan?"

Deklan sat on the bed beside Grace since there were no other chairs. "I think it will take us two days to reach Bexhill and another half day to find Vixen's grave. We'll need to meet up with you on the third day. A quick handoff of the crown. We part ways again. The question is where do we meet to hand the crown off to you?"

"I'm thinking Eastbourne," Donal said. "It is close to Bexhill, yet far enough away to raise no suspicions. You and Grace can also hire a boat out of Eastbourne to sail you up the coast back to London."

"No, I'll be hiding Grace elsewhere." He intended to take her to Brighton since he happened to have a house there. But only his cousin, Finn, knew of it. Finn took care of the family's financial matters and had acquired this manor house overlooking the water in Finn's own name as nominee. No one, not even members of his family, knew the house actually belonged to Deklan.

"Care to tell us where the two of you will be in hiding?" Lorcan asked.

"No. It is better you don't know. I won't make liars of you when Wooton asks. And I know he will ask. You need to respond truthfully."

Lorcan rarely broke into laughter, but he did so now. "So we can stand by innocently and watch the steam pour from his ears? Gad, Dek. You are diabolical."

"You give me too much credit."

"Give us at least a hint," Donal said, trying to suppress a chuckle. "How do we get hold of you? We'll have to warn you if something goes wrong. But Deklan, Wooton is now related to me by marriage. He is Lucy's father, after all. Will you please try to go easier on him? You have him apoplectic and twitching whenever you ignore his orders which you happen to do all the time."

"He ought to know by now that he cannot manage me. I am carrying out my assignment and that is all he needs to know. But here's a clue to where I'll be hiding Grace, and do not follow up on it unless it is necessary." He glanced from one cousin to the other. "Finn will know."

Donal arched an eyebrow. "That's it? Our cousin? Finn will know?"

"Yes, don't ask for more." Deklan had quietly contacted Finn after his last assignment and asked him to purchase this home with a lovely view of the sea. It was not far from the Royal Pavilion. "By the way, you are all welcome to use this hideaway in the summer. It is quite an elegant house. Grace, I think you will like it."

She nodded. "I'm sure I will. I'm not in a position to complain even if it turns out to be a hovel, am I?"

"I suppose not."

Her expression softened. "I would not complain. You know I

am grateful to you for all you are doing. This extends to the Quinton and Brayden families, too. I don't know how I can ever repay you for the kindness you've shown."

Deklan took her hand and gave it a light squeeze. "None of us wishes to see you hurt. Anyway, I hope you like our hideout. And I hope my cousins do make use of it at some point in the future. I'm not sure how often I'll get to enjoy it if Wooton keeps assigning me to the Continent."

"Generous of you, Deklan," Donal said. "So we are talking about a summer retreat on the coast? That narrows it down to about a thousand possible locations. But are you sure about keeping Grace out of London? Wooton wants her returned there as soon as possible."

"He does not get Grace back. I do not trust his motives and cannot risk his trading her to that foreign government even if their crown is returned."

"I don't think he would ever sink so low as that," Donal said. "Lucy would never allow her father to pull such a dirty trick."

"I'd rather not put him to the test. Grace stays with me until the affair is completely resolved."

"Got it," Lorcan said. "I would do the same if Cammy were at risk. So where in Eastbourne specifically do we complete the handoff?"

Deklan gave his cousins the name of a popular tavern. "Then it's up to you to lose whoever may be following us and get back to London as fast as possible."

"While you take Grace into hiding at an unknown location," Lorcan said, cracking a grin. "I bet I can figure it out in under five minutes."

"Maybe you could, Lor. But don't try. Wooton will demote the lot of us to filing clerks, he'll be that angry if he thinks you are abetting my misbehavior."

"Fine, I'll let the matter drop. I think you are the only one who ever riles him. Sometimes, I think it is a game the two of you play. With everyone else, he is the Duke of Ice. Nothing shakes his composure. But at the mere mention of your name…" Lorcan emitted a hearty laugh. "They'll hear Wooton's angry roar throughout the Home Office when I tell him what you've done."

"It'll do him good not to get his way. Builds character. Modesty. Humility." Deklan grinned as he crossed his arms over his chest. "Are we done? Anything else to discuss?"

His cousins rose.

"No, Dek." Donal gave him a quick hug. "Take care of yourself. I'm sorry you won't be with us for the holidays."

Lorcan did the same. "I don't know who I fear worse when breaking the news, Wooton or Aunt Miranda. She'll be disappointed to have you miss yet another family holiday."

Deklan nodded. "I know. I'll make it up to her…and to Rafe and Sam and my mother. I know I've let them down. But they'll understand."

He ought to have kept his mouth shut because Grace was fretting again.

Was she worried about his missing Christmas with his family?

Blessed saints.

She wasn't going to talk him into returning her to London, was she?

CHAPTER ELEVEN

WHILE BEING ON the run from foreign agents and a blisteringly angry Duke of Wooton was not quite the same thing as an enjoyable countryside ride, Grace still felt her spirits lifted to be thundering along the well-traveled roads at full gallop toward Bexhill. She finally felt as though she was doing something helpful for England and her own family.

Deklan, it galled her to admit, was right when he insisted she did not have the coldness of heart or the brute strength to physically fight off enemy agents. But she had been the one to figure out where this elusive crown was buried and it felt good to be able to contribute something toward ending this sad affair.

The further south they rode, the less snow they encountered. By the time they reached Bexhill, there was no trace of a blizzard ever having touched upon the ground. This was likely because they were so close to the water. However, this close to the bay one felt the biting wind with particular intensity, each gust carrying tiny grains of ice which struck her cheeks.

Despite the cold, she wanted to press on. Indeed, she would never stop now, for they could not be far from the house her family had let that long ago summer. "Vixen's grave," she whispered, determined to find it even after all this time.

"Grace, how are you doing?" Deklan called, riding beside her and easily keeping pace even though she was an excellent rider and not holding back on her reins.

But she held back now, slowing her horse to a trot because she knew they were close. The landmarks were familiar to her and the turnoff to the manor house had to be coming up soon. "Eager to have this over and done."

Two days had passed without incident, although sleeping beside Deklan's sinfully divine body every night was quite the incident in itself. She was inexperienced in the act of love, but certainly not dumb as rocks, and felt the dangerous attraction simmering between them.

Not merely simmering.

They could not be in the same room together without sparks igniting.

Of course, she felt the attraction because she was in love with Deklan.

He felt it because he was a low brain male in a frenzied need to bed her as he would any woman who pleased his senses. His strictly disciplined mind and the fact she had never performed *that* act with a man before was all that stood between her and true ruination.

"Deklan! There it is! The house. I know it is the one." She spurred her mount toward a graceful manor appearing to have seen better days. An aged beauty standing proudly on a hill overlooking the bay. While she had seen it in the summer when the foliage was lush and green, there was no mistaking the property even though everything now looked sparse and dying.

Grace tugged on the reins to hold back her horse as they were about to ride up the rutted drive. "I did not think of this before, but what do we say to the owners? Do you think they will allow us to dig up the grave? Should we ask them or just do it and run off? Well, we'd have to properly bury Vixen again...and say a prayer for her."

"A prayer?" He sighed, emitting a breath of vapor that danced in the air between them. "All right, just tell me what to say and I'll say it. As for the owners, we had better let them know we are here. I don't want their groundskeeper mistaking us for trespassers and shooting us."

"You have a point."

"But you are to let me do the talking. I have a very impressive badge that I carry with me whenever on official business. The badge does not have my name on it, so you and I are still Captain and Mrs. Adam Driscoll. I am here on official Crown business and not at liberty to say more."

"They'll be curious and want to know why you are digging up a dog's grave."

"As I said, official matter. Cannot say more."

"And why is your wife with you if you are on official business?"

"My orders came as you and I were on our way to visit family in London for Christmas. Stop asking questions, Grace. Let's get this done." He turned up the drive and spurred his mount to a loping pace.

She easily kept up with him. "But is it not important for me to know what to say? Wouldn't you be asking questions of me while my husband was digging up your grounds?"

"Distract them with meaningless conversation. You know, what a lovely house. Have you always owned it? If their name is Smythe for example, ask them if they are related to the Dover Smythes."

"Why Dover? Do you know of any Smythes in Dover?"

"No, it is just a meaningless example. Name a city. London, York, Weymouth. It doesn't matter. Just toss something out and they'll go on for hours telling you all about their family history."

She laughed. "You seem to have experience with this."

He smiled. "More often than I care to admit. You have no idea how people love to talk about themselves. Sometimes, it takes all my disciplined training to stifle a yawn."

They dismounted when they reached the porticoed entry. Deklan strode to it and knocked on the massive door knocker affixed to the sturdy oak door. No one responded. "Perhaps the house is closed up for the winter," he muttered. "That would be convenient for us."

He knocked again.

When there was still no response, he peered in the window and then walked around the house, doing the same by peering through the various windows into each room. "Did you notice anything?" Grace asked when he'd circled back to the front.

"Furniture covered and not a soul to be found, not even in the kitchen or the caretaker's cottage. I checked inside that cottage and there's no sign of a fire having been lit recently."

"Does this mean we have the house to ourselves?"

He nodded. "But we're only staying long enough to find that crown. That's it, Grace. No sentimental walk along the grounds or reminiscing about how you and your mother drank lemonade on the terrace while your father went boating and Richard swam. And I do not care where you carved your initials in a tree."

"How do you know I did that?"

He arched an eyebrow. "Didn't you?"

She sighed. "Yes, you irritating man. Do you not even want to see–?"

"No, none of it. Not where you collected frogs or fished off the dock in the early morning. Not the slightest interest."

"Deklan! That is cruel."

"No, Grace. We are not out for a morning stroll. We are here on official business for one purpose and one purpose alone, to retrieve that crown. All right? Are we clear on this? Crown. Prayer. Ride out before someone comes along and does start asking questions."

"All right," she muttered, for he was wringing every bit of joy from that summer. It had been a beautiful time marred only by Vixen's passing shortly before the month came to an end. She could not remember her family ever being together and laughing with such carefree spirit again. "Hold on a moment and let me get my bearings."

She had just started to walk the grounds when Deklan suddenly left her side and sprinted to a small mound beneath an enormous ash tree. "Grace, is this it?"

The breath caught in her throat.

How could he possibly know?

She ran to his side and gripped his hand partly out of fear and partly out of excitement. Her heart pounded and she took several deep breaths. "Oh, Deklan. Yes. This is exactly the spot."

A ray of sunshine struck the damp earth as though shining a beacon to guide them.

Deklan was in his leopard stance, his eyes scanning the area, and all his senses on alert as he knelt and lightly touched the ground. "The grave has been disturbed."

She inhaled sharply. "How recently?"

"When was your brother's last trip home from the Continent? Three months? Four? That's probably when he dug it up to bury the crown."

They had stopped to purchase a shovel in one of the small towns along the way and Deklan now went to retrieve it.

When he returned, Grace watched him dig into the hard ground. The earth was frozen and it took all of his impressive strength to break through.

She had not meant to cry while watching him, but so many feelings rushed to the surface the moment she saw Vixen's bones and her tears would not stop flowing. Since she did not want to distract him from his purpose, she stepped back and quietly withdrew the handkerchief she had tucked in her sleeve.

"Grace?"

"Don't mind me." She dabbed her eyes and tried to stay silent as a mouse while Deklan worked.

Several times, she tried to peer over his shoulder, but all she saw was earth and bones. "The crown isn't here."

"It is, Grace. It has to be. He's buried it deeper, no doubt beneath the remains. Don't worry, I'll treat Vixen's bones with reverence. I know this is important to you."

"Thank you, Deklan." She appreciated the extra effort not to disturb the grave, and stood by quietly as he carefully dug around and then beneath it.

"Here we go," he said at last, setting aside the shovel and removing a large tin container from the hole. He unfastened the lid to reveal a blue velvet cloth bag. "Ready to see what's inside?"

She merely nodded, for her heart was beating so rapidly, she could not speak.

He reached in the bag and withdrew a magnificent, jewel-encrusted crown. "Blessed saints," he muttered, holding it with exquisite care. "How did your brother ever sneak this massive thing out?"

"Oh, my heavens. I have never seen so many jewels in all my life. Our Crown jewels pale in comparison. Do not tell His Majesty I said that."

He glanced up and grinned. "I wouldn't dream of it. He's quite vain about our royal treasures and will lock me in the Tower for uttering the blasphemy. He'll be green with envy over this prize. No wonder everyone wants to get their hands on it."

"Yes, I can see why." Sunlight reflected off the gemstones creating prisms of light in a dazzling array of colors. Ruby red, sapphire blue, emerald green, and diamonds in crystal white and subtlest pink. The gems were attached to an artfully crafted frame of gold, and the crown was finished in dark velvet with ermine trim.

Deklan held it out to her. "Care to try it on?"

"No!" But after a moment she knelt beside him. "Really? You would let me?"

"Yes, princess." He cast her a tender smile that melted her heart as he placed the crown on her head with exquisite care.

She steadied it so that it did not slip off. "It's heavy."

"Henry IV thought so, too. *Deny it to a king? Then happy low, lie down. Uneasy lies the head that wears a crown.*"

"Shakespeare."

"The man understood his monarchs." He carefully removed the crown from her head and tucked it back in its velvet bag. "Wooton will dance a jig when Donal and Lorcan present this prize to him."

"Will he be happy enough to forgive your ignoring his orders?"

"Are you fretting about that, Grace?" He placed the wrapped crown back in the large tin. "He and I have been butting heads for years. He always forgives me and would have done so even if we had not found this crown."

"Truly?"

"Yes. Oh, he will be angry as blazes at first and give me a blistering lecture about ignoring orders and doing things on my own. He will excoriate me on why I must learn to accept authority and how I must always answer to my superiors. Then he will thank me for a job well done and hand me another assignment."

He tossed the displaced earth back atop the grave.

"And what of me?" Grace asked as he tamped down the dirt.

"I told you, I am with you to the end. I do not leave your side until I am certain you are safe. We are not going back to London until I know that foreign government has been appeased."

This wasn't what she had meant by the question.

Perhaps what she ought to have asked is, what about us?

He had been going on about not following orders and doing as he wished. She thought he had made some progress in changing this attitude, at least toward a future wife. They had spent hours talking about feelings, about spouses being considerate of each other and accepting to deal with their problems as a couple.

But he must have taken none of it in.

He was the leopard again.

Alone. Apart from everyone. Hiding up in his tree.

She ought to have known he would not change, but he had been so attentive to her while on this journey. Was this all she would have of him? "How will you know it is safe to return me to London if we are in hiding? Who will send word to us?"

"Something will turn up in the newspapers. No mention of

the theft, of course. Perhaps the papers will report on a grand feast to celebrate strengthening ties between our two nations."

"Can you tell me the nation in question?"

"No, Grace. I have not been given leave to reveal that information yet. Irritating my superiors is one thing, but revealing secret information is quite another. It is something I will never do, not even to confide it in you." After uttering a brief prayer along with her, he tucked the tin under one arm and placed his other arm about her waist to escort her back to their horses. "Why are you suddenly so quiet?"

She forced a smile. "Just taking it all in."

He nodded. "It is quite a lot to absorb. You have been splendid throughout. I mean it, Grace. I could not have accomplished any of this without you. Now, all we have to do is meet Lorcan and Donal as arranged, hand this thing over, then it is off to Brighton for us."

"What if I wish to return to London?"

He did not mask his surprise. "No, love. I dare not take you back there yet. The risk is too great."

She did not argue because she trusted his judgment and he had explained the dangers.

Although not experienced in matters of war or politics, she had read enough in the newspapers to understand how delicate negotiations could be and how often outrageous demands were made.

Anything could happen, especially if that foreign power was still seething over her brother's theft.

She could be tossed in as part of an agreement to secure peace.

Why anyone would want the daughter of a notorious thief was beyond her, but it was not outside the realm of possibility this demand would be made to spite her father and brother.

Only she would be the one to suffer.

Then Deklan would come after her because this was just the marvelously reckless sort of thing he would do. Ignoring Home

Office instructions. Ignoring promises made from one king to another.

Keeping to his promise to protect her.

She said no more about London.

A few hours later, they met Donal and Lorcan in Eastbourne at The Salty Dog, a seaside tavern of questionable reputation that seemed to attract a respectable working crowd during the daylight hours. She was not the only woman dining there, and her sturdy woolen gown was no more remarkable than the garments worn by the other ladies who must have been local shopkeepers. She was rather proud of the way she blended in.

"Bloody hell," Donal muttered when Deklan passed the tin over to him. "Sorry, Grace. Pardon my language. But how big is this thing? It won't fit in my pouch."

"No, you'll need to stow it in a valise or a sailor's duffle."

"I noticed a shop up the street," Lorcan said. "We'll find suitable luggage. Then we're going to hop on the next mail coach from Eastbourne to London. It's the fastest way to get us back there. As soon as we arrive, we dump this thing on Wooton's desk and return to celebrating with the family."

"But what about your horses?" Grace asked. "Will you just leave them behind?"

"No," Donal said. "We'll make arrangements to have them returned to Ronan's stable. They are his horses, after all. He won't be too pleased with us if we simply discard them."

Deklan took her hand again and gave it another squeeze. "Grace, we deal with this all the time in our work. Those horses will not be neglected. I promise you."

Their meeting broke up soon after.

She and Deklan immediately rode off because he wanted to get her out of Eastbourne as quickly as possible. They would have no more than an hour or two of daylight left, not enough time to get them to Brighton. However, he had mentioned a nice little place along the coast where they would spend the night.

Another night pretending to be husband and wife.

Any woman would be thrilled to be spending time with Deklan, sleeping in the same bed, and likely doing a lot more than merely sleeping.

But it was truly wearing on her heart.

He must have sensed her dismay, for he glanced over at her and arched an eyebrow. "Grace, you are fretting again."

She sighed. "Being on the run is starting to get to me."

"Be brave a little while longer. You have been wonderful throughout this assignment."

Yes, she was merely an assignment to him.

They reached an inn off the beaten path just as the sun was setting.

Grace ought to have been used to the pretense of passing as a married couple, but she still felt the shame of it so deeply and had to keep herself from crying as Deklan introduced her as his wife. "Right this way, Mrs. Driscoll," the innkeeper's wife said, pointing to a set of narrow stairs leading to the guest chambers.

She followed the woman while Deklan took a moment to attend to their horses. "It is our finest room. You won't have much of a view now that the sun's gone down, although you might catch the last rays of light on the horizon if you look quickly. Come morning, it will take your breath away."

"I look forward to it. My husband spoke highly of your inn and its charm."

"Oh, Captain Driscoll has stayed here before, has he? It must have been when I was off visiting my mum. I visit her regular because she's old and ailing. And we're usually quiet here after the summer months. No, I would have remembered someone as handsome as him if I'd been here."

Grace followed the kindly proprietress as she lumbered up the stairs and continued to chatter even though the climb left the woman a little breathless. "We're very quiet here tonight. Not that we have a lot of rooms. We're a small establishment. Five guest rooms in all. Yours will be the only one occupied tonight. We do a brisk business with our kitchen though. Local fishermen mostly. And our taproom is quite popular no matter the time of the year. Our specialty is fish soup. Doesn't sound like much, does it? But it is quite hearty and as thick as stew. Like a bouilla-baisse, the French call it. It's very popular."

"Sounds delicious."

"Will you be dining in your chamber or do you prefer to have your supper in the common room?"

"I'll let my husband decide."

"You look tired, love. Been traveling far?"

"Yes, a bit. It has been a busy week for us."

Deklan returned before long and they shared supper in their quarters. The inns he chose were all of fine quality, even this small one, and they had no lack of comfort. But this made Grace think of her mother and siblings, which saddened her all the more because she knew they were suffering and there was nothing she could do about it yet.

Also adding to her unsettled feelings was the realization that her time with Deklan would soon come to an end. He seemed to think it could take weeks and perhaps as long as a month for the matter of the stolen crown to resolve. Were it not for the need to assist her mother, she would not care if they were in hiding for an entire year.

Or a lifetime.

But her time with him was going to end and she had to decide what she was going to do about it.

Was there anything she could do?

After their meal had been cleared and they were getting ready for bed, Deklan spoke up. "Grace, you need to tell me what is bothering you."

"It isn't important."

"Obviously, it is." He had been unlacing her gown, but he stopped after only partially completing the task and turned her to face him. "You have been fretting all day."

"Not fretting exactly."

"Then what is it, love?" He gave a little grunt when she

frowned. "You did not mind when I called you that before. Why the change? Because you think I am using the endearment too casually?"

"Aren't you?"

He tipped her chin up so that she met his gaze. "Is this what your frown is about? You think I am going to leave you as I did Genevieve and not think of you again once this assignment is over?"

"Is this not what you do?"

"I may have been guilty of it in the past." He released her chin with a mirthless laugh. "You and she are nothing alike."

"She was a *ton* diamond and I am the daughter of a thief."

"The beautiful, sweet, kind, intelligent, compassionate daughter of a thief."

Grace could not help but laugh. "Well, the latter part of that statement is true."

"All of it is true." He began to pace like the jungle cat he was at heart. "I am not perfect. In truth, I can be incredibly insufferable at times. Perhaps most times," he said, tossing her an endearingly wry grin.

He really was not insufferable, just so comfortable being on his own and doing whatever he liked without answering to anyone.

"I reject authority and do stupid things like having a massive snake tattoo inked on my arse."

She laughed despite her quiet turmoil that was perhaps not so quiet since he knew she was overset. "I would sneak a closer look but it would require me to stare at you when your trousers are down."

"Dear heaven, we can't have that," he teased.

"The glimpse I had of it was fascinating, the way it wrapped around your thigh and seemed to move as though it were alive. As I learn more about you, I begin to understand why the tattoo is obviously such a *you* thing to do. There is no one like you, Deklan. I am going to miss you very much when this stolen crown crisis is over."

"This assignment will end, but it does not mean we must." He drew her into his arms and took a deep breath. "Well, here goes. Keep in mind I am inept when it comes to feelings. I hide them. I hate talking about them. But here goes…the only way I am leaving you is if you decide you do not want me. It is your choice."

"Mine?"

"Yes, I am yours if you will have me."

Her eyes widened in surprise.

Have him for what?

For a husband?

Was it possible? Could she believe his words?

"Are suggesting you love me?" Or was he saying this to ensure her cooperation? But for what? The crown was safely on its way back to London.

She regarded him dumbfounded.

Well, he had not said he loved her.

"Bollocks." He released her. "You don't believe me, do you?"

"I…" She sank onto the bed with a groan. "I'm not even sure what you are talking about. We've known each other less than a week. How can I trust you to commit yourself to me when you are so entrenched in your leopard ways?"

"For pity's sake. I am not a jungle animal." He emitted a low growl, obviously one of frustration with her, but did that growl not prove he was exactly that?

The lone leopard.

"You are a solitary creature. Will you deny it? You flaunt authority. You flaunt rules. You *enjoy* flaunting them. You cherish your independence. You dismissed a *ton* beauty because you did not want to be tied down to anyone, not even the most beautiful, charming, eagerly sought after young woman in all of London."

"She wasn't you, Grace."

"What is so special about me? Pauper. Disgraced family. Overly demanding when it comes to marriage. You take nothing to heart and I take *everything* to heart. How does this not irritate you?"

"Because I do not see you as you describe yourself."

She shook her head. "How else can someone like you see me?"

"Someone like me?" He raked a hand through his hair. "What's that supposed to mean? And since you raised the topic of *seeing* clearly, I suggest you work on that a little harder. You are in love with me and–"

"How dare you presume to know my thoughts."

"You are in love with me and so scared to admit it to yourself that you are tossing every hurdle you can think of in the way to avoid confronting your feelings."

"My feelings? Well, I've learned from a master, haven't I? You toss those hurdles about with remarkable ease. You've strewn them around you so effectively, no one has ever broken through."

"No one? Is this what you think? Do you trust nothing I tell you?"

He strode to the door without awaiting her response. "Latch this after me. I'm going for a walk."

He was out the door and disappeared downstairs before she had the chance to stop him. Nor could she follow since he had earlier unlaced the ties of her gown. The sleeves were slipping off her shoulders and her bodice was loose enough to provide a clear view down her bosom.

She had taken off her boots, too.

Well, there was no point in chasing after him.

He was angry because she did not tumble into his arms and joyfully admit she loved him.

She buried her face in her hands. "I do love him."

What had she done?

CHAPTER TWELVE

DEKLAN STRODE DOWNSTAIRS to the inn's taproom and ordered an ale. There were a few men at the bar, local fishermen by the weathered look of their faces. Otherwise, the place was quiet. He took a seat at a corner table with a clear view to the stairs.

Despite his irritation with Grace, he would never shirk his duty. He would be on his feet in a trice if anyone but the innkeeper's wife went up those steps. There were no back stairs to worry about either, for the place was small. While comfortable, it was also old and not built for finer folk who employed a staff of servants and wanted to keep them out of the way with use of hidden doors or separate stairs.

Grace.

He sighed.

She wasn't the problem, he was.

He knew she was in love with him and was scared witless because of it. She wasn't a timid mouse, but she was a girl with a badly battered heart. After the family upheaval and suddenly becoming a pawn between two countries on the verge of war, she could not bear another ordeal.

Loving him would certainly be an ordeal.

Was he not everything she had accused?

Independent.

Aloof.

Disdainful of authority.

He had spent a lifetime doing things his own way and answering to nobody. Making a point of boasting about it. How did he think this sweetheart of a girl who wanted her husband to be more than a mere coin purse would react to his declaration?

But it was not something he was going to discuss with her tonight. Some old houses were sturdily built and had thick walls that rocks hurled on catapults could not destroy. This inn had paper-thin walls and he was not going to engage in a conversation on love and marriage with a woman he had already passed off as his wife. The risk of their being overheard was too great, especially now that the taproom was emptying out and had turned quiet.

He downed his ale, nodded to the innkeeper on his way out, and mounted the stairs. The door was latched when he tried it. Well, he wanted Grace to think of these added measures of security, even if she had latched it only to keep him out.

He knocked lightly. "Grace?"

"I'll be right there." He heard her soft footsteps approaching. "I did not mean to shut you out. I was putting on my bedclothes."

"You did right to be careful. I should not have stormed off the way I did. Just proves what an arse I can be."

"Deklan, I–"

"No, let's not talk about what I said. Let's not say anything to each other tonight. All right? I do not want to discuss that mistake."

She nodded. "Yes, a big mistake. As you wish."

He watched Grace slip under the covers and curl herself up in a tight ball on her side of the bed. After securing the door, he readied himself for bed and fell in beside her. But he did not like that she was setting herself away from him.

He put an arm around her waist and drew her up against him. "You need my body's warmth, Grace."

And he needed her body's softness.

This is how they fell asleep, wrapped in each other's arms.

This is how he wanted it to be for the rest of their lives.

Their silence continued into the morning, broken up only by the sound of waves crashing along the nearby rocky shore, and an occasional comment by each of them on how beautiful the sunrise looked upon the water.

They left the inn and did not stop until they arrived in Brighton at the twilight hour. Deklan was excited to show Grace the house he had acquired, a beautiful, stone manor nestled atop a hill with a view of the sea. They reached it just as the sun was fading, its last rays of golden-pink light illuminating the elegant structure to magical advantage.

Of course, it was better viewed during the day when the light was more natural. He would give Grace a tour of the place tomorrow. Right now, they needed to settle in before night descended. In another few minutes, they would be stumbling around in the dark, the only thing visible being moonlight upon a black expanse of sea.

"What do you think, Grace?"

She took in its height and breadth. "It is stunning. Takes my breath away."

"A step above living in a tree, is it not?" he teased, knowing she thought of him as a leopard. He hoped showing her this house might convince her that he was capable of putting down roots.

"Yes," she said, smiling at him for the first time in hours.

"I have yet to see the inside. After Finn helped me with the purchase, I left him in charge of restoring this house to its original condition."

"Finn decorated it?"

Deklan laughed. "No, he gave the plans over to Ronan's wife and asked her to work on it. Dahlia has an artist's eye. He knew she would be able to restore it to the magnificent structure it had once been. However, she did not know it was mine. He only told her the project was for one of his clients. No one but Finn knows I own this house."

"Why did you keep it a secret from your family?"

"I wasn't ready for them to make a fuss over it or me." He raked a hand through his hair, realizing how bad that sounded. Had he become so detached, he could not reveal something as innocuous as a house purchase to the family he loved? "Just more of my leopard ways, I suppose. Shall we see what it looks like inside?"

"Don't you have any idea?"

"No, I haven't been here since I purchased it."

She stared at him, her eyes wide and her expression mildly chastising. "Then you never even saw sketches of what Dahlia designed for you?"

"I knew she had talent and I could trust her judgment. She hasn't seen the house either. She resides in London with Ronan and was not about to come all the way down here. Finn provided her with a set of detailed plans and asked her to formulate ideas. Dahlia then engaged a local designer to take measurements and supervise the actual installations. But the ideas were all hers."

There were no servants about.

The door, when he tried it, was locked. "Wait here, Grace. I'm going to find a way in."

"What if the house is completely sealed up?"

He shrugged. "There's always a way in."

It took him little time to find an entry used by delivery men. It had a weak lock, easily pried open without damaging the lock or the door. He then made his way through the house to the entrance and let Grace in. "Welcome to my humble abode, Miss Montford."

He took a moment to light the sconces affixed to the entry foyer walls, and then looked on with pride as Grace's expression turned to one of marvel.

He watched her as she peeked in the nearby rooms.

From what he could see in soft candlelight, everything was tastefully done. The furniture and furnishings were of the highest quality. The entry hall had an exquisite Italian marble floor and the dining room floor and furniture, visible from where he stood, was of finest dark wood.

A large, crystal chandelier dominated the entry hall. The dining room also had a chandelier centered over the large table.

"Look, Deklan. There's a visitors' parlor and a larger formal parlor. Light the sconces in there, too. I'd like a better look in there."

Deklan did so, then looked around the room and groaned. "Floral drapes."

"They're beautiful." She walked toward the two glass doors framed by these drapes. "Do these doors lead out onto a terrace? And is that the sea beyond?"

"Yes, you'll have a better view of it come daytime. Gad, what did she do to this room? There are flowers on everything."

Grace turned to him, her eyes glittering with amusement. "Don't you like it? Makes me feel as though I am walking through a garden. I'm sure this is the effect she wanted to create. It must be lovely in the summer when the doors are open and a light sea breeze blows into the room."

"But she put them everywhere. On the walls. The chairs. And drapes. What if she's done the entire house this way?"

Grace laughed. "Whose fault is that? You could have worked with her to get exactly what you wanted. But I suppose leopards don't do this. Well, I love it."

"I'm glad you do." This house was as much for her as it was for him. He found wood neatly stacked beside the hearth and took a moment to light a fire. "Finn hired a local couple to live in and maintain the house in my absence," he said as he stoked the flames. "Not sure where they are just now."

"Well, they did not know we were arriving. It is likely they are at a church service or dining with family."

"Perhaps. I hope they've left some food around. I'll see what I can scrounge for us in the larder. You must be famished. We haven't eaten since early morning."

She joined him by the hearth, holding her hands by the fire to warm them. "I am a little hungry. But what about you, one of Miranda's wildebeests? You must be ready to chew the furniture."

"I'll settle for anything that does not eat me first," he said with a grin. "Do you mind if we hunt for food before I show you the rest of the house? The bedrooms are upstairs. I have no idea what Dahlia has done with them or whether those have been furnished beyond my own bedchamber."

"Dear heaven, do you involve yourself in nothing but your work? Never mind, I suppose we'll find out soon enough whether those bedrooms have been left empty."

He nodded. "Grace, about our sleeping arrangements…we need to discuss this before the couple returns. Will you be sharing my bedchamber?"

"I will have to if the others have not yet been furnished. But are you giving me the choice?"

"Yes. However, I would still insist on keeping you in the room closest to mine. We are in my home and no one knows to look for you in Brighton. The danger ought to be minimal, but on the chance something happens, I need to be within easy reach of you. As I said, the choice is yours. As for the hired couple, I don't think they will find it odd for us to sleep apart. It is not unusual for husbands and wives to maintain separate bedchambers."

"Then we are to keep up the ruse of being a married couple?"

"Yes, and I am still Adam Driscoll, captain in the Royal Navy. You are my wife. We are newlyweds. Same story how we met in Bath. Nothing changes until the crown is back where it belongs and no one is asking you to be shipped out of England as their hostage."

"Wait, are you telling me the people you employ do not even know who you are?"

"Why should they care who pays them? Their names are Joseph and Letitia Hyde, by the way. I do know this much. But to get back to the topic. If we sleep separately, I will insist on keeping the door between our rooms open. I need to hear your breaths and listen for the light swish of your sheets as you toss and turn."

She still stood beside him, her cold hands held close to the warming fire.

Blessed saints, she felt so right and perfect next to him. He was a big man and she was merely of average height for a woman, but it felt to him as though their bodies were made to fit each other. Their hearts, too. Somehow, she filled in all he lacked. "Grace, do you realize we have never spent a night apart since meeting each other?"

She nodded. "I was thinking the same thing. We've done it all backwards, haven't we?"

"Sleeping together first and then getting to know each other? Well, the circumstances are unique." He studied her, caught by how pretty she looked in the firelight's reflection.

He also noted fatigue in her eyes, for they had been riding hard all day in the cold and she had to be completely worn out. But nothing seemed to detract from the delicate beauty of her features.

They had kept their cloaks on until he got the warming fires going. He now removed his cloak and then helped with hers, tossing both onto a nearby chair for now. "It will feel odd to be apart from you," he said. "I won't like it."

"It will feel odd for me, too. You are better than a warm blanket. You give off heat like a stoked furnace." She cast him a surprisingly tender smile.

He laughed. "Glad to be of service."

As for him, sleeping with her in his arms was heaven.

He did not want to give up his taste of heaven. "Stay with me, Grace."

She cast him that distraught, you-will-think-me-a-hussy stare, because sleeping with him, even though he had not touched her beyond a few kisses, was still utterly crushing to her spirit.

They had shared a room and then a bed out of necessity, but this did not diminish the embarrassment she must have felt slipping between the sheets with him each night.

He should have understood this.

The fact she enjoyed lying beside him, curling up against him, gave her no solace and only made her feel worse.

"You are right. I'm sorry. I'll put you in the bedchamber next to mine, assuming it is furnished. Is this what you prefer?"

She sank onto the sofa and buried her face in her hands.

He settled beside her. "Grace, do whatever it is you wish to do. Expressing my preference was not meant to put you in agony. You know I cannot get out of my low brain whenever I am around you. Ignore it. Your comfort is all that matters."

She surprised him by throwing her arms around him.

"Grace, love." She was twisting him in knots. He wanted to do right by her, but everything he said seemed to upset her. "Are you not sure? I thought it would be an easy choice for you."

"What if I wanted to stay with you?"

"It would delight me."

"But what will you think of me?"

"Because you want to sleep in my bed?" Gad, had he not just mused about her feelings of shame. She was such a sweet thing. "It does not make you wanton. A wanton is someone who flits from bed to bed with a string of partners. You want to stay with me because you love me to the depths of your soul."

She looked up at him in alarm.

"You cannot hide your feelings. There may as well be a big sign written across your forehead that says *I love Deklan*. You do not hide your feelings well at all. Why deny them to yourself?"

She buried her face in her hands again. "Oh, what am I doing? You even said yourself this is all a big mistake."

He did not know what she was talking about.

He groaned. "Tell you what, if that adjoining bedchamber is properly furnished, then this is where you'll sleep. But the door will be open between us and you can come into my bed any time you wish. Or ask me to come into yours. Or not. Whatever you decide is fine with me."

"Truly?"

"Yes, Grace," he said, now laughing softly. "Well, my body will be wracked in torment because it will miss yours. I think I am always going to feel this way about you. But it is more important that you are comfortable and not caught up in the pain of guilt come morning. You first, Grace. You will always be my first concern."

He slapped his hands to his knees. "None of this will matter if we expire from hunger. I'll find us some food."

She quickly shook off her distress and nodded. "I'll unpack our pouches. What about the horses?"

"I'll take them to the local stable once you are settled in. You first, Grace. As I said, you are always my priority."

He was about to leave the parlor in search of food when he heard voices by the front door. He withdrew his pistol and moved with a predator's silent steps to stand behind it as it opened and two people stepped in. "Coo, Lettie. Better run for the constable. I think someone's broken into–"

Deklan stepped out from his hiding spot. "Stay where you are, Mrs. Hyde. And I presume you are Mr. Hyde," he said to the older man who was staring at his pointed pistol with his mouth agape.

"Yes, sir. I am. And just who might you be?"

Deklan placed the pistol back in the lip of his boot. "Captain Driscoll, owner of this house."

Grace emerged from the parlor with fire iron in hand.

"All is well, my dear," he said. "You needn't worry about coshing our intruders. This is Mr. and Mrs. Hyde, the couple who takes care of our house when we are not in residence. Remember? Mr. Brayden advised us he had retained them on our behalf."

"Oh, yes." She cast the pair a gracious smile. "A pleasure to meet you."

Mr. Hyde's eyes widened at the sight of Grace and he puffed out his chest. "Will you look at that? You've got yourself a very pretty bride, Captain Driscoll. Look at them, Lettie. Aren't they a match? So, you are the mysterious owner?"

"Yes," Deklan said, putting a possessive arm around Grace's waist. The gesture appeared affectionate, but was mostly because he wanted to be able to subtly signal her if she started to give something away in their conversation.

Mr. Hyde shook his head and said in a whisper they all heard, "My wife was certain the house had been acquired by the king himself for one of his mistresses. Meaning no disrespect, Mrs. Driscoll. We are relieved to know we are working for a properly married couple."

"What a sweet thing you are," Mrs. Hyde added. "You look newly wed."

"We are," Deklan said. "Two weeks."

Grace blushed.

Mrs. Hyde cooed over her. "Oh, what a dear. She is still the blushing bride."

Deklan needed to put an end to that conversation before Grace burst into tears. Not that she was one to cry at the drop of a hat. Her eyes did mist up on occasion. But the only time he'd seen tears pour down her cheeks unrestrained was at Vixen's grave.

However, being unmarried and sleeping with him, then also lying to everyone about it, was never going to be anything but a humiliating torment for her. "Mrs. Hyde, would you mind preparing a light repast for us? We have traveled a long distance today and my wife is exhausted."

Grace cast him a look when Mrs. Hyde eyed her belly as though she might be in the family way.

Deklan cleared his throat. "Mr. Hyde, our horses need attention."

"Right away, sir. Mr. Gambol's stable is close by. I'll take them over and see they are properly fed and quartered. What about your belongings? Have those been brought in yet?"

"I'm afraid we have little with us at the moment. Our baggage cart is miles behind. We'll make do with what we have for now. Mrs. Hyde, might we trouble you for some tea? Or cocoa if you have some in the house. It is Mrs. Driscoll's favorite. She could do with a little warming up."

Mr. Hyde guffawed. "Aw, I'm sure ye'll have no trouble warming her up. The two of ye cannot seem to let go of each other. Mrs. Hyde and I were just like you. Lovebirds we were and still are. Married going on thirty years and I love her more each day."

His wife rolled her eyes, but it was obvious she was pleased. "Get on about your business, you old goat."

"You are right, Mr. Hyde. Ours is a love match." He turned to Grace and took the fire iron out of her hand. "We don't need this. Let's put it back in its place."

Within the hour, their horses had been tended and so had they. Mrs. Hyde had put the kettle on for tea and fixed them a broth with bread for dunking which was more than ample to hold them until morning.

While they were eating, Mrs. Hyde ran upstairs to freshen their bedchamber, merely assuming they would share. He meant to correct her mistake, but Grace gave his hand a light squeeze. "It is all right," she said when they were momentarily left to themselves. "I will jump at every creak on the stairs or rattle of windows if I am alone in my bed. The damage is already done and I'd rather have you beside me. We only need the one."

He set down his spoon and regarded her. "It is a good idea, Grace. I would not have slept a wink for worrying about you."

Mr. Hyde brought more wood in and immediately went upstairs to light a fire in the hearth in their bedchamber. The pair walked back down together just as he and Grace finished their meal. "Our quarters are just off the kitchen," Mr. Hyde said. "There is a bell cord at the side of your bed, Captain Driscoll. Just tug on it if you wish to summon us."

Deklan nodded. "You've been most accommodating, Mr. Hyde. Thank you."

Mrs. Hyde offered to sit with Grace in the morning to review the list of supplies they would need now that they were in residence.

"An excellent suggestion," Grace said, her smile sincere. "Shall we say ten o'clock? I usually wake earlier, but I would like to sleep in tomorrow."

Deklan bid the Hydes a good evening, dismissing them with a nod. He then led Grace upstairs, but neither of them was prepared for the sight they beheld upon entering the bedchamber. "Blessed saints," Deklan muttered and began to laugh. "It is fit for a bloody king."

Grace was also staring at the canopied bed dominating the large room. It was draped in dark emerald velvet and jutted out into the center of the chamber. Its dark wood headboard abutted the wall. The fireplace mantel appeared to be from a fourteenth century chapel and the carpet was of an oriental design that could have been from a sultan's palace.

She turned to him, obviously stunned. "It is beautiful. Masculine, and yet warm and inviting despite its grandeur." She ran to peer out the window. "It overlooks the sea. The view will be spectacular come morning."

Deklan was still chuckling. "Can you see yourself as mistress of this house? And by mistress, I do not mean my unmarried concubine. I wish to be clear on this point."

"Well, since we are keeping up the pretense for now, I would not mind at all. It is a lovely house. Dahlia did a superb job of decorating it. I would very much enjoy being mistress in such a home. This is what my years of training were for, to run a household. Although I never understood why it was referred to as that when the lady of the house never actually *runs* anything. A proper lady has a housekeeper, cook, maids and butlers, at her beck and call to do all the work. There is little left for her to do other than look charming and pour tea in a cup with casual ease when entertaining guests."

"You shouldn't dismiss the importance of your role."

"It is not a very demanding one, is it? What does a lady have to do but smile charmingly throughout the day and greet her husband when he returns home…or in your case, greet him whenever he deigns to reappear after months of absence?"

She sighed. "No, that is unfair of me. You are important to England and the wife you choose must understand this and not put you ill at ease for doing your duty."

"Could you do this, Grace? If this were not a pretense?"

"But it is." She turned her back to him. "Will you help me with my laces?"

This was it? All the response she was to give him?

Was she being purposely dense and not understanding his point? Or was he being purposely elusive because he did not want to make her any promises until the crisis of the stolen crown was over and done? "Grace—"

"No, do not go on about this when you've already said marriage to me is a big mistake."

"What? Where did you ever get that idea?" He groaned, recalling his words last night. "Bollocks, you misunderstood. I was not referring to you as a mistake. I was talking about myself and the way I left you to cool my anger. I was angry with myself, not you."

"Why were you angry with yourself at all?"

"Because of who I have become. You have seen me clearly all along. I am that leopard who looks down upon everyone from his high perch in the trees. I come and go as I please. I answer to no one, not even my loved ones. I even kept this house purchase quiet from them for no reason at all. And having done that, I then proceeded to have Ronan's wife design and decorate it from London. My own house, for pity's sake. I put none of myself into it. No wonder you are so afraid to love me."

He led Grace to the bed and sat her on his lap. "Bollocks, I was not planning on having this discussion with you yet."

"Because you wanted to be done with this assignment first?"

"That's right. But I wish to be done with *it* and not *you*. Did we not read that book together? Are we not now experts on the topic of senses, expectations, and flaws? Well, you have no flaws."

"That is nonsense. Of course, I do."

"No, not a one," he said, knowing he was being stubborn about it. But how else would he make her see how perfect she was for him and all he would ever want?

"But I have expectations."

"Yes, Grace. We have to talk about that. You have very high expectations in your requirements for a husband."

She skittered off his lap. "I am already pretending to be your wife. We are sharing a bedchamber and this massive bed. My life is in ruins and my family does not even have a goose for Christmas. I do not need to now be lectured by you on my impossible standards and how ridiculous they are for a husband who will never come along because no one will ever come near me after the family scandal."

"Grace–"

"No, I do not even have a shred of pride left. An unmarried woman sleeping with you and I cannot even hide the fact that I like it. And who will ever believe I am still untouched? One look at you and they will assume I leaped into bed with you and never wanted out of it." She made a sound of utter frustration. "Do not say you will marry me. In all the misery my selfish brother and deluded father have caused, I have not yet sunk so low as to be willing to accept crumbs from you."

"We are still on crumbs, are we? Is this all you think I am offering?"

"I have no idea what you are offering or why you are offering me anything at all." She turned away and struggled with the lacings of her gown. "The horrible thing about it is I do love you. You are right. My heart is bursting with love for you. I can hardly think or breathe, I love you so much. And truth be told, I am on the verge of giving in and accepting you because having crumbs of you is better than having nothing of you at all."

She stopped struggling when he put his hands on her body and started to untie them for her. "Hold still, you've got them all knotted."

"Just like my heart."

"Oh, Grace...do not put yourself through this. I am not going to leave you once this assignment is through."

"Well, you are not going to marry me either."

"Yes, I will."

She shook her head as she turned to him. "Deklan, I am only nineteen. I am not of age to marry without my father's consent. Do you think he gives a care for my happiness? He will demand his freedom and more in exchange for it. He will not hesitate to use me as his bargaining chip. So let us not even have this conversation. Even if you were truly willing–"

"Damn it, Grace. Of course, I am."

"Says the leopard desperate to climb back in his tree. Even if you were, what do you think the chances are of my father ever agreeing?"

CHAPTER THIRTEEN

THE NEXT FEW days passed uneventfully and it was now the morning of Christmas Eve. Deklan knew his cousins must have reached London and handed the crown over to the Duke of Wooton by now. Not only handed it over to him, but negotiations were likely underway to return the crown to its rightful place.

For all he knew, the foreign agents had already been called off and told to return home. Even if not yet, those orders would be imminent. Grace was safely out of sight in Brighton while frantic political maneuvering was going on elsewhere.

Where was Grace?

He went in search of her and found her reading in the library. That he had any books in the house was a fortunate circumstance. Dahlia had thoughtfully supplied some to fill his empty shelves. "Ah, there you are."

She glanced up from her cozy nook and set her book aside. "You're back. I did not hear you return."

He had done a quick turn about the area to make certain all was quiet, something he did often throughout the day, not only to scout the streets, but also to get out of the house.

He was not good at staying in one place too long, even with someone as tempting as Grace to keep him close. Well, she would always keep him close. It was his restless nature and the confinement of four walls that had him tense and prowling.

Waiting for danger to happen only made things worse. "The Bramsons are throwing a party tonight," he said of their neighbors. "I encountered their son off on an early morning errand and he invited us."

She looked at him with a mix of hope and surprise in her expression. "Did you accept the invitation?"

"No, of course not. I politely declined. Too much of a risk to have you seen yet. Not only from those foreign agents."

"I know," she said, obviously disappointed. "I'm in as much danger being recognized by society acquaintances. I may be able to tolerate their ridicule most times out of the year, but not at Christmas. This is a time of charity and good cheer."

"What does it say of those who would show you none? It speaks worse of them than of you."

"I do not even want to think what they'll say when they find out I have been traveling with you. Unmarried and in close quarters."

"Grace, all this will pass."

"The foreign agents, yes. But the scorn of society? That will take another decade. Even then, it will require some other shocking scandal to knock it out of everyone's memory."

He put his hands on either side of her chair and leaned close. "And scandal always does come along. That is the beauty of a man's low brain, always getting him into trouble whether he is a butcher, baker, duke or prime minister."

She smiled, but there was not much mirth in it.

He could not blame her. She had also been trapped inside for days, and although it was a lovely house, one could only stare at the walls for so long before growing bored enough to climb them.

He had gone out a few times to run some errands in addition to regularly searching the area, but Grace had not even been allowed to stick her head out the window.

He gave her cheek a light caress. "Only a few more weeks, then it will all be over."

Pain etched her eyes.

Bollocks, she still thought he was going to leave her at the end of this assignment.

Well, hopefully his plans for tonight would convince her otherwise.

Rattling aimlessly about the house had left her with nothing to do but fret. Grace's nature was not to indulge in her own misery but to worry about the comfort of others. In this instance, it was for her mother and siblings and their deprivation.

He hoped Donal and Lorcan had been able to do something for Lady Montford. While outside of Grace's hearing, he had asked for their help and given them funds to apply for her benefit and that of her children.

He dared not say anything to Grace about his efforts, for his cousins had the crown to return and plenty of Brayden family obligations to occupy them. They might not have been able to do anything for her mother yet.

Christmas was tomorrow.

It could not come soon enough for him.

If his plans for tonight did not work, he wasn't certain what else to do.

He took Grace's hands and nudged her out of the chair. "Come on, I am taking you out."

She laughed. "Are you serious? Where?"

"You are in need of a new gown for tonight. Our excursion ought to be safe enough at this hour. Just one shop. We'll slip in and out fast. I'm sure Mrs. Hyde will know of the best dressmaker in town."

"Deklan, have you forgotten this is the day before Christmas? Even at the quietest times of the year it is impossible to simply walk into a shop and out with a gown." Even though she was shaking her head, he could tell by the sparkle in her eyes that she was delighted at the prospect.

This is all he wanted, to see her smile and be carefree for a little while.

"Besides, why would I need a new gown?"

"I may not be able to take you anywhere, but there is no reason we cannot have our own elegant party right here."

"You really are a leopard lost up in that tree of yours. Do you know what goes into preparing for a party? Or properly dressing a lady? The modiste will never be able to finish even one of her simplest designs for me by tonight, not even if she engages a team of seamstresses. It is an impossible task."

He still had hold of her hands. "We'll see. Come on, we are wasting precious time."

"Well, if you are going to be stubborn about it. All right."

Her laughter touched his heart.

He began shouting through the house for Mrs. Hyde. The woman came scrambling out of the kitchen, worried something was wrong. Then she shook her head and gently chided him for alarming her when she noticed their broad smiles.

"We need the name of the best dressmaker's shop in Brighton. My wife must have a new gown for tonight."

"Captain Driscoll, that will be Mrs. Galbraith's shop but I doubt she will be able to–"

"She'll get it done. Just give us the direction. Grace, love…get your cloak. I've hired a carriage and driver from the stable. He's waiting for us outside."

"You've planned this out?" She blushed and ran upstairs to get her things.

He turned to Mrs. Hyde and spoke quietly. "Has your husband purchased the decorations?"

"Yes, just as you requested."

"Good." He and Grace were going to spend the night putting up holly boughs and red velvet ribbons to celebrate the holiday. He knew Grace would enjoy it and get into the Christmas spirit because she was a traditional girl at heart. "And the wassail bowl?"

"All will be done to your instructions. What a sweet thing you are doing for your wife."

He rubbed a hand across the back of his neck. "In truth, Mrs. Hyde, I would do anything for her."

The woman smiled. "It is obvious."

Although wassail was traditionally a Twelfth Night drink, it was not unheard of to have it at the start of yuletide celebrations as well. The drink was a particular favorite of his and held treasured memories from his childhood when his mother would set out the hot mulled cider and add her secret spices. Nutmeg, cinnamon, and he did not know what else, other than she would also put brandy or mead in it.

As boys, he and Rafe could not wait to drink it. Of course, they would wake with a blistering hangover the next morning because it was always a contest between them as to who could drink the most.

"I'm ready," Grace said, her cheeks pink and her words a little breathless as she returned to his side.

The shop was not far from their residence and the carriage ride proved short. He had the driver wait for them even though the day was sunny and surprisingly warm. They could have walked the distance home, but he was already taking a risk merely having her out. A minimal risk, but he did not want their neighbors prying.

"Are you certain we ought to be doing this?" She spoke in a whisper, as though they were about to do something naughty.

"Quite, and you needn't whisper," he said, putting his hands around her waist to help her out of the carriage and across a patch of mud by the shop's door. "I am going to spoil you, Grace. It is about time I did something nice for you."

"In addition to saving my life? And being wonderful to me in every way? You needn't, but thank you."

The shop was more elegant than he expected, resembling the finer salons in London. Then again, the well-heeled set had followed the king to Brighton, so it should not have been all that surprising for merchants to follow as well.

While Grace browsed the various fabrics on display with one

of the shop assistants, Deklan took the proprietress aside. "The finest for my wife and I need it ready by this afternoon." He then placed an obscene amount of money in her hands and told her where to send the gown once it was finished.

"She'll need matching accessories," Mrs. Galbraith said, eyeing him shrewdly. But she must have seen something a little terrifying in his expression to understand he was not going to be an easy mark. "What you've given me should cover all of it. You have been most generous."

"Just treat my wife well, that is all I ask."

"Of course," she said, now looking more closely at Grace and then back at him. "Captain Driscoll, she will need proper jewelry to complete her outfit. But she has delicate features, so I think you can get away with something small such as a string of pearls or a simple diamond necklace. Nothing elaborate. Just tasteful." She gave him the name of a nearby jeweler.

He took Grace there next.

She held him back as they were about to enter. "Is this not too much?"

"No, Grace. It is not enough, if you wish me to be frank about it. Choose something lovely and do not stint on yourself or I shall be forced to choose for you. I can assure you, it will be something gaudy and crass since I have no idea what I am doing when it comes to buying jewelry for women."

She laughed. "I do not believe that for a moment."

He cast her a wry smile. "Well, I haven't done it in a very long time."

"I suppose you bought something nice for your Lady Genevieve."

He sighed. "Yes, but it wasn't the same thing at all. She expected gifts from her suitors, wanted diamonds mostly. It was all part of a courtship game, more of a competition than a courtship for me since I was not serious about her. It was not well done of me, but I stepped back when I realized she was not someone I could ever love. Come inside and let's find something perfect for you."

They ended up selecting a necklace with a pink diamond stone as its centerpiece to match the pale rose hue of the gown she would wear tonight. The necklace was not too big because Grace had a slender throat.

Nor was she very big herself, just nicely rounded in all the right places.

He turned to her as the jeweler was wrapping it up in a pretty box. "Just to be clear, the necklace is yours. Do not attempt to return it to me. I will not accept it back from you. All right?"

"All right. But I wish to be clear as well. If you change your mind, all you have to do is ask."

"Put it out of your head, Grace. I am not doing that."

"Your mother warned me you were stubborn." But she was all smiles by the time they hopped in the carriage for their return home.

Yes, he did consider it their home.

He hoped Grace would in time as well.

To everyone's surprise but his, the gown was delivered on time.

Mrs. Hyde assisted Grace in donning it and doing up her hair.

He had little to do other than shave and put on the naval uniform loaned from Ronan which Mrs. Hyde had aired and brushed clean.

When Grace was dressed and her hair fashionably styled, he brought in the necklace earlier purchased for her. Mrs. Hyde could not contain her smile as she darted out the door to give him privacy.

"There, love," he said, fastening it around Grace's neck and planting a kiss at her nape. "You look beautiful."

She turned to face him, her smile radiant. "You clean up well for a leopard," she teased. "I'm not sure what you have in mind for tonight, but I look forward to it. Thank you for taking me out today and for all this."

"It is my pleasure, Grace."

She cast him an admiring look. "Every young lady in Brighton will be green with envy. Truly, Deklan. You are so handsome."

He gave her a light kiss on her lips. "Come on downstairs. You can swoon over me later."

"Do I smell chestnuts?" She caught the scent of them as they made their way downstairs to the parlor.

"Yes, Mr. Hyde tossed a few onto the open fire to roast while we work."

"You are putting me to work?" She glanced down at herself and laughed. "I am wearing silk and diamonds. Just what sort of work have you planned for me to do?"

He pointed to the boxes set out beside the settee overflowing with holly boughs, ribbons, and other decorations. "We are going to decorate the parlor."

She went to the boxes and peered in them. "Oh, what a wonderful idea. Is that mistletoe? Where did you get all this?"

"I left that to Mr. Hyde while we were out shopping. Of course, I insisted on mistletoe. I'll hang some in every doorway and kiss you whenever you walk under it."

The Hydes joined them in time to hear his remark.

"Young love," Mr. Hyde remarked with a guffaw.

The men strung the boughs and put up mistletoe while the ladies tied ribbons to all the greenery.

Warmth flooded through Deklan whenever he heard Grace's gentle laughter.

Once the decorations had been put up, they all helped themselves to wassail and chestnuts. Perhaps it was not the best combination, but it filled the room with familiar scents of winter. Mulled cider, nutmeg and cinnamon. The char of roasted chestnuts.

The Hydes then excused themselves to go to church. "I'll set out your meal for you before we go," Mrs. Hyde assured. "Leave the dishes once you've finished. Mr. Hyde and I will clean up on our return. I'll prepare meals for you for tomorrow as well since

Mr. Hyde and I will be spending the day with our daughter. She and her husband live close by. We'll enjoy our grandchildren. Seven of them and an eighth on the way."

Grace's eyes widened. "Oh, my."

"Well, you need only look in the larder to find whatever you need."

"Thank you, Mrs. Hyde. It all sounds wonderful. I hope you have a lovely time with your daughter and her family." Grace turned to him when they were once more alone. "You did this for me. I cannot thank you enough."

"Well, we could not attend our neighbor's party. I thought we would have one of our own." He opened one of the doors that led onto the terrace just a crack and wrapped her in his arms to keep her warm when she joined him in peering out. "Listen, Grace. Do you hear it? Their guests are arriving. The son told me they engaged musicians, so there will be dancing later. Come on, let's have our supper."

He shut the doors and then brushed his hands up and down her arms because she was shivering after standing in the cold. It was a warmer night than usual, but still winter. He was comfortable in his naval uniform, but she wore delicate silk which would not even protect a flea in this weather. "Better?"

She nodded.

"Mrs. Hyde worked hard to prepare a holiday feast for us." He led her out of the parlor, but stopped in the doorway and glanced up.

Grace laughed. "Mistletoe."

"I ought to hang it over our bed, too," he said and swept her into his arms for a decadent kiss.

Hot, deep. Grinding.

As ever, their mouths sank perfectly into each other, hers soft and yielding. His possessive and demanding. Yet his kisses could never be harsh or bruising because his need to protect her was ingrained in his blood and in his soul.

Whatever heat he put into their kisses was always tempered

by his love.

They were both struggling for breath by the time they drew apart. "That was nice, Grace."

"Nice and wicked, you naughty man." She was blushing but also laughing, and she looked quite pleased.

He grinned at her. "There'll be more of that tonight."

But after a moment, he sobered. "You are beautiful. Truly, Grace. You are the loveliest thing I have ever seen. I shall be the envy of every man in Brighton."

"If I am ever permitted to venture out."

"You will soon."

Their supper was a private affair just for them in the elegant dining room. The table had been set with all his finery, none of which he had chosen or had any idea he possessed. *Bollocks.* Everything about the house was a reminder of how much he had separated himself from society and his own beloved family.

But having Grace beside him was a mark of his determination to make things right.

"You really did not have to go to all the fuss, Deklan."

"Are you enjoying yourself?" He wanted Grace to remember this special night.

"I am loving every moment." She cast him a heartwarming smile. "You are doing very well for someone who has spent his life in a tree. But all jesting aside, this is the nicest thing anyone has ever done for me. You have a very kind and romantic heart."

He shook his head. "Only with you. I'm still insufferable to most people."

They started with a delicious white soup which he ladled out of a tureen into bowls for them. Next was the fish course, smoked and encrusted in salt. He broke apart the hard, salt shell and served the haddock to Grace. Between courses, they ate sweets of almond paste and some of honey which had also been set out for them. Their final course was a refreshing *glace a l'orange* kept cold inside an ice sculpture.

Grace could not stop admiring the sculpture which was

shaped like a fish.

She peered at it from all angles.

Finally, she stood up and held out her wassail glass in toast. "I've had years of training in how to host a perfect party. Years, I tell you," she said with a hiccup and cast him the sweetest, lopsided smile.

He stifled a chuckle.

Grace was tipsy.

He should have realized she could not handle anything stronger than ratafia. The mead alone was potent enough to knock a man on his arse. Added to the mulled cider, the drink had gone straight to her head.

"Years, I tell you," she repeated. "I could not have done better."

Her smile was still adorable and completely lopsided.

"You made it look effortless and everything was delicious. Top marks for you, Deklan. No wonder you are the Crown's best agent. You would have made an excellent debutante, too."

He laughed. "Grace, you may not have noticed but I am a man."

"Oh, I noticed every blessed sinew and muscle on you. I'm surprised I did not melt from the heat radiating off your exquisite perfection. And you would have made a spectacular woman, too. A diamond of the first water."

"Oh, good grief."

"Suitors bearing all manner of flowers and chocolate sweets would have beaten a path to your door in hope of courting you."

"Am I that impressive?" he teased.

"Yes, and even more so. I mean it sincerely and I am not drunk," she said with another hiccup. "Despite appearances, I am not. I can see what you are doing, the consideration and tender effort that went into making this night special for me."

"Grace, it was my pleasure."

"I cannot tell you how long it has been since I've felt happy. My body is singing and my heart is dancing, and…"

She was sloshed.

On less than two cups.

"And I shall never forget this beautiful night you have given me."

"Nor will I, love." He rose and came around to her side. They had finished their supper and it was time to return to the parlor.

He gave her his arm, more to be sure she would not trip over her own two feet. She gasped as they entered and rushed to the doors leading onto the terrace, opening them slightly. "The Bramson's orchestra is tuning up. Listen."

"I hear it. Sounds like they are about to play a waltz." He took off his jacket and wrapped it around her shoulders to keep her warm. It was far too big for her and swallowed her up so that all he saw was her beautiful face.

He led her onto the terrace, for the stars were bright and thousands were visible on this clear night. The moon was big and splendid, reflecting on the water with its silver shimmer. Was it merely the effect Grace had on him? Or did the sky and water sparkle particularly brightly tonight?

Nothing could match the sparkle in Grace's eyes.

The music started, the gentle refrains carrying on the night breeze.

"Dance with me, love."

She beamed like a ray of moonlight and set his jacket on the balustrade before walking into his open arms.

He slowly began to twirl her around the terrace. "Do you remember this, Grace?"

She nodded. "We waltzed like this on the night we pretend met on that made up summer in Bath."

"This dance will be real for us." He drew her closer in his arms, holding her up against his body not only to keep her warm, but because he loved the feel of her against him. "We have the evening to ourselves. The music, the moonlight, and all these stars are out for us alone."

She nodded again. "Because the world has melted away for

everyone but us."

"That's right. No one exists but you and me." He kissed her as they waltzed, claiming her soft mouth. She tasted so sweet, of honey and mulled cider, and the orange ice they'd had for dessert. "I love you, Grace Montford. This is real. No pretend words on a make-believe night. Here and now. You are everything to me."

"I love you, too. Deklan, I am so sorry for every dismissive thing I said about you. There is no one with a better heart than yours. Can you forgive me for being such a fool?"

"I gave you so much cause to doubt. How can I blame you for all that was my own fault? As soon as it is safe to bring you out of hiding, I am taking you to Gretna Green. I want you to be my wife. Will you, Grace? I am asking you to marry me."

She took a deep breath and smiled up at him. "Well, you have done it now. Made every wish of mine come true. Made every dream of mine come true. I am joyful and grateful, and my heart is bursting with love for you."

"Is that a yes?"

She nodded. "You have made this a magical moment for me. Yes and yes again. Can you ever forgive me for being so wrong about you? *The Book of Love* spoke of sacrifices and compromises, and seeing clearly what is before your very eyes. I was blinded by my high ideals, just as you warned."

"You wanted a husband to share your life."

"And I almost lost the perfect man because I was too foolish to understand what truly matters. It isn't the number of days we are together. It is the quality of them that counts. What am I holding out for? Why would I change you when I love everything about you? I may not have you at home as often as I would like, but what you offer me will never be crumbs. *Never.* I'm so sorry I ever accused you of that. Your love is precious and every day you share with me is a priceless gift."

He kissed her again. "I was born a stubborn and irreverent arse, and shall always remain so. Hopefully never beyond your tolerance. I never want to hurt you."

"Speaking of your arse, I shall have to get used to that snake of yours." Her lopsided smile reappeared and she seemed a little unsteady on her feet. Well, that blast of cold air as they danced could not have been good for her. "Hideous fanged thing on your rump, but I am sure I shall grow to love it as much as I love you."

Bollocks, had he ever had a stupider idea than that tattoo?

But it seemed to fascinate women and arouse them.

Sweet Grace would likely be no exception. "Never mind about the snake, as long as you enjoy its tail. However, it will not be making an appearance for you tonight."

"Why not?"

"Because you are a tipsy virgin and we are still unwed. But rest assured, it is very much alive and eager to entertain you. We shall find other ways to amuse each other tonight." He lifted her in his arms to carry her upstairs. "Miranda would be smacking me on the head if she had any idea what I had in mind to do to you next."

"Indeed, she thinks you are a very naughty fellow."

"I am, love. But from now on, it will only be with you."

She leaned her head on his shoulder and sighed.

"Grace, how are you feeling?"

"Excited and dizzy," she said, nuzzling his neck. "Mostly dizzy, I think. The mulled cider went straight to my head. But I'll be fine. I am determined to have my night of pleasure with you."

Assuming she did not pass out first.

He set her on the bed and knelt beside her to remove her pink satin slippers that were a perfect match to her gown. "Oh, the bed is spinning. It feels as though we are floating on the water. Rocking in a storm."

"That cannot be good," he muttered, grabbing the basin and setting it close before helping her out of all but her chemise. He removed her necklace and put it back in its pretty box, then took a moment to place it in her bureau drawer.

She was still sitting up, her cheeks pink and her bosom in a steady rise and fall as she took deep breaths to steady herself.

Probably not a good idea.

Inhaling air in those deep gulps was more likely to put her out than sober her up.

He took the pins from her hair and ran his fingers through her golden curls. The tumble of tresses flowed like silk between his fingers.

He moved away a moment to remove his clothes, although there was no need to hurry. Despite her willingness, Grace was in no condition to do anything with him tonight.

They'd kept the fire going in their bedchamber all day to warm the room, but it also cast plenty of light. They were surrounded in a gentle, amber glow and Grace looked like an angel on his bed.

She watched him as he stripped down to his breeches. "Close your eyes, Grace."

"Why?"

"I am taking these off now. But it is only to change out of them into the pair I have been wearing to bed."

"Not on your life. I am not closing my eyes. I am not missing this."

He did not know whether to laugh or groan.

She had accepted his marriage proposal, so they were in effect officially betrothed. Never mind that her father would never consent. She had given her consent and this is all that mattered to him. They had pledged their hearts to each other. It was time they moved beyond merely sharing a bed.

However, not the *deed* itself.

Even if she were sober, he would not have claimed her. He intended to wait until their wedding night because Grace, being Grace, needed it to be this way whether she realized it or not.

In the meanwhile, there were a thousand ways to explore her body, to evoke her breathy moans and teach her about passion.

"All right, Grace. Fair warning. The breeches are about to drop."

He set them beside the other garments he'd shed.

Grace came to his side as he dug out the pair he intended to wear from his bureau drawer. "May I touch your snake?"

He closed his eyes and shuddered. "Depends what part."

He was going to shoot off like a cannon if she touched its tail.

But she ran her fingers lightly along his thigh, stroking the body of it, fascinated by the way it wrapped around the upper part of his leg. "That's a little too close, princess."

He lifted her in his arms and set her gently back on the bed. "Stay right there. Try not to look so beautiful."

"I look beautiful to you?" She touched her hands to her face. "My cheeks are on fire."

"You are either reacting to my magnificent body or the mulled cider. I am afraid it is probably the cider. Is your head still spinning?"

"Yes. And my heart is racing, but I would blame that on your body. Are you going to put your breeches on?"

"I had better."

After doing so, he propped her pillow against the headboard and did the same with his. "Your stomach is not going to make it through the night if you lie flat."

He settled in bed, took her into his arms, and held her warm body against his until she fell asleep.

Grace often spoke of miracles…a miracle they had found the crown. A miracle that he loved her. A miracle they were to share the rest of their lives together.

He would add another miracle, that she had not cast up her accounts in this big, lovely bed they shared.

Chapter Fourteen

DEKLAN AWOKE THE next morning to the sound of Grace's light snores. "Happy Christmas," he said in a whisper, laughing as he placed a kiss upon her cheek.

She looked delicious.

Pink and warm, and displaying a tempting length of leg because her chemise had ridden up her thighs. A sinful amount of breast was peeking out from the bodice because the sheer fabric had also twisted and ridden downward as she tried to curl herself into a comfortable position against him.

She was now sprawled half atop him, her hair somehow twisted around his arm.

He tried to unravel himself from her with painstaking care, but it did not work. She stirred and opened her eyes, smiling when she looked up at him.

"I did not mean to wake you, love."

"Thank you for a wonderful night. I'm sorry it didn't end quite as you hoped."

He cast her a lazy grin. "You were in my arms. I have no complaints. There's always tonight."

"What do you have in mind for us tonight?"

"Nothing, if you prefer." As for him, it was all he could do to keep from devouring her right here and now. Women were usually the ones desperate to marry, but seeing her wake with a smile just for him brought forth this very feeling in him.

He needed Grace, her smile and her sweet, warm body.

As well, he needed her earnest goodness and deeply caring heart to balance out the hollowness of his after all his years as a Crown agent. Taking on the most dangerous and often dirtiest assignments had taken its toll on him. "Truly, Grace. We need do nothing, if this is what you wish."

Her lips curved upward in a sleepy smile. "Oh, no. I am not missing out on any of your leopard love."

"For pity's sake." But he laughingly growled as he set himself over her and began to tease and lick her as though he were that beast.

What started out as playful soon turned hot.

There would be no waiting for tonight.

"I knew it," Grace said, stroking her fingers through his hair. "The jungle cat is aroused and now giving me his leopard stare."

He groaned as he kissed her on the nose. "How do you think I am looking at you?"

"With a sharp and hungry eye, as though you want to pounce on me and eat me."

"Well, I am always hungry for you and you do look quite delectable this morning." He sat up and curled one arm around her waist, drawing her up against him as though she weighed nothing. "How do you feel?"

"Much better than last night."

"You look better." He could tell by the brightness of her eyes and the pallor of her skin that the effects of the mulled cider had worn off.

She had imbibed less than two cups.

The effect could not have been all that bad, although she was a slender thing, not very much meat on her bones to absorb the potent mead.

Sunlight streamed in through the window, so he guessed it was sometime after eight o'clock. Normally, the household would be stirring, but he had given the Hydes the day off for Christmas and they had gone off last night to spend their time in church and then with their daughter.

He and Grace were alone in the house and no one was going to interrupt them.

Why should they not spend it in bed?

She appeared content to be nestled in his arms. "I am going to kiss you, Grace."

"Why do you feel the need to declare it?"

He shrugged. "Just making sure you are all right with it."

"More than all right, I am eager for it. But it feels different now that we have decided to marry, does it not?" She began to fret her lower lip.

He understood exactly what she was suddenly worried about.

He had made a commitment to her.

Would he now have regrets and run away as he did with Genevieve?

"Grace, I was never afraid of marrying you. I am not going to change my mind and hide up in my leopard tree. Are you having second thoughts?"

"No, but I have nothing to lose. I gain everything by marrying you."

"I feel the same about you."

"But it isn't true for you. It is the other way around. You would lose by marrying me."

"I gain everything," he insisted. "I could no more give you up than I could give up my own heart. This is what you are to me, my very heart."

"That is a lovely thing to say."

"It is the way I feel about you. May I kiss you now?" He started with gentle butterfly kisses along her throat and shoulders. Light, sweet kisses falling upon her body like droplets of a summer rain.

The scent of her body aroused him and his kisses grew wilder and untamed. He was waiting for Grace to accuse him of being a jungle cat, for this is how he now felt. Eyeing her as prey. Wanting to make a meal of her.

Tasting her on his tongue.

Licking the tips of her creamy breasts, drawing them into his mouth and suckling each in turn.

He had tugged the chemise down and now fully slipped it off her body.

She did not resist, but she was shy and tried to cover herself.

"Don't, love. Let me look at you." It was a big step for her, to be exposed like this to his view. He took a moment to soothe her, although he was barely able to breathe himself for the loveliness of her form.

He traced her delicate curves with the pad of his finger. "You are so beautiful."

He ached for this girl.

She was more exquisite than he had ever imagined.

Pink and soft.

Lush in the bosom.

She put him into low brain spasms. "I never stood a chance. My heart was lost at the first sight of you."

Had she been his destiny all along?

Had he ever had a choice but to love her?

She moaned when he took the bud of one soft mound into his mouth and began to gently suckle. He meant to go slowly, but Grace was a little ball of heat.

She responded passionately to everything.

Yes, this was Grace. Honest and compassionate.

He loved that she would not hold back.

She purred and moaned, clutched his head, then cried out when he moved his hand lower and began to stroke the golden curls between her legs. "Deklan!"

"Trust me, Grace." Lord, he'd longed to touch her like this since that first night. "Trust me."

She nodded. "I do. Oh, dear heaven."

He felt her nether curls moisten beneath his fingers.

She arched her body, yearning for him.

He was not a romantic by nature, would not spout flowery

words to describe her, but poetic thoughts now filled his head.

She was a swan.

A dove.

An angel.

His perfect rose.

He watched her lick her lips.

She purred like a kitten in her soft, breathy way.

Her eyes were beautifully wild when she opened them and looked at him. "Deklan, please."

"Let yourself go, love."

She gave her lips another lick. "I…something's happening…"

"I know, sweetheart. You are almost there." He knew the moment her body erupted in flames, for he caught the hot, sweet scent of her arousal and felt her body shudder as he held her in his arms.

Heat tore through him as he watched her soar heavenward.

But he'd promised himself he would wait before claiming her innocence. So instead of succumbing to his animal need, he held her and caressed her until she collapsed against him, now in her final throes of passion.

She said nothing for the longest moment, spent and simply holding onto him.

Nor did he speak, for it took all his effort to contain his own throbbing ache.

"Oh, my heavens. Deklan, is it always like this?"

He kissed her on the lips. "Always for you and me."

Once her breaths calmed, he released her and rolled out of bed to toss more logs onto the fire.

Grace watched him, her eyes so filled with love for him he almost could not bear it. In truth, his feelings were just as unbearably strong for her. He climbed back into bed and drew the covers over them. "It is early yet. No need for us to get up."

"Deklan…" She cuddled against him.

"Yes, love?" He had never been one to cuddle, but everything was different with Grace. He loved having her in his arms.

Breathing in the scent of her on his sheets and on his skin.

"How long do you think before the news of the crown is out?"

What he suspected she was really asking was, how long before they married and Grace was legitimately his wife? "I don't know. Soon, I'm sure."

They spent a quiet day which turned into a quiet week.

And then another week passed without a hint of anything going on in London.

If the Hydes thought it was strange he and Grace never went out or made any attempt to meet their neighbors, they did not remark on it. Nor did they comment when their supposed luggage cart never arrived.

But finally, the notice Deklan had been waiting for did arrive.

Two notices came at once, to be precise.

He received a letter from his brother on the same day the newspaper reports of renewed ties between the two countries made headline news. He scanned the newspaper account first, a report of a grand feast to commemorate signing the treaty of amity between England and the Kingdom of Silesia by their top diplomats. "Grace! Grace!"

He went in search of her and found her standing on the terrace looking out across the sea. It was a windy day and the waves were more turbulent than usual, striking the rocky shore with considerable force.

But his attention was not on those white-crested waves or their smash and roar as they broke upon the shore.

He had eyes only for Grace.

Gad, she was beautiful.

The sun shone down on her, bathing her in golden light. The wind whipped several strands of her long hair loose and they now brushed against her cheeks.

She turned to him, her smile stealing his breath away.

"It is done, Grace. We are free to return to London." He lifted her in his arms and twirled her around.

He thought she would be delighted by the news, but her smile faltered. "Oh, that is wonderful. When will we be leaving?"

She wore one of her sturdy woolen gowns and had a wool shawl wrapped around her shoulders, but he felt shivers shoot up her spine as he held her in his arms. He understood what was worrying her, what had always worried her from the first night they had shared a bed. "We are not going straight to London. Gretna Green first. As I've told you, you will always be my priority. I am bringing you home as my wife."

She hugged him fiercely, and then began to laugh. "Hurrah! I have been in agony, waiting to get my hands on your Olympian-god body. I was willing, Deklan. Shockingly eager to be claimed by you on Christmas Eve and then Christmas day. I thought for sure you would...then you didn't...and you never did...I didn't know what to think."

"I am reckless and irreverent about many things, but never about you. First of all, you were tipsy on Christmas Eve so I was never going to take advantage. Even if you had not touched a single drop, I would not have claimed you then or now."

"Why ever not?"

"For your sense of pride. You may want me, and I assure you I ache with wanting you. But you have been deprived of everything since your family's downfall. I was not going to deprive you of your virtue as well. That is for you to give me on our wedding night."

He noted the relief on her face.

"This was your reason?"

He nodded.

"I had no idea leopards were so moral. Thank you, Deklan. I am yours for always. I am yours for the asking. But you are right. I would have carried that regret in my heart if I came to our marriage bed with nothing at all to offer."

His laugh was more of a groan. "You have plenty to offer. I will never have enough of you. Even now, I cannot look at you without my eyeballs throbbing."

She grinned. "Only your eyeballs?"

"No, you wicked seductress. But my other parts are unmentionable. We have gotten off the point, and that is, the crisis has passed."

He led her inside and they sat together on the settee while he showed her the newspaper account.

"Silesia? So this was the foreign country? And King Stanislaus the monarch who lost his crown?"

"Yes, love. But everyone is happy now."

Graced wriggled closer to him. "What is that envelope you have in your hand?"

"A letter from my brother."

"And you did not think to open it first? Why hold off? Aren't you eager to read it?"

"Not if it contains orders I intend to ignore anyway. My priority is to get us married." But he did open his brother's letter at Grace's amused, but determined, insistence. It contained nothing more than confirmation the stolen crown had been returned and the demand to hold Grace hostage rescinded.

"Oh, thank heaven." She let out a trembling breath.

The rest of the letter asked about Grace and sent good wishes to her from all the family. It ended with a paragraph admonishing him for keeping his Brighton house a secret from his own brother.

Deklan laughed as he read on. *"I had to learn not only your whereabouts from Finn, but that you actually owned a home. You are such an..."* He glanced at Grace. "I cannot say aloud what he called me."

She shook her head, thoroughly amused. "Do not hide it from me. I want to see what expletive he used."

"Not on your life."

She giggled. "You know you deserved it."

He kissed her on the nose. "I am a reformed man now, Grace."

"I doubt it, nor would I want you to be. I love you, my jungle cat. You are a very good man in all the important ways." She kissed his cheek and tucked her arm in his. "What else does he say?"

"Mother is angry and hurt." He paused and groaned. "Right, he is still going on about my purchasing this house and keeping it a secret. That was not well done of me. Rafe says she'll get over it as she always does."

"Because she loves you."

"Aunt Miranda is another matter."

"Let me see." Grace took the letter out of his hands and read the last part. *You had better approach her wearing full body armor or you will lose limbs.* " Grace clapped her hands. "I adore Miranda."

"So do I, even if she is going to lop off my head. Grace, will you be all right with our leaving for Scotland tomorrow?"

"More than all right. I would run upstairs to pack but we've hardly got anything here with us. Oh, what shall I do with my elegant gown and the beautiful necklace? And what about the book? I think we had better take it with us. We must return it to your family."

"Take the book. Leave the gown and necklace. We'll be back soon enough for those."

"How soon? Once we are married, you'll need to report back to the Home Office and I'll need to see my mother and siblings. I cannot leave them where they are. But I dare not bring them to London. The children will never understand why they are treated so cruelly by our former friends."

He set aside the letter and the newspaper. "I've given it thought. Why not bring them here? New life. New friends. And under our protection. They will keep you company whenever I am gone."

"You would agree to have them live here with us?"

He grinned. "Do you not understand me yet? I would do anything for you."

"Oh, my brave husband-to-be. If they irritate you, we can always settle them in a pretty house not far from us. How is that for a compromise?"

"Perfect, love." He eased back against the settee and shifted her onto his lap.

She threw her arms around him. "Deklan, I love you."

Mrs. Hyde walked in just then to announce luncheon was ready. But the words stalled and her mouth gaped open.

Grace had let down her guard and called him Deklan within her hearing. She was now making it worse by trying to cover up the error. "Oh, ha, ha...you heard that, did you? This is my pet name for my husband..." She paused and groaned.

He sighed.

Pet name?

Love. Sweetheart. Dearest. Those were pet names. But Deklan? Really? "Mrs. Hyde, summon your husband. I would like to speak to both of you."

"Yes, Captain Driscoll...I mean...begging your pardon, but who exactly are you?"

CHAPTER FIFTEEN

DEKLAN DID NOT intend to reveal more than his name to the Hydes because the rest was none of their business and they were not going to question too closely while in his employ. All he needed to tell them was that his *wife*, Grace, had to go along with their false name in service of his duties.

He showed them his Crown badge, and that would have put an end to all questions had Grace not fled the room in obvious distress, putting more doubt into their heads. They all heard her scrambling up the stairs, and then heard the slam of a bedchamber door.

She was decidedly overset because they were unmarried and yet shared a bed.

"I gather you and the lovely lass are not husband and wife," Mr. Hyde said cautiously.

Mrs. Hyde shot her husband a frown. "It is none of our business. Can you not see he loves her?"

"Indeed, Mrs. Hyde. I do. We will be married by the end of the week. If either of you dare cast her a disapproving look or ever utter a disparaging word against her, I shall sack you on the spot."

"Mr. Quinton, it never even crossed our minds," Mr. Hyde assured. "Why, Mrs. Hyde and I...well, let us just say, he who is without sin...and so forth."

Mrs. Hyde nodded. "Mr. Hyde and I could not keep our

hands off each other. Our daughter was born…um, early. It is common enough. But may I ask you a question, Mr. Quinton?"

He sighed. "Go ahead."

"She seems very much a lady, not the sort to run off with you even though she obviously loves you in return. Nor do you strike me as the sort to steal off with a young lady and set her up in your home if you were not married. It seems to me there must be more going on than two lovebirds running off together."

"There is, Mrs. Hyde. I am not at liberty to tell you most of it, but Grace was the one in danger and I was assigned to protect her. Her life was at risk and it was vital to keep her hidden. Traveling as husband and wife was the only way to ensure her safety while on the run. Several attempts were made to abduct her. For this reason, I could not let her out of my sight even for a moment."

"And you fell in love while on the run?" Mrs. Hyde asked, obviously swept away by the romance of it and not the actual danger of the situation.

He cast her a wry smile. "Yes, Mrs. Hyde. This is exactly what happened. But we received word today the threat has been addressed. My priority now is to marry her."

"Oh, my," Mrs. Hyde said, "the poor dear. No wonder she would jump at every unexpected creak and thump."

"And she kept very much to herself," her husband added.

Deklan nodded. "For Grace's sake, I will ask you to maintain the pretense of our marriage. As I said, she will be my wife by next week and I will not see her shamed when none of this was her fault."

Brighton had been a quiet port town until Prinny, now king, plunked his Royal Pavilion in its midst. Recently, it had become a favorite summer retreat for the London elite. But they were still in the midst of winter and could get away with maintaining the pretense of husband and wife without anyone recognizing Grace and knowing she was a Montford or unmarried.

Grace would have to face the social slings and arrows sooner or later. But by next month, they would be back here, lawfully wed, and with her mother and siblings to support her if snide remarks were made.

He did not think there would be much resistance to her or her family here. Grace was too charming to be reviled for long, if at all, by the local population. She could start going out, join ladies' clubs, begin to gain allies before the weather warmed and her elite friends descended.

He went upstairs and knocked lightly at their door. "Grace, I'm coming in."

She was not weeping but looked quite miserable. "Why did you knock? I would never bar our door to you."

"I know, love. I simply did not want to charge in like a regimental cavalry." He opened his arms to her and she did not hesitate to fly into them. "The truth was bound to come out eventually. There is no harm in revealing it to the Hydes."

She nodded. "Yes, all the deception felt…"

"Awful?"

"But how can I face them now that they know?"

"They are not going to say anything. Mrs. Hyde thinks it is the most romantic thing she's ever heard, my falling in love with the woman I was charged to protect."

"You were charged to find that crown."

He shook his head and laughed softly. "I did not tell them that part and you should not either. It may require divulging information that is still sensitive and meant to be kept secret. Besides, most people are not interested in the political intrigue."

"They want the romance?"

"Yes, love. And we've provided plenty of it." He cupped a finger under her chin. "We'll leave for Scotland tomorrow and be married by next week. From that moment on, you will have the protection of my name and the support of my entire family. In truth, you already have their support. I'm sure they like you better than they like me."

She smiled despite her reluctance to be put in good humor.

"They must adore you as I do. All right, I will try my best to develop a thicker hide. It just might take me a while."

"You are soft and sweet. I would not want you any other way. But it destroys me to see you hurting."

"It isn't your fault and there is little you can do about it for the moment. I will be fine. I don't mind that the Hydes know the truth. They are kind people and it hurt me to lie to them. So, no more fake names. You are Deklan Quinton and I am Grace Montford. No more lying to the Hydes, the shopkeepers, or our neighbors."

"Grace, you are not chaperoned. We need to keep up the pretense of marriage until I can legitimately claim you as my wife. So do not start running to the Bramsons or the dressmaker and pouring out a confession. The Hydes know, but it is no one else's business."

She nodded. "I wasn't going to do anything so foolish. All I meant was that I would not hide from the truth if it came out, especially not deceive good people. I would love to shout it from the rooftop, but I won't. Instead, I will do no more than hop about quietly in our bedchamber and cheer."

"All right." He kissed her on the nose. "So long as you keep your hops in here for now."

"Does this mean I am not allowed out yet at all? Not even for a discreet celebration? I love this house. It is the most beautiful house in all of England, but I am going to scream if I stay hidden inside another moment. Can we not even take a walk?"

"I have a better idea. But here are my terms. I shall give my real name if asked, but we must keep up the pretense of you as my wife. You are Grace Quinton. I will not budge on that requirement. All right?"

"You will have no objection from me. Yes, as your wife. Where are you taking me?"

"The Pavilion Hotel. Their tea room ought to be fairly quiet on a Monday afternoon in winter and I hear they serve an excellent tea."

"Sounds lovely." She reached up on tiptoes and kissed him with touching innocence.

Several hours later, he wished to be anywhere but in that tea room.

Had he thought it was a good idea?

Seemed The Fates were conspiring against him.

Having spent almost a month worried about foreign agents stealing Grace away, he did not expect to encounter a more vicious nemesis here.

He could protect Grace against those foreign agents, for he had the prowess to defend her from physical attack. Threats from shooting or stabbing were nothing to him. Throwing punches and watching a villain fall to his knees was commonplace in his line of work.

But how was he to protect Grace from the wrath of Lady Genevieve de Clare, the woman he had courted and might have married had he not had second thoughts and run away as fast as his legs would carry him?

She was marching straight toward them as they sat in the Pavilion Hotel's tea room, a vindictive gleam in her eyes. "Oh, hell."

He and Grace were to leave for Scotland first thing in the morning. Why had he not simply kept her hidden for another day?

Until this moment, they were enjoying their elegant tea. The chef was renowned, and even though the hotel drew an elegant crowd, those who remained in winter were mostly on the fringes of society and no threat to Grace.

The elite were not supposed to arrive with their fine carriages and haughty airs until summer.

What was Genevieve doing here?

Grace had been watching the stewards bring out more cakes and other delicacies, but now turned to him. "What's wrong?"

He reached for her hand as Genevieve and her companion, the sharp-eyed woman from the Blue Moon Inn, approached. He remembered why she had seemed so familiar. She was Genevieve's waspish cousin, Velda de Clare.

Of all the bad luck.

He had met her only the once at a crush of a party held at the country home of Genevieve's parents several years ago. Velda was unremarkable then and remained unremarkable now, a drab woman with a sour smile and a mean spirit.

He had not recognized her because she had aged considerably since their only meeting. She was Genevieve's toady and always ready to do Genevieve's bidding.

What were these two doing in Brighton now?

Velda cast him a gloating smile. "I told you I'd seen him with the Montford girl. They were traveling together and sharing a bedchamber."

Genevieve's gaze was filled with malice. "Indeed, you did."

How had he ever thought this woman beautiful?

Well, Genevieve had classically beautiful features and those had not dimmed over the years. But that sneer and the venal look in her eyes revealed how petty and vain she had become. In truth, she had always been this way.

Why else would he have run?

Grace tried to slip her hand out of his, but Deklan refused to let her go. He did not want her leaving his side to hide in shame when she had nothing to be ashamed about. Society's conventions were nothing but hypocritical rules often flouted and ignored by the very people who would use them as weapons against innocents like Grace.

He was not about to let Genevieve hurt Grace.

He politely rose to acknowledge the pair, hoping to take the brunt of their anger and move them on their way. "I am surprised to see you here, Lady Genevieve."

"Oh, heavens," he heard Grace mutter as she realized who the haughty beauty was to him.

Genevieve had perfected the art of condescension. "I am Lady Somerset now, not that you would care."

No one could look upon another person with such convincing disdain.

Of course, back then she had been all smiles and sweetness toward him. Her true nature had come out as he got to know her, for her lack of kindness or compassion toward those she deemed below her station was not something she could easily hide.

Not that he was any prize.

He was detached and aloof, but he would never ridicule or humiliate a person in public for the sport of it. "My congratulations on your marriage. I hope you and Lord Somerset will be very happy together." The man was rich and an earl, so she had landed on her feet and done nicely for herself.

Her eyes glittered with intense anger.

She had not forgotten a moment of his rejection and intended to make him pay for it now.

"I would congratulate you as well," she said, glancing at Grace before turning back to him, "but I know of your companion's reputation and she is no one you would ever marry."

"You are quite wrong about that." He introduced Grace as his wife.

"Do not take me for a fool. You really ought to stop consorting with the dregs, my darling. But I suppose *Lady Disgrace* is easily bought now that her family is in ruins. Even you must know it is terribly bad form to bring your mistress to a respectable establishment."

Grace tried to leap to her feet, but Deklan held her down. "I will not stop you if you now wish to walk back to your table, Lady Somerset," he said, his voice a soft menace. "Indeed, I urge you to do so before I lose patience and bodily toss both of you onto the street where you belong."

"How dare you!" Genevieve now had her claws out. "How long has Mr. Quinton engaged your services for, Miss Montford? I hope you demanded more than that cheap necklace from him. He is quite wealthy, you know."

Grace looked angry as bloody murder.

Although he was glad she responded with outrage and was not shrinking back in tears, he remained determined to keep her out of this exchange.

Genevieve was purposely provoking her.

Every patron in the dining room was now staring at them.

Every member of the serving staff had frozen in place.

Lord Somerset approached. "Quinton? Is that you? What is going on here?"

"Take your wife home, my lord." He had never hurt a woman and would not start now. But if Genevieve took it further and demanded Somerset take action against him, that was a more serious situation. He had no intention of hurting the man, but neither was he going to back down if he insulted Grace.

"Return to our table at once," he ordered his wife. "You as well, Velda."

Apparently, Somerset knew of him and what he did in service of the Crown. The man was known to be arrogant and a bit pompous, but he was obviously no fool.

Genevieve's wasp of a cousin did not look pleased. "My lord, he insulted your wife."

"Be quiet, Velda, or I shall assist him in hauling you out of here. My apologies, Quinton. My wife seems to have forgotten she is married to me. But you have found yourself a lovely young bride. Lockbridge will be sorry he ever let her go. We shall not disturb your tea any further."

He then called over the maitre'd. "Mr. Quinton and his wife are my guests. I will settle their account."

The man bowed obsequiously. "Of course, Lord Somerset."

"Do not contradict me, Quinton. Consider it a wedding token from me and my wife. I hope this makes us square." He grabbed his wife and her cousin by the elbow and steered them back to their party of friends.

Grace was trembling, obviously overset after the rude confrontation. "Let's go, please. It was a mistake to come here."

"There will always be one or two vindictive wasps trying to

stir trouble. They will not stop if they think they can get to you."

"Well, they can. Is it not obvious? Deklan, please. Everyone is looking at us."

"If you run, Lord Somerset's support of you will be for naught. Do not take it lightly, Grace. He may have done it to admonish his wife, but all anyone in the tea room will remember is his acceptance of you." He glanced around. "They will quickly lose interest now that there is nothing to see. This isn't London, love. Most of the tea room patrons are not *ton*. As far as they are concerned, they are looking at Deklan Quinton and his wife because I said you were mine and so did Lord Somerset."

"But Somerset had to know the truth."

"Of course, he did. I owe him the favor for his support. We have to stay, Grace. Just listen to the whispers."

"What do you mean?"

"You may be a viscount's daughter, but you were not out in society and most of them don't know anything about you beyond the gossip rags mentioning your viscount father had a daughter about to make her debut. Beyond this, we are not that interesting. They are more curious about Lord Somerset and his misbehaving wife."

She leaned forward to better overhear the chatter at the surrounding tables.

She was in love with Quinton but he chose the quiet, pretty one instead. They say Lady Somerset never got over him. Poor Lord Somerset. How humiliating it must be for him.

Who is she? A Montague, did Lady Somerset say? Hmm, Montague…that name is familiar. She might be an Italian relation of my aunt. But the girl does not look Italian, does she? We were there just this summer on the Amalfi coast. The climate is so much more tolerable than in England. We really ought to go back, but it is quite vexing. So few of them speak English.

Isn't she lovely? Did Lady Somerset say Montford? I wonder if she's related to the viscount who got into a spot of trouble. And the viscount's son, awfully nice looking fellow. He threw a good party. Haven't seen much of him lately. I did enjoy his last party. Have you ever been?

Lady Somerset is green with envy. Has she forgotten she is married to an earl? Never seen that Montague girl before. Quinton obviously noticed her and wasn't letting her get away. He's sharp as a crack, that one.

No wonder Lady Genevieve lost him. That Montague girl is quite beautiful. I'm sure she is related to my aunt. We really ought to return to Amalfi in the spring."

Poor Lord Somerset, his wife is obviously not over that Quentin fellow.

Grace covered her mouth to hide her amusement. "That Quentin fellow?"

"And you are the beautiful Montague lass. Italian ancestry?" He placed his hand over hers. "Grace, most people are in their own worlds and do not care what goes on around them unless it affects their comfort. There will always be wasps like Lady Somerset's cousin who have nothing better to do with their days than spread malicious gossip. Most people don't care beyond the initial titillation and will soon overlook it. Do not be surprised if we are suddenly flooded with invitations."

"Why would anyone invite us?"

"To liven their parties, of course. Nothing can be worse for a host or hostess than to be considered drab." He called over one of the tea room stewards. "Another pot of tea. And what are these cakes you just brought out?"

"Turkish delicacies," he explained. "Our chef has introduced them to England in honor of His Majesty and the Royal Pavilion built here in Brighton. Of course, they are not traditionally served in English tea rooms. But our patrons seem to enjoy them. We have our array of traditional cakes as well."

"Oh, I would love a small piece of each," Grace said, pointing to one the steward called *baklava* and another he said was *konife*.

"Of course, Mrs. Quinton."

"Have you ever tried these before?" she asked Deklan. "The dough is crisp and thin, and coated in honey."

He nodded. "I had these particular sweets in Constantinople.

They have been popular for centuries throughout the Ottoman Empire. But do not let on about that. The London elite will rave about these exotic delicacies because they have been presented as delights served only to kings. They will not be pleased to learn these sweets are available to commoners as well."

"Well, they are delicious. I would love to hear about your adventures, those you are at liberty to divulge. You must have seen and done so many interesting things, met so many interesting people. Perhaps even changed the course of history."

He reached over and dabbed her lip with his table linen. "You have some honey on the corner of your mouth. I could kiss it off you."

"Don't you dare," she said with a gentle laugh. "I would rather not be barred from coming here again because of your scandalous behavior."

"Very well, I shall be as pious as a choir boy."

She began to smile with each bite she took. "I thought the Royal Pavilion was designed after the royal palaces of India. Are these desserts traditional fare of theirs, too?"

"I don't know, but I hardly think it matters. Anything foreign to the English palate is lumped together as one."

Her smile was irresistible.

Even the maitre'd was now beaming at her.

She glanced over and cast him a gracious smile in return. "Deklan, you were right. I'm glad we stayed. This was my first hurdle, and thanks to you I have gotten over it. Well, hopefully we shall have no more trouble once I am truly your wife."

"Now you know why I could not marry Genevieve. Had the situation been reversed, my choosing her over you, something that would never happen in a million years, by the way. But had I momentarily lost my mind and chosen her, you would have come over to wish us every happiness. You would have done this even if your heart was breaking."

"She behaved badly, but I cannot blame her for loving you."

"I think it is more that she cannot get over anyone rejecting her, especially a commoner like me."

"But is this not more reason to forgive her? She cared for you, not for a title."

"She cared for my wealth, no doubt something her family needed to maintain appearances. She is not like you, Grace. Her heart does not work the same as yours."

The lady was haughty and vengeful, and that was a bad combination. He did not expect her to give up meekly, so he kept an eye on her.

Somerset, however, had handled himself well by showing surprising tact and consideration. Perhaps he was not as bad as reputed to be in his younger days. Men grew up. Became responsible.

Too bad Genevieve did not appreciate what she had.

He kept an eye on Velda, too. He did not trust that conniving woman for a moment, and was immediately suspicious when, after a brief conversation with Genevieve, she suddenly excused herself and left Somerset's table.

She returned several minutes later, giving Genevieve a subtle nod as she sank back in her chair.

That sly smile again.

No, he did not like it at all.

He decided it was time to get Grace away. "Love, are you ready? We ought to return home now. We'll be getting an early start in the morning."

"Oh, yes." She rose as he drew out her chair, and then waited for him in the hotel foyer while he retrieved their cloaks.

He had just taken the cloaks in hand when he heard Grace scream.

He raced to the foyer in time to see her stumble and then clutch her throat.

For one mad moment, he thought someone had slit her throat. But he quickly realized a wretched thief had merely snatched her necklace.

"I'm fine," she insisted. "He pushed me as he grabbed the

necklace. Go after him, Deklan. I promise you, I am not hurt."

He tore after the man, catching up to him as he was about to disappear into a nearby alleyway. He tackled the culprit with a flying leap, and smashed the man's hand when he attempted to pull out a knife. But it turned out not to be a knife at all, just a coin purse. "No, m'lord! It was a prank. Don't break m'hand. Here. I'm givin' you the necklace and what I got paid."

"You idiot. Who put you up to it?"

"Lady Somerset's friend. You know the one. She looks like a wasp. The lady said yer wife's necklace was a fake and she meant to prove it. Said I'd come to no harm. Ye're fast as lightning, m'lord. No one ever catches me. I wasn't stealing it, just going to turn it over to the lady. She was going to give it back to your wife, she told me."

"And you believed her?" This boy was fleet of foot but utterly lacking in brains. Only a complete dolt would have failed to understand it was a theft and Velda was never going to stand by him. Nor would Genevieve put in a word for him, even though this had obviously been done at her urging.

That vindictive pair had not counted on his catching the boy, but were more than willing to let him take the fall for their predatory antics.

"Yes, m'lord. She said she would return it. Truly, I meant no harm by it. She paid me to do it. Just a prank. That's all it was meant to be. No harm done."

"I suppose pushing my wife was also a prank." He hoisted the man to his feet and dragged him back to the elegant hotel. "Summon the constable," he told one of the stewards.

"At once, Mr. Quinton. Why, that's one of our kitchen scullery boys. William Penny, what do you think you were doing?"

"It was a prank," the young man repeated, still trying to talk his way out of a prison sentence. "The fine lady paid me."

He pointed to Genevieve's cousin who was just now walking out of the tea room with the Somerset party. "There! Ask her. She'll tell ye."

Two of the hotel's burly footmen arrived to assist.

Deklan handed the lad over to them. "Hold him for the constable."

The hotel's manager hurried forward, wringing his hands and offering apologies. Deklan took a moment to relate what had happened. "Have Lord Somerset speak to the boy. He might recognize the coin purse."

Of course, Velda would accuse the boy of stealing it from her.

The authorities would accept her denial because this is how social conventions worked. A scullery boy would never be believed over the cousin of a countess.

But Somerset would understand what had really gone on.

That idiot boy.

What had he been thinking?

Did he understand yet his life was in ruins?

Well, toiling in a scullery could not have been much of a life.

The hotel's foyer was suddenly crowded as the tea room emptied out amid the commotion.

He needed to find Grace.

One helpful woman pointed to the door. "She walked out with an old lady."

What the hell?

Deklan stepped outside and saw Grace slowly escorting a hooded figure in a cloak toward a waiting carriage.

Was this another ruse to lure Grace away from him?

More of Velda's mischief? Or was it something more serious? An abduction attempt by those foreign agents even though the crown had been returned and the treaty signed? Perhaps not all their agents had received the word.

When Grace and her companion turned to him with a smile and a wave, he breathed a sigh of relief for he recognized the lady. But that relief was short-lived when he saw a man standing across the street.

Something about him did not feel right.

Deklan crossed the street for a closer look at him.

The man's attention was fixed on Grace and her companion as he withdrew a pistol hidden within the folds of his cloak. Deklan was on him before he could take proper aim. In the struggle, the villain managed to get off a shot that ricocheted off a lamp post and must have nicked the ear of one of the carriage horses near where Grace and her companion stood. The horse reared in fright, upsetting the rest of the team of matched bays and causing the carriage to tip precipitously.

"Grace!" he shouted, trying to issue a warning over the clatter of a wildly rocking carriage and the shrieking neighs of bucking and kicking horses.

She was already acting on her own, quick to grab her companion and pull her away from the tottering carriage and the frightened horse's flailing hooves. In pulling the old lady out of danger, both of them fell backward, the woman landing safely atop Grace because Grace had purposely shifted her body to take the brunt of the fall.

He hastily subdued this man, too, and turned him over to the hotel's footmen. Once he was securely in custody, Deklan ran to Grace's side. "Love, are you hurt?"

"Winded, that's all." She was almost hidden beneath the elderly Duchess of Dunfell who was sprawled atop her.

He helped the duchess to her feet.

"Who fired that pistol?" Grace asked, now able to get up on her own.

"I don't know the man's identity yet." But he surmised it was one of William Penny's scullery mates, the pair of them paid to carry out Genevieve's so-called pranks. He would deal with this dolt later.

He now turned with concern to the elderly duchess. "Your Grace, are you hurt?"

"No, Mr. Quinton. The lovely lass saved my life."

"Hardly," Grace said, slowly struggling to her feet and brushing dirt off her now stained gown.

"Do not contradict a duchess, my dear," Her Grace said. "You were very brave. I am not a small woman and might have squashed you. But you saved me from getting run over, and at the very least, breaking several bones. I hope I did not crush you."

The duchess's own footmen, having finally subdued the horses, now hurried forward to assist her.

She shooed them away. "Utterly useless. Go question whoever fired that shot."

"But Your Grace—"

"Question him and do not let him escape. I am in good hands." She turned to Deklan. "You must recognize those two since they are Crown agents and not really footmen. I do wish they would assign you to me again. That culprit would never have gotten this close if you were guarding me."

"Perhaps in the future."

"No, Wooton relies on you for the truly dangerous assignments. Are you on duty now?"

"I was. It resolved only this morning. A few loose ends to tie up now, nothing more."

"I assume those loose ends involve Miss Montford. Yes, I know exactly who you are, my dear. I knew it before that unpleasant Lady Somerset shouted it out to one and all."

Grace groaned.

"Never you mind. I can guess most of what Wooton called upon your Mr. Quinton to do. I warned King Stanislaus he ought to have better security for his crown jewels. Put his entire kingdom at risk because of a stolen crown. Oh, he wrote to me crying about it."

Deklan grinned. "He ought to engage you as his security advisor."

"Nonsense, I am an old lady. What do I know? Well, it is good to see you again, Mr. Quinton. You and I need to have a little talk."

"With pleasure, Your Grace. But I am leaving Brighton first thing tomorrow. I expect to be back in another month."

"Taking your pretty lady friend?"

"She is my…" He was not going to lie to the Duchess of Dunfell. The old besom was one of the sharpest women he had ever met, and he knew her well from prior assignments because she and her husband were constant targets and often in need of protection. "Miss Montford will be my wife by the time you and I next meet."

"I thought that might be the situation. You are not going to run away from this one, are you?"

Deklan grinned. "Not a chance."

"Clever boy. Come see me when you and Miss Montford return to Brighton. I shall hold a tea in her honor."

Grace inhaled sharply.

"Your grandmother and I were childhood friends. I hope we shall become friends, too." She patted Grace's cheek. "If anyone dares disparage you, just send them to me. I shall deal with them."

He and Grace watched as her Crown agents disguised as footmen returned and the duchess was helped into her carriage.

"That pistol shot by the horse's ear was either another bit of mischief courtesy of Genevieve," Deklan mused, "in which event we shall quickly get the truth out of her cousin or the scullery boy who stole your necklace."

"You have it back?"

He nodded. "The clasp is broken and a few of the diamond chips fell off. But otherwise it is intact."

"Thank goodness. You said either…do you think the shot scaring the horses was something else?"

"Possibly another attempt on the life of the duchess. The timing of it could have been mere coincidence."

"*Another* attempt on her life? Good gracious."

"You aren't the only lady to have villains after her. But we know of hers and usually keep close watch on them. I'm not sure how this man slipped through her protection and got that close. She berated those Crown agents, but they are good men and not easily fooled. That indicates to me this was likely more mischief planned by Genevieve. A shot only meant to be fired in the air to scare you, perhaps hoping you might be kicked by a startled horse."

"But she might have hurt the Duchess of Dunfell."

"She did not count on that, did she? And now she's made an enemy of that tough old bird."

"Dear heaven."

"Serves her right. She's brought it on herself. Somerset will be steaming mad."

"What will he do to her?"

He arched an eyebrow as he put his arm around her. "That's between them. Come on, love. Give me a moment to question this lad, then I'll take you home."

She nodded. "Who knew taking tea on a Monday afternoon in Brighton could be so exciting?"

CHAPTER SIXTEEN

THE FOLLOWING DAY, Grace found herself in a mail coach with Deklan and four other passengers, all of them crammed together on their way to Scotland. She rode most of the way crushed against Deklan since the man on the other side of her had shoulders as broad as Deklan's, only he was not nearly as fit or his scent as appealing.

She did not mind these tight quarters nor the bouncing and jouncing as the carriage tore northward at precipitous speed. They stopped only occasionally to change horses. "Twenty minutes to eat and tend to yer necessaries while we hitch the new team," the driver called out when they pulled up in front of one the many coaching inns along the way.

This was their routine for the next few days because making good time was more important than comfort. As for her, it still was not fast enough. If she could have sprouted feathered wings and flown to Scotland, she would have done so without hesitation.

On the day before they reached the borderlands, Deklan surprised her by having them descend the coach. "We'll take the last leg of our journey in a private carriage," he said, then turned to the driver and asked him to hand down their pouches.

The driver seemed to know Deklan and his cousins. "Send my regards to Lor and Donal. What is it with the men in your family? You seem to latch onto the prettiest ladies."

Deklan glanced at her and grinned. "She is an angel, isn't she?"

"Aye, she is." The driver laughed, and with a flick of the reins, drove off.

She watched as the coach clattered out of sight and hearing.

"Come on, love. Let's get you settled at the inn."

They had stopped in Penrith, a lively market town not too far from their destination. Since Deklan seemed to be familiar with every town in England, she was not surprised when he secured a room for them at one of the finest lodgings to be found in Penrith. Nor was she surprised when the innkeeper hurried forward to greet him. "Mr. Quinton, good to see you again."

Deklan then introduced her as his wife.

She was not certain the innkeeper believed him, but the man said nothing. Since they had gotten off the mail coach and were not far from the Scottish border, it was not a stretch for him to recognize they were en route to be married tomorrow.

But not married yet.

Deklan sighed as the man hurried off to summon a maid. "Grace, he is not thinking of us at all beyond the nice fee he will make from me. I've asked for his best guest chamber, ordered our meals sent up, and ordered baths for each of us. He is already counting the coins that will shortly be jingling in his pockets. As for me, I can hardly breathe for all the pounds of dust on me."

She nodded. "I dare not pat my gown for the ball of dust certain to rise from it. But–"

"No fretting, love. I could have brought along a goat instead of you and he would not have asked a single question."

"Deklan! That is ridiculous."

He tweaked her chin. "My point is, you are the only one feeling the burden of our situation. Grace, I promise you. We shall be married by tomorrow." He then finished signing them in as husband and wife. "I'm sorry it will not be a finer wedding. You deserve the best, but in this instance, I dare not wait before making you mine."

"Nor do I. The first blacksmith's shop we find upon crossing into Scotland is perfect." She reached up and kissed him on the cheek. "It will be the best ceremony ever performed. I do not care if we are caked in mud and smell like a pig farm…but thank you for ordering baths. I might choke on this dust if I do not get it off me soon."

She could not deny it felt good to retire to bed having been scrubbed clean and her hair thoroughly washed. An added touch was the scented soaps, and although her favorite was a Farthingale strawberry scent, the lemon one provided for her was also nice.

Deklan's had a bay rum scent that had her silently wishing the inn's helpful staff would disappear so she could ravage his body, which she would have done had she not fallen asleep before her head hit the pillow.

She must have been more tired than she realized.

No doubt the excitement of their journey had worn her out.

She spent the night dreaming of Deklan.

She awoke the next morning to his kisses and playful nudging. "Good morning, my sleepy love. Still want to marry me?"

"Good morning." She kissed him and wasted no time in tossing off her covers to ready herself for the day ahead. "Oh, Deklan, can you believe it? This is our wedding day. I am going to hold my breath until the ceremony is over."

"Worried that some bounder like the Duke of Wooton might interfere with our plans?"

"Do you think he would?"

"No, love."

To her relief, no one did.

By early afternoon they crossed into Scotland and their carriage stopped in front of a blacksmith shop in Gretna Green.

A light mist fell and the day was gray and dreary.

To Grace, it was the most beautiful day they'd had all year.

They entered the blacksmith's shop and could take no more than two steps in because of the other couples ahead of them.

These ceremonies moved fast and it was soon their turn.

This was not the wedding Grace had ever planned on, but she had not a single complaint because she was about to become Deklan's wife.

"I do," she said in response to the blacksmith's question and breathlessly awaited Deklan's turn.

He took her hand and cast her an appealingly tender smile.

He was so confident and had the most reassuring touch.

"And do you, Deklan Quinton, take Grace Montford to be your lawful wife?"

"I do."

After a few garbled words in the officiant's thick brogue, the ceremony was over. Several quick signatures, and the blacksmith moved on to the next waiting couple.

Deklan laughingly helped her into their private carriage and settled in beside her. "I've taken pisses longer than that ceremony," he joked.

"Ugh, Deklan!"

He cast her a wicked smile. "Sorry, love. How do you feel?"

"Joyful. Relieved. Euphoric. I doubt there is a happier woman in all of England. Well, we are in Scotland at the moment but we shall soon be back in England."

She squealed as he drew her onto his lap.

"You are now my wife, love."

She pressed kisses to his freshly shaven jaw. "Can you believe it?"

He wrapped his arms around her. "Yes, and I am never letting you go."

"Until your next assignment. But hopefully it will not be right away." She shook her head in wonder. "You are my husband. The best man in all of England. Why you chose me is still a mystery, but I will not question my good fortune. An enormous weight has been lifted off my shoulders. I am starting to gain my life back."

"A life I hope will be long and happy, and shared with me."

"Forever with you. I will never give you cause for regret, and I will always cherish your brave and caring heart. I promise. Nor will I ever complain about your duties to the Crown. If we must be apart for a time, then so be it. I will always be waiting to welcome you home."

"For my part, I'll try never to be away too long."

"The work you do is important. You better the lives of others. So many families have it worse than what befell mine and will never have the chance to better their lot."

"No more talk of that today. Only good thoughts on our wedding day."

"Well, had we Montfords not taken a fall, I might never have met you. I cannot imagine what my life would have been if our paths had never crossed."

"You would have married that dolt, Lockbridge, and been a duchess."

"I shudder to think so. That is one mistake avoided. I am now your ball and chain."

"You are my miracle, Grace." He kissed her with an unexpected depth of longing. Deklan was never one to let others into his heart, but this kiss was an outpouring of raw feeling. "As you are mine, so am I yours."

He regarded her thoughtfully for a long moment. "You have to let me know if I ever disappoint you."

She nodded. "Oh, I will open my mouth. But you needn't worry. I don't know that you can ever let me down. Truly, I will be happy so long as you make room for me in your leopard tree."

He laughed. "Always, love."

She sighed. "Grace Quinton. I like the sound of it."

"So do I. We'll be stopping tonight at an inn just outside of Carlisle. Would you like to do the honors and sign us in the register?"

She nodded. "I would love to. How sweet it will feel to look the innkeeper in the eye and proudly proclaim I am your wife. Deklan and Grace Quinton. Mr. and Mrs. Deklan Quinton."

"Sounds nice, Grace."

"I hope your family will be pleased. It is one thing to take in a stray and show her kindness, but quite another to find she has married into the family."

"They will welcome you with open arms. I have no doubt of it. The Duke of Wooton might not take it quite so well, but he will come around in time. In any event, he has nothing to grouse about. England is safe. King Stanislaus is happy he got his crown back. None of it would have been possible without you. Who knows? Wooton might even offer you a position as a Crown agent."

Her eyes glittered with mirth. "Oh, he'll never ask me. I think he likes having you all to himself, an agent with undivided allegiance to the Crown and answering only to him."

Deklan's chuckle was more of a groan. "No, love. I give him fits with every assignment. I never answer to him as he wishes me to do. Indeed, I will continue to ignore his wishes if I deem them foolish. No one tells me how to handle an assignment when it comes to my service for the Crown. If anything, he is relieved you have managed to tame me. It gives him hope that someday he might, too."

"Will he?"

"Probably not. You, on the other hand, can always tell me what to do."

"Nonsense. I wouldn't, unless you were completely dense about something important."

"Grace, I bought a house and did not even tell my own mother. I think that qualifies me as dense."

She chuckled. "All right, I see your point. I'll tug on your leopard leash and bring you to heel if it should happen again."

He stretched his legs and leaned back against the squabs, looking quite relaxed. "I like having a wife."

She arched an eyebrow. "Just any wife?"

"No, love. I would not bind myself into eternity with anyone but you. Marriage to anyone else would feel like a noose pulled taut around my neck. With you, I feel as though I have landed in a soft bed of rose petals. Speaking of bed…"

That night, Grace watched Deklan slowly disrobe by the soft light of their hearth fire. Their inn was another charming one, built of sturdiest stone and existing for centuries. The guest chamber they occupied was their finest and contained every amenity for their comfort.

She held her breath as Deklan removed his shirt with casual ease, his muscles taut and flexing as he lifted the garment off his shoulders and over his head in one fluid motion.

He tossed the shirt aside, leaving him only wearing breeches. *Blessed mother.*

She had only a vague idea of what the act of love entailed, but she was hungry for it with this man. Perhaps standing by firelight enhanced his features, for his body appeared sculpted bronze amid the flames and shadows.

Oh, my heavens.

Her heart beat faster as he prowled toward her with slow, determined steps.

His attention remained fixed on her as he put his hot, rugged hands on her body and began to remove the last of her clothing. She sighed as his supple fingers worked the lacings of her corset. She melted when he slid the rough pads of his palms up her thighs to lift the chemise off her.

She expired from anticipation when he put his lips to the peak of her breast and began to slowly lick it.

He had given her a taste of passion that one time on Christmas morning and the memory of it was enough to turn her wanton.

The heat of it still scorched her.

Was there an inch of her not ignited?

"Deklan," she whispered, running her hands over his body. She felt the outline of thin scars, noticeably pale against his golden skin. There were also a few thicker scars, puckered and pink, perhaps still raw. These were the result of deeper, more serious wounds. "Do they hurt you?"

He took her hand and placed a soft kiss on each of her fingers and then along her wrist. "No, love."

Up close, his muscles seemed daunting.

Touching them was like touching granite stone.

They stood facing each other, nothing between them but sparks of attraction that filled the air and drew them inexorably closer.

His snake was plainly visible and she stared at its sinuous form, fascinated by the way it wrapped around his thigh and the thick heat of its tail.

Her eyes widened.

Deklan laughed. "Oh, love. Trust me, we shall fit."

She wasn't certain.

But women had been amenable to coupling since the dawn of time. Too amenable, if what she'd been warned was accurate. Hence the need for vigilant chaperones. Few would be eager to toss caution to the wind if the act were something unpleasant.

She decided to have faith in his assurance.

He lifted her in his arms and carried her to bed, settling her gently atop the mattress.

"Grace, we can take it slow. I needn't–"

She stopped him with a kiss. "I am not a porcelain doll. If you must know, I am in a low brain frenzy over you at this very moment. I did not realize ladies could feel this way, but they must. Does it mean I have two brains? The unthinking one is now firmly in charge and all it wants is you."

"Blessed saints, I have been in a taut coil of agony over you ever since we first met." He eased her onto her back and settled his large frame over her, propping on his elbows to avoid crushing her with his weight while he positioned himself between her legs.

She did not mind at all.

In fact, she liked their intimacy and found it most arousing.

"I love you, Grace," he said, his voice ragged and raspy as he prepared to claim her for his own. But she needed little encouragement. She was eager for him the moment he touched her.

Her response seemed to please him and he quickly fell into a gentle rhythm with his first cautious thrusts.

She felt a pull and a pinch.

"Love," he said with concern, wanting to withdraw when she cried out softly.

She held him back. "You didn't hurt me. It was the enormity of the moment. We are now bound in heart and body as husband and wife."

His tension eased and he smiled. "Forever, my beautiful Grace."

He tried to proceed slowly, but Grace wanted all of him and no halfway measures would satisfy her. Deklan was a beast who survived on feral instinct. Rugged and untamed. He wanted to be gentle with her, but she wanted his savage heat.

She wanted her leopard.

Lean. Powerful. Dangerous.

Not the civilized shell of him.

He was never meant to be tugged on a leash.

Nor was she afraid of setting him loose, for she was his mate and he would always come home to her. He would always protect her and never be the one to hurt her.

She cried out again as he seemed to know what would pleasure her and took command of her body with kisses and more determined thrusts. The pressure began to build inside her, for they were kindling to each other and together created a perfect flame.

She clasped his shoulders, needing him to anchor her as a blazing heat suddenly tore through her and scorched her soul.

This man ensorcelled her, turned her molten.

Hot, liquid lava streamed through her.

She called his name, cried it out in a string of breathless moans.

He wrapped his arms around her, his embrace exquisitely

tender. "Grace, I am wild for you."

His voice was still raspy and hardly recognizable as he soon joined her in the flames, the liquid heat of him thick and explosive as he poured himself into her.

For Grace, the moment lasted forever and at the same time was too short.

They stayed wrapped in each other, he atop her and inside her, his muscled arms around her and their bodies damp from exertion.

Her heart beat erratically.

She could feel the pounding of his while they remained enlaced in each other's arms.

When they had wrung every drop out of each other, he eased himself off her and fell back against the mattress with a deep and resonant laughing groan. "Blessed saints, that was good."

His grin revealed his pride of conquest.

She could not stop smiling. "Did you really like it?"

"Love, I have never felt so spent. Yes, I liked it. How could I hide it? Do not smile at me that way, you wicked enchantress."

"How am I smiling?"

"As though you have conquered me and I am your ever obedient jungle cat."

"You are my leopard, to be precise. But I would not cage you for the world. I like that untamed part of you."

He kissed her softly. "Grace, you are in my heart. I will share everything I have with you. I will always come home to you."

She rested her head against his chest, unable to recall when she had ever felt so content.

"Just don't expect me to invite the rest of the world in."

"No, Deklan. I never would." He would not change the essence of himself. This solitary creature is who he would always be, simply no longer perched alone in his high tree. He would allow her to share it…or he would come down, ready to make a life with her.

"I love you so much, Deklan. It is a miracle."

"A miracle that you love me?" He arched an eyebrow and cast her a deliciously irreverent grin when she glanced up to look at him. "Or that I am still alive after that bout of lovemaking?"

She laughed, knowing he was in jest.

He had all the experience and she had never been loved by anyone until this moment. "I am sure it was tame in comparison to your other…times. Any man with a snake on his rump has to have a streak of wicked."

He caressed her cheek. "It has never been better than with you. Coupling is not about the act itself, it has no meaning unless with the right partner. Do you know what is the true miracle? Your smile. It is the loveliest thing imaginable and what will always draw me home to you."

"My smile? That does not sound very low brain of you."

"Oh, I'll always have plenty of those mindless urges about you. But my high brain chose you because of your smile. It is pure sunshine and you shone your light into my soul the moment I met you. I did not read *The Book of Love* to discover the right woman for me. I knew it was you. Never a moment's doubt."

She pursed her lips, now confused. "Then why did you read it?"

"To learn how to be the *right* man for you."

"But you were. You've been wonderful to me all along."

"Because I am in love with you, Grace. But I am also that leopard who wants to hide in his tree, happy to be on his own and answering to no one. I knew this had to change or I would lose you. For you, I will always come down from my perch in the tree. I want to make you happy. And I will, I give you my sacred promise."

He rolled her under him again. "Do not get mawkishly sentimental and give me your sacred promise in return. I do not need it. I know you will never give me less than every drop of love in your heart. But there is something you can do for me now."

"Anything, my love. What is it?"

He whispered in her ear.

She gasped and burst out laughing. "Deklan! Seriously? You truly are a naughty man. I do not even want to know where you learn these things."

"The question is, are you willing to let me teach you?"

She nodded. "Your utterly wanton and delicious pleasure tricks? Yes, but I have one question."

"What is it, love?"

"Can we start now?"

"Blessed saints, yes."

She closed her eyes and sighed in pleasure as he began to trail kisses down her body, his touch gentle and divine, as she knew it would always be.

CHAPTER SEVENTEEN

Brighton, England
June, 1822

DEKLAN STRODE THROUGH the Duchess of Dunfell's garden in search of Grace amid the crush of London elites who mixed with the local gentry on this fine summer day. The duchess was throwing another of her much anticipated and always well attended garden parties. Everyone who was anyone in Brighton had been invited, he and Grace always among the first on her list since Grace, having saved the duchess from trampling by one of her frightened carriage horses last winter, was now a favorite of the grand dowager.

She had taken to inviting Grace to accompany her everywhere and treated her with as much indulgence as she would her own daughter had she and the duke ever been blessed with children. The duchess also kept true to her word about holding a tea in honor of Grace. It was held shortly after they returned from Scotland, Grace happy as a sparrow because they were newly wed and there was no more need to deceive anyone about her marital status.

He loved Grace more each day.

At times, he could not think straight because she filled his thoughts.

As for her, she was now much sought after in Brighton society. All her fears of being an outcast were firmly squashed now that she had the Duchess of Dunfell's support. That she was everyone's darling came as no surprise to him.

Did he not fall in love with her at first sight?

The duchess noticed him and waved him over.

"Your Grace," he said, coming to her side and bowing over her hand. "It is good to see you looking so well."

"Ah, but you are such a charming liar," she teased. "You are looking as handsome as ever, you devil. Not here five minutes and already the ladies are in a swoon. I've never seen so many fans suddenly fluttering all at once."

"I'm sure it is merely the heat of the day," he said, shrugging the comment off with a wry grin. "Where's Grace?"

"Still have eyes only for your wife?"

He smiled. "Can you blame me?"

"No, it is impossible not to adore her. Did she know you were returning today?"

"I finished my assignment early and rushed home. She has no idea I am back."

"Well, she will be eager to see you. But spare me your displays of affection. Draw her inside the house to somewhere private if you are going to insist on kissing her as though she is the very air you breathe."

He laughed. "I am not going to hold back kissing her. But I shall spare your delicate sensibilities and find a quiet alcove to have my wicked way with her." He could not wait to drink in Grace's lovely smile or hold her in his arms again. Three months was too long to be away from her and he would not accept such a lengthy assignment again.

He found her seated on the grass in the shade of a willow tree, her younger brother and sisters seated beside her, their little faces glowing with happiness as they ate their tea cakes and chatted with her. Those three, James, Serenity, and Hope, had thrived since coming to Brighton and he expected Grace would ask him if they could remain permanently.

He would agree, of course.

He could deny her nothing.

Besides, those little ones needed to be kept away from the family mess still going on in London.

Grace leaped to her feet when she saw him stride toward her. "Deklan!"

He caught her in his arms and kissed her thoroughly before setting her down. Her brother and sisters giggled and ran off to grab more cakes. "Love, I missed you so much."

She laughed, the soft trill of her voice carrying on the light sea breeze. "I missed you every moment of every day. Thankfully, I have the children to keep me busy, but our bed is awfully big and it is lonely at night."

"I'll do my best to remedy that," he said and kissed her again with all the ache and insatiable longing built over a three month absence. "I'll be home for a while this time, perhaps the entire summer."

"Truly? I hope so." She cleared her throat. "I've invited your mother and Sam to join us for the month of July. Miranda, too. Well, any of your family who wishes to join us is more than welcome. I may have need of your mother to return in about four months." She patted her stomach. "I should think the reason is obvious by now."

If hearts could glow, then his was surely glowing brighter than the light of a thousand suns. "I noticed. You look beautiful. Only four months before our little delivery?"

She nodded.

"I'll be here. I am not leaving your side."

She appeared relieved. "Good, because if your mother cannot come, then I will need you more than ever. I don't think my mother will join me."

He caressed her cheek and frowned. "She is foolish to be angry with you. Your father and Richard brought their problems on themselves. They could have worked out a lesser punishment had they cooperated with Wooton. But they did not and lost any advantage in negotiating their way out of their self-imposed troubles."

He saw the wobble of her chin and took her back in his arms before she started crying. "You did not betray them, Grace. You did the right thing in helping me find that crown. We are all better off for your honesty and good sense."

"But it still hurts. My mother will not forgive me and this is what cuts my heart to ribbons. I did not expect her to side with my father and Richard against me."

"None of them should ever be against you. Being supportive of your father is understandable. She loves him and will stand beside him as a loyal wife should. But to dismiss you and blame you? That is unacceptable. Your father ought to be showering you with gratitude, for he retained his title through your efforts alone."

"He assumes it is because of his privilege of peerage."

"More the fool, he. Everyone else understands it was you who fought for him. He will soon be released from house confinement because of all you are doing for him."

"My parents do not see it that way."

"Which is a flaw in them and why your father got into trouble in the first place. It is always easier to blame others for the ills brought on by their own failings. Did your parents think they were going to waltz back into society, be invited to balls and theater outings after the enormity of the scandal? It will take years for them to be accepted again, but it will happen in time because of your sacrifice on their behalf."

"They only see I could not help Richard."

Deklan shook his head in frustration. "He dug himself too deep a hole. There is little anyone can do to help him. But I will call in a few favors. I hate to waste them on your brother, but I can see it is eating at you and that cannot be good for you or the babe."

"I try very hard not to let it affect me." She sighed. "But it does, too often. Even something as insignificant as that Christmas goose. It meant so much to me for my mother and siblings to have it. I am so grateful to you, Donal, and Lorcan for getting it to them in time. She will not even acknowledge the gesture."

He kissed her on the forehead. "Never mind, love. You did the right thing and your siblings appreciated it. Your heart is generous and sweet. I am going to hold on to you with all my might and love you to eternity."

She shook her head and laughed. "I love you, too. You are my wonderful leopard."

He groaned. "Do leopards take one mate for life? They must, because there is no one for me but you. Even now, I cannot take my eyes off you. You're so beautiful."

She laughed again. "*The Book of Love* at work."

"What do you mean?"

"My body has changed because I am with child. Have you not noticed?"

"Yes, your smile is brighter and there's a sparkle in your eyes. All right, your breasts, too. They've grown to the size of melons and–"

"Deklan!"

He put his arms around her and drew her up against his chest. "Do not be angry with me for loving you. I am going to lick you all over when I get you alone tonight."

He heard giggles behind them.

Grace burst out laughing.

"Blessed saints, they heard me. Didn't they?"

She nodded. "But they can be bribed to keep quiet. James can be bought for a shilling and a cherry tart. The girls will settle for ribbons and ginger cake."

"Done. I know when I am defeated." He sent the children off again to fetch cakes for him, then turned serious a moment later. "I'll talk to Wooton now that he has had a few months to calm down. I think he will agree for Richard to be sent into exile. Your parents won't be happy, but surely your brother will appreciate regaining his freedom, albeit outside of England. He will eventually be permitted to return since he is heir to your father and will inherit the viscountcy on his passing. He's forfeited the baronial title inherited from his mother's side, though."

She nodded. "I did not think His Majesty would allow him to go unscathed. It is small punishment considering all he's done."

"If he does get a new start in life, hopefully he will not muck it up. But he'll have to change his ways. He cannot revert to his old habits. I doubt there is anything anyone can do for him if he does."

Later that night, they climbed into bed together.

Deklan held her in his arms.

He slept without clothes, but Grace had not overcome her shyness and wore a thin nightgown over her luscious body. He was not going to coax it off her or make love to her because of her delicate condition.

She would likely punch his shoulder if he dared call her delicate, but he could not help feeling overwhelmed and wanting to protect her and their child. Was this not the time she would need him most?

He knew she had spirit and determination, had taken on the care of her siblings and become involved with charitable work in Brighton. Some people had even started referring to her as the little duchess because she and the Duchess of Dunfell often worked on these charitable endeavors together.

She did not need him to hover over her and treat her like a fragile flower, but she was the sweetest wife any man could have and he wished he could protect her from all the ills, all the stupidity, all the hurt in the world.

"Did you see your Aunt Miranda when you were in London?"

He nodded. "Of course. Miranda first, then His Majesty and Wooton."

Her eyes lit up with mirth. "And what does she say about *The Book of Love*? Has the family decided on who gets it next?"

"Not yet. She's handed it over to Sophie Farthingale for safekeeping until the next victim comes along."

"There are no victims here, only fortunate men whose eyes

are opened to love. So no one yet?"

"No, sweetheart." He arched an eyebrow as he studied her. "Do you have someone in mind?"

"Yes...no...not really. He is married already and miserable about it, but I do not think the book works that way."

"Who are you talking about?"

"You will think my brains utterly scrambled if I tell you. But I've met him at the Duchess of Dunfell's several times now. He never says a disparaging word about his wife, but you can see the misery reflected in his eyes. I am speaking of the Earl of Somerset."

"Genevieve's husband? Grace, keep away from that pair. She will eat you alive if you interfere in their marriage."

"I have no intention of interfering. She is back in London with her society friends. He is here in Brighton at his country estate. I think he was already unhappy with his choice of wife before that incident at the Pavilion Hotel. The scene she and her cousin Velda caused merely confirmed his worst fears. Well, it is too bad. He is rather a nice man, but I would never wish ill on his wife. Never. All I am saying is that if he is ever free to marry again, I would like to give him that book."

"Should I be jealous of him? You seem to have become quite friendly with Somerset."

"No, good gracious. I am in the arms of the only man I ever want. I've found my love match and now you are stuck with me forever."

"That is no chore for me, love."

She kissed him lightly on the lips. "I am so proud of you, of the man you are and the sacrifices you quietly make to keep us all safe. There is no one better, and I am certain our children will feel the same. By the way, I know it is too early to be sure, but I think there are two sets of feet kicking inside me."

He gasped. "Grace...truly?"

"Yes, I am sure we will have twins to add to our family come October."

He laughed wholeheartedly. "Two baby leopards?"

"Yes, isn't it just grand?"

"It certainly is, love." He gave a low growl and nuzzled her neck. "We'll have to make room for them in our leopard tree."

The End

Also by Meara Platt

FARTHINGALE SERIES
My Fair Lily
The Duke I'm Going To Marry
Rules For Reforming A Rake
A Midsummer's Kiss
The Viscount's Rose
Earl Of Hearts
If You Wished For Me
Never Dare A Duke
Capturing The Heart Of A Cameron
Tempting Taffy

BOOK OF LOVE SERIES
The Look of Love
The Touch of Love
The Taste of Love
The Song of Love
The Scent of Love
The Kiss of Love
The Chance of Love
The Gift of Love
The Heart of Love
The Hope of Love (novella)
The Promise of Love
The Wonder of Love
The Journey of Love
The Treasure of Love
The Dance of Love
The Miracle of Love

The Dream of Love (novella)
The Remembrance of Love (novella)

DARK GARDENS SERIES
Garden of Shadows
Garden of Light
Garden of Dragons
Garden of Destiny
Garden of Angels

LYON'S DEN SERIES
The Lyon's Surprise
Kiss of the Lyon
Lyon in the Rough

THE BRAYDENS
A Match Made In Duty
Earl of Westcliff
Fortune's Dragon
Earl of Kinross
Earl of Alnwick
Pearls of Fire
Aislin
Gennalyn
A Rescued Heart
All I Want For Christmas (novella)

DeWOLFE PACK ANGELS SERIES
Nobody's Angel
Kiss An Angel
Bhrodi's Angel

About the Author

Meara Platt is an award winning, USA TODAY bestselling author and an Amazon UK All-Star. Her favorite place in all the world is England's Lake District, which may not come as a surprise since many of her stories are set in that idyllic landscape, including her paranormal romance Dark Gardens series. Learn more about the Dark Gardens and Meara's lighthearted and humorous Regency romances in her Farthingale series and Book of Love series, or her warmhearted Regency romances in her Braydens series by visiting her website at www.mearaplatt.com.

9 781960 184009